# WHITEWASHED

# WHITEWASHED

A Novel

SANDY BERMAN

*In Memory of Erin*
*And in Honor of Annie*

# Acknowledgements

I would like to thank all of my readers who added their suggestions, insights, and editorial comments throughout the process of writing this novel. I would also like to thank my family and friends for their unwavering support and encouragement.

# Author's Bio

S ANDY BERMAN IS an archivist and museum curator. Sandy's debut novel "Klara with a K," received the bronze medal for historical fiction from Independent Publishers Book Awards. "Whitewashed" is Sandy's second novel. She lives in Atlanta, Georgia with her husband and enjoys spending time with her children and grandchildren.

# AUTHOR'S NOTE

WHITEWASHED IS A work of fiction. With the exception of actual historical figures, the characters in this book are entirely the product of the author's imagination. Any similarity to persons living or deceased is purely coincidental.

# TABLE OF CONTENTS

# PART I

---

# REMEMBRANCE

# 1

---

# 1968

THE MORNING BEFORE my high school graduation the body of my best friend, Ben Lowe, was found hanging from a tree. My boyhood ended that day in 1950 and so did any attachment to Huntsville, Alabama, the city of my birth. Once Daddy died and Mama joined me in Atlanta, I had no thought of returning—not in body or in spirit.

Over the last eighteen years I had worked hard to banish the memories of that long-ago morning. I moved away, went off to college and then to law school. The distance helped, but for a long time, a word, a scent, or seeing someone push up their glasses, in the same way as Ben once did, was all it took to transport me back to that awful day. The nights were hell. I had no control over the demons that lay in wait, destroying my sleep and leaving me wide-awake with a pounding heart and drenched sheets. With time, the nightmares grew less frequent, and for the most part, Ben stayed in the past, where he belonged.

On an early March morning in 1968, all of that changed when the shrill ringing of the telephone prompted me to roll over, reach for the receiver and grumble hello. To say I was blindsided by the call from the Huntsville Police Department would be an understatement. Long-buried feelings resurfaced the moment I heard the voice on the other end. Someone had come forward with new information about Ben's death.

"Why now?" I asked.

"Can't answer that, Tommy."

No one called me Tommy anymore. Then I remembered my mother telling me that Cole Preston, one of my brother's old buddies, was Huntsville's chief of police.

"Hey, Cole," I said.

"Hey yourself, Tommy."

"So why now?"

"Just get yourself over here. This person will only speak to you."

"I need a little more information," I said. "I can't just drop everything and drive to Huntsville."

"Suit yourself Tommy but knowing that Ben was your best friend and all, I thought you'd bust ass to get here. But like I said, suit yourself, cause that's all I can tell you over the phone. I'm sorry for all the mystery, but I already told you this informant will only speak to you and it has to be in person."

"Thanks for clearing up the mystery," I said before hanging up.

*What in the hell was going on?* I really didn't have time for this. I had a trial starting in three weeks, and I was up to my neck in work. The ghosts from the past had already sabotaged my morning but with two cups of coffee and a hot shower I forced them aside and drove to the office.

"Good morning, Mr. Stern."

"Morning, Helen. Any messages?"

"They're on your desk."

Helen O'Boyle was fifteen years my senior and had been my secretary for the last seven. We were a good fit. We both knew I couldn't get along without her, and she had no reservations about voicing her opinion whenever she felt the need.

"You look tired," she said.

"Is that a euphemism for saying I look bad?" I asked.

She smiled.

"No, but your hair, it's…"

"What about my hair?"

I automatically reached up and tried to figure out what she was talking about.

"You've also got a little twitch above your left eye, and that only happens when you're exhausted or worried about something. Do you want to talk about it?"

"For God's sake, Helen, I'm fine. I'll be back in a minute."

The thing was, she was right. I didn't feel fine. I escaped into the men's room, hoping she wouldn't follow me in. I didn't put it past her. I walked over to the sink and splashed cold water onto my face and stared into the mirror. No wonder she had commented on my appearance. I looked like a damn porcupine. I was a partner at Hubbard, Whitney and Barns, one of Atlanta's most prestigious criminal law firms and my usually parted and slicked down hair was sticking out in every direction. I had also missed shaving a small patch of stubble on my chin and another under my right sideburn. I wetted and combed my hair, but there was nothing I could do about the leftover stubble or about controlling that telltale nerve above my right eye from working overtime. The phone call had rattled me. My demons were beckoning, inviting long-suppressed childhood memories to launch a surprise attack on my defenses.

For the rest of the day I immersed myself in work. At seven that evening I finally convinced my mother hen to go home and poured myself a much-needed drink from the small bar in the corner of my office. I settled into one of the leather chairs, usually reserved for my clients, and thought about the day when the idylls of my childhood began to lose their magic.

# 2

# 1941

Decermber 7 started out like any other Sunday in my hometown. My friends were heading to church, and I was on my way to Sunday school at B'nai Sholom, the Jewish church, as some liked to call it. I was glad that I too had something to do when everyone else was busy praying. I liked my teacher that year, and since my older brother Joe usually drove me over there it was one of those rare occasions when I had him all to myself.

I guess you could say I idolized my big brother. He was seven years older than I was and was already driving and dating. The day he turned sixteen, Daddy bought him a used truck. Once that old Chevy pickup came into his life, Joe was home less and less.

"So little brother, how come you like Sunday school so much? I couldn't wait for it to end so I could get over to the ball field and be outside."

"I like the Bible stories," I answered. "Some of those guys are just like superheroes. I mean look at Samson or David when he slew Goliath."

"Tommy, somehow you always manage to make me laugh."

He reached over to tousle my hair.

I knew I was a little different from the other kids. Yeah, I liked playing ball and riding my bike, but sometimes, if I had the choice, I would rather stay indoors and read one of the books my father bought for me. He ordered them special, straight from the publisher. They were Scribner's Classics, and as my collection grew Daddy placed a bookshelf in a corner of my room and told me that he would keep buying books as long as I kept reading. I had already finished eight of them, including *Treasure Island, Kidnapped, Robin Hood,* and the *Black Arrow,* and I was planning to spend a couple of hours after Sunday school at home so I could finish up reading *Quentin Durward,* a book about a Scottish archer in the service of King Louis XI. I never spoke to my friends about my reading. I knew better. None of them were into books like I was, and I wanted to fit in because, once in a while, I felt this underlying difference between them and me. It was nothing we ever spoke about, but except for Ben Lowe everyone in my fifth-grade class was Christian of one sort or another. I never did figure out the difference between the Baptists, Methodists, and Lutherans, and I knew none of my friends were the least bit interested in what went on in my small little syna-gogue building on Lincoln Street. On Sundays, we all went our separate ways and usually met up later. That's how it was, at least until Ben came to town.

"Joe, do you ever feel different, you know, because we're Jewish?" I asked. "Do you lay awake at night thinking about stuff like this?"

"Sometimes," I answered honestly.

"Yeah, well I suppose I do too, sometimes. It can't be helped. We are differ-ent. We don't go to church and we don't celebrate Christmas or Easter."

"We do too," I answered. "We always have a tree in our house, and every year Daddy puts up an eight-footer in the front window of the store, and during Easter, he helps to buy all the eggs for the hunt held at the park. Remember that time he dressed in that smelly white rabbit suit and passed out candy?"

"Okay, you got me there."

We both started laughing at the memory of our slightly overweight father prancing around in a bunny suit. It wasn't until years later, when I went up north to college that I really understood that most Jews who lived above the Mason-Dixon Line didn't partake in the two biggest Christian holidays. It was more of a southern thing. We were such a small minority, and it was important to fit in.

"But," Joe continued, "even though we may join in the fun we don't go to church on those days, now do we? And we still light the Menorah and get pres-ents on Chanukah, and Aunt Ruth's entire family always comes to Huntsville for

Passover, and none of our other friends celebrate those days. What I'm trying to say is that, sometimes, that sets us apart."

"My friends treat Ben differently than me," I said.

As soon as I said it, I wished I could have sucked those words right back in.

"Ben Lowe? What do you mean?"

"You know, different. He speaks with an accent, and his parents hardly speak any English at all."

"He's young. He'll start speaking like everyone else before too long. Did you know that Daddy was the one who sent the Lowe family money and signed the affidavit to help them emigrate from Germany?"

I wanted to say, '*Then I guess I'll have to thank Daddy for bringing Ben Lowe into my life,*' but I didn't. Instead I said, "What's an affidavit?"

"It's a paper promising that Ben's father would have a job waiting for him once he came to America. That was the only way the Lowe family could get out of Germany. That's why Mr. Lowe does the tailoring in our store. It's bad for Jews over in Germany. There are all these laws making it hard for them to work or for kids to even go to school. Daddy heard about the Lowe family from one of the Jewish agencies down in Atlanta. They were looking for a storeowner who might be willing to hire a tailor. People in this country are hard-pressed for money right now, and there aren't too many like our father who try and help complete strangers. There are even some folks, right here in Huntsville who probably didn't take too kindly to Daddy hiring a foreigner since so many Americans are looking for work."

We sat there, not saying anything for the next few minutes. I was squirming, hoping the conversation was over. We only had one more block to go before I could get out of the car.

"Tommy, do your friends pick on Ben?"

*How did he know?* I didn't want to look at my brother. I was embarrassed.

"Tommy?"

"Kind of," I answered.

"Do you?"

"No."

"But you see it happen, don't you?"

"Yeah, sometimes."

"And you don't do anything to stop it?"

"I can't. I just can't."

Joe shook his head, and I could tell he was disappointed in me.

"Tommy, if you don't stand up for Ben, who will? Think about what that kid's already gone through. I know you're only ten, but I see you listening when Mama and Daddy talk about what's been happening in Germany. Did you know that Ben and his family were stripped of their citizenship? Men and women can no longer practice their professions or even go to concerts or movies. What if our government decided to take away all of our rights?"

I didn't answer him. Instead, I just stared out the window sulking and thinking about what Joe had said. He didn't get it. Everybody loved my brother. He was the quarterback of our high school football team. Whenever Mama's sister from Atlanta visited she always talked about how smart and how handsome he was. Daddy would often say, "Bethy, did you just spit that boy out? Surely I had something to do with it." Then the two of them would smile leaving me slightly confused about what was so funny. Joe did look like my mother. He had the same blond thick hair and dark blue eyes. He was funny, smart and made every team he tried out for. Joe could stand up for someone like Ben Lowe without threatening his social standing. It wasn't like that for me. I was small for my age and ended up with my father's mousy brown hair and mud puddle eyes. When I looked in the mirror all I saw was ordinary. I didn't think I'd ever measure up to Joe in height or anything else. Sometimes, I felt like I was holding onto my friends with a frail rope. One wrong move would break the strands, and I would be picked on too.

When Ben Lowe moved to town, it made everything harder for me. He set himself apart right from the beginning. On his first day of school, Ben walked through the door wearing leather shorts and knee socks. When Miss Richman, our fifth-grade teacher, introduced him to the rest of the class, he barely looked up. What I remember most was how ghostly pale he was. It was early September, and most of us boys still had scabbed noses from summer burns and tan lines peeking out from the sleeves of our T-shirts. The only color on Ben came from a few freckles scattered across his face. To make matters worse, his lunch box consisted of unknown foods that filled our classroom with strange and disgusting smells. No one, including me, wanted to be anywhere near Ben when he opened it. Before he came hardly anyone ever thought about me being Jewish or about Jewish people at all. On my father's side, our family had been in Huntsville since before the Civil War. Daddy always said the South had been welcoming to our family since they first arrived in the late 1830s, and we should always remember that and give back. For most folks, my great-granddaddy was the first Jew they'd ever met. When the war ended, he threw a pack on his back and started peddling across Alabama. Daddy kept that old pack in a trunk up in our attic, and every once in a while he would take it out and tell Joe and me tales about great-granddaddy's service and about how he started the family business.

My mama hailed from Atlanta, and from what I've heard, my grandparents were none too pleased when she met my father and decided to marry him and move to Huntsville. It's not that they didn't like him, but she was only eighteen and they hoped she would go to college and then settle down with a nice Jewish boy closer to home. As they often pointed out, she could have had her pick. They were probably right, because in my eyes, my mama was the prettiest woman in the whole town. Mama was just as proud of her family as my father was of his, and at bedtime, she would sometimes tell me about all the parties and dances she attended at the Jewish country club in Atlanta. In fact, she met my father at one of those parties. It was called the Ballyhoo and was held every winter so Jewish boys and girls in the South could get to know one another. Daddy always said it was love at first sight. Mama said it took her a little more time.

Daddy had one of those appealing personalities that made folks feel welcome. Everyone shopped at Sterns. Even members of the local Klan gave their business to our store. Daddy often laughed about how, during their parades when they thought their hoods disguised their true identities, he recognized each and every one of them. They all bought their shoes from Sterns my father knew who they were by what they wore on their feet.

The big day for shopping was on Saturday. That's when all the farmers drove in. In the late 1930s, a lot of them still came to town by horse and wagon. That's when my brother and I helped out and worked alongside our parents. Joe, at sixteen, was already Daddy's best salesman. Sometimes there were three or four girls lined up, all waiting for Joe to take their money. I mostly worked in the stockroom unpacking the new merchandise. I knew our father hoped that one day Joe would take over the running of the family business, but even as a kid I sensed my big brother was destined for other things.

"We're here," Joe announced. "I'll pick you up in a couple of hours."

"Okay," I yelled, already hopping out and slamming the door.

"We'll talk more about Ben later."

That was the last thing I wanted to do. Ben seemed like a nice enough kid, but I didn't feel a kinship or the need to be his only friend just because he was a fellow Jew.

There were only fifteen of us in the entire Sunday school, and we were divided by age into two separate classes. Being almost eleven, I was with the older group that included everyone from nine to fifteen. Ben Lowe was also in my class, but hadn't shown up in the last few weeks. Until that morning's conversation with Joe, I hadn't wondered why, but now I did.

"Mr. Stern, you were supposed to have been here fifteen minutes ago."

"Sorry, Mr. Arnstein. My brother and I got a late start."

We didn't have an actual rabbi. The congregation was small and Daddy said they could never find anyone who wanted the job. He thought Mr. Arnstein knew as much as any rabbi, so it didn't matter. He also ran the services on Friday night.

"Well, you're here now; that's all that matters. Now where were we? Oh yes, I was telling you about Judah Maccabee."

Two hours later, I was sitting on the front steps of the synagogue waiting for Joe to pick me up. I had already forgotten about Ben and was thinking about the first night of Chanukah that was only one week away. In fact, it was all I was thinking about.

Since most of the pieces and half of the money were missing from my old Monopoly game, I was pretty sure I was getting a new one. But what I really wanted was a Veda The Magic Answer Man game. I left countless hints all over the house. All the ads on the radio promised that Veda could tell the future, and since I was still at the age where I believed that the world was a good place and that the rest of my life would be as perfect as the first ten, I wasn't frightened by what the Answer Man might reveal.

"So how was it today?" Joe asked when I hopped into his car.

"Good. Mr. Arnstein spent a lot of time talking about the Maccabees. They were Jewish warriors that defeated a much bigger army."

I started telling Joe the story about Judah Maccabee and about the oil that was only supposed to last one day but ended up lasting eight, but after a few minutes I could tell he wasn't listening. When I turned quiet, he finally looked over and realized I was slumped down in my seat sulking.

"Sorry, Tommy. I have a lot on my mind."

"Like what? You can trust me."

"I know, and I will tell you, but not just now. I need to think a few things through. Then I promise I'll spill my guts."

It seemed as if Joe had forgotten our earlier conversation about Ben, and that was okay by me. We spent the rest of the car ride talking about the Atlanta Crackers baseball team and their prospects for the coming season. I didn't remember until several days later to ask my big brother what was troubling him. He told me not to worry about it. He had worked a few things out and felt better. Later, I found out that Joe was planning to enlist in the Canadian army so he could join the British in their fight against the Nazis. He told me that he couldn't stand what was happening over in Europe to Jewish families like the Lowes. He was worried about telling our parents. As it turned out, he wouldn't have to go to Canada.

That day, when Joe and I got home, we expected to smell the familiar aromas of our dinner coming from the kitchen. Selma was our maid, and I thought she made the best fried chicken in the entire state of Alabama. She had worked for my parents since before Joe was born, and I didn't remember a time when she wasn't in our kitchen, humming or singing along with the tunes on the radio while she was getting all her special fixings together. But on that Sunday, instead of singing and music, all I heard was the soft buzzing of words coming from the living room.

"I'm starving. When's dinner?" Joe yelled.

The screen door banged shut behind him.

"Me too," I echoed.

When there was no response we found our parents oblivious to our arrival, sitting in front of the Philco radio. Selma was sitting there too, listening.
*Sammy Kaye's Sunday Serenade,* my parents' favorite show, had been interrupted
by world-changing news. That morning at 7:53 a.m., the Japanese had attacked
Pearl Harbor, the US naval base in Hawaii.

Joe and I grabbed a couple of kitchen chairs and sat down with them. No
one spoke.

My parents and Selma had tears in their eyes. I was scared and a little excited. We were going to war, and all I could think about was how we were going
to pay back those dirty Japs.

# 3

# 1968

I HAD TO admit, that phone call from Cole had unnerved me. I finally left
my office around ten and drove the short distance to Buckhead, an older
neighborhood north of downtown, where I had lived for the last seven years.
From the outside, my stately brick home looked good enough for the cover
of *Architectural Digest*. The inside was another matter. My ex-wife Donna
and I had purchased the fixer-upper a couple of years into our marriage and
dreamt about returning it to its former glory. Within a year, her passion
had waned for the house as well as for me. When we divorced, I bought her
out. Once I was inside, I walked directly into the library. I had inherited a
collection of first editions from my father and the books were a reminder of
the man who had died too young and whom I still missed. It was the only
room I had managed to restore. I then poured myself a hefty glass of Jack on
the rocks and tried to relax. I sat down in Daddy's worn and frayed oversized chair, drank in the rich scent of the old leather bindings, sipped on my
whiskey and hoped for enlightenment. I was torn between ignoring Cole's
phone call and driving to Huntsville in the morning. In less than an hour, I
gave up and went up to bed. It had been a while since Ben's last minutes had
haunted my dreams, but that night I woke up in a cold sweat, unable to stop
the onslaught of the ghoulish images of my best friend hanging from the tree
behind the high school.

With no hope of going back to sleep I got dressed and packed a bag. I was at my office by seven, but couldn't concentrate on anything other than what awaited me in Huntsville. My stomach was churning, and I searched around for a Rolaids. I was becoming addicted to antacids. I had a trial looming and a shitload of other appointments, but in my gut I knew, even before I threw my suitcase in the back of my car, I would be leaving for Huntsville before the day was out.

"I quit!" said Helen. Her formidable figure dressed in a dark blue polyester suit, and what Sterns would have advertised as sensible shoes, was standing before me.

I had just told her that I was heading out for a day, two at the most. Helen threatened to quit on a regular basis, but since we both knew it wasn't going to happen, I ignored the comment.

"Helen, come on. I'll bring you back a present. Cancel tomorrow's appointments. I'll probably only be gone one night."

Helen outweighed me by a good twenty pounds, and with her hands on her hips she looked like she was actually going to bar the door. I grinned, shaking my head.

"I don't like this one little bit," she said. "Not one little bit. Where should I say you went if anyone asks?"

"Tell them I went home. That's all anybody needs to know."

I was nervous as hell about the trip. I thought about calling my mother for her opinion. She was the only person, other than my ex-wife, who would understand what a trip down memory lane might cost me. She might want to tag along but I nixed that idea. Huntsville held too many painful memories for her as well. I then thought about calling Donna. As ex-wives went, she was the best. We were still friends and got together every couple of months to catch up. One night, after a few too many I had told her about Ben. I knew she would help me sort things out, but she was happy in her new life, and the last thing I wanted to do was to drag her back into my unresolved issues and disturbing memories from my childhood.

In the end, I didn't call anyone and headed out to the parking lot. It would take me about three hours to drive the hundred and eighty miles separating my home in Atlanta and the one of my youth in Huntsville. I never even turned on the radio. I thought the quiet and solitude would help me figure out who in the hell I was going to see at the police station. It didn't. Cole had been deliberately cagey about his mystery witness, and I still had no idea why that person would speak only to me.

I had no time to tell anyone in Huntsville that I was coming, and truth be told, I was hoping to avoid seeing any of my old friends. One relative, a much older first cousin, still lived there, but I was too embarrassed to contact him, since I hadn't reached out in over a decade. When I pulled into town everything was eerily familiar. I drove by my family's old department store but stopped myself from conjuring up any seductive memories from my boyhood. The fronts of all the old businesses, including Sterns, were there, but the names on their brick facades were mostly different. For a moment I felt disoriented, no longer sure where the police station was located, no longer sure if I should have come. I was ready to bolt—to turn around and drive back to Atlanta—to the safety of my uncomplicated life, but in the end my curiosity got the better of me, and I pulled into the curbside spot directly in front of the station.

# 4

---

# 1942

I N THE DAYS that followed the bombing of Pearl Harbor all Joe spoke about was signing up. It turned out that the attack was devastating to our American forces. More than two thousand sailors and soldiers were killed, and another one thousand were wounded. We were glued to the radio, always hoping for more updates. Over the next several days we learned that in addition to the loss of life, twenty American naval vessels including two enormous battleships and almost two hundred airplanes were destroyed. The day after the attack President Franklin Delano Roosevelt asked Congress to declare war on Japan. Congress approved, with just one dissenting vote. Three days later Japan's allies, Germany and Italy, declared war on the US, and again Congress returned the favor. My brother was just seventeen. He begged my parents to lie for him and say he was a year older so he could join up. They were equally proud and terrified, but insisted he wait out the year and finish high school. I think they hoped the war would end before he would have to go. It didn't. The day Joe turned eighteen he joined the Army Air Corp, newly renamed as the United States Army Air Forces. At the time, the requirements were pretty loose. They were desperate for airmen. All you needed was a high school diploma, which, thanks to my parents, he had. Within days, he was sent to the aviation-training center in Montgomery, a little less than two hundred miles from our front door.

It was Joe's first time away from family, and the first time I didn't have my big brother sleeping in the bed next to mine. For a while, the room still smelled like him. On the day I discovered that Selma had stripped his bed and put on new sheets, I cried like a baby. He wrote often, and I always answered, but it sure wasn't the same as him being at home. There were times, during those first few months, when my stomach ached from missing him. Every day there were dozens of subjects that I wanted to talk to him about, but by the time I finished my schoolwork and sat down to write him a letter, most of them had been forgotten, and I simply wrote about the daily meanderings in the life of a small town boy.

"Mama, when will Joe be coming home?"

I asked the same question every day. Mama was a patient woman.

"As soon as he's finished with training he'll be coming home for a few weeks," she answered.

"Then what?"

"Then, I suppose he'll be sent somewhere overseas, either to fight the Japanese, or heaven help us, the Germans."

She said that every time.

I didn't get it then. I was too immersed in my own misery, my desperate yearning for my brother, to understand or more importantly to ask why my mother was more afraid of the Nazis than of the Japanese. After all, it was the dirty, sneaky Japs who had attacked Pearl Harbor. They were the enemy most often destroyed while being grotesquely portrayed on the front covers of my comic books. I was still a child, and once we entered the war, I was no longer interested in the long-ago escapades of Quentin Durward or Robin Hood. World War II changed all that for me. I was now consumed with new heroes—ones found in the stories and pictures of the cheaply-made comic books that I ravenously devoured. Every night my mother walked into my room and told me to turn off the light and go to bed. A month earlier, she had confiscated my flashlight. Perhaps, my parents worried about my change in reading habits, but they never said so. I supposed, like everyone else fighting the good fight, annihilating Tojo and Hitler were all my parents cared about. I read them all; every issue of *Batman*, *Superman*, and *Captain Marvel* I could get my hands on, but at least for me, no superhero compared to Captain America. He was the only one who had the courage to sock Hitler on the jaw right on the front cover, and he did it even before the US entered the war. He was my favorite, because the more enemies he annihilated, the more battles he won, the faster my brother would come home.

Joe wrote daily from the training center. He had already made it through Classification, the one week of testing when it was decided whether or not an enlistee had the smarts and the athletic ability to continue as a flight cadet. It was also the time when you were designated as a navigator, bombardier, or pilot. If you failed, you were sent back to the regular army. Joe, who had graduated at the top of his high school class, passed easily and had been classified as a pilot. Within days, he sent home a couple of snapshots showing a smiling newly- processed cadet all decked out in his military uniform. My mother put one of the pictures in a place of honor on the living room mantel. The other was framed and stood on the nightstand next to my bed. I'm not sure what Joe wrote about in his letters to my parents, but the ones to me were filled with colorful stories about his fellow trainees, disgusting descriptions of the food he was eating, and an accounting of the regimen he was following in order to get through the next two stages of pre-flight. The first six-week period concentrated on military training and athletics, followed by four weeks of academics where the cadets were taught the mechanics of the physics of flight. If he passed the sessions, including a ten-hour evaluation in a flight simulator, he would be promoted to Pilot School.

I wasn't worried. Just as I had hoped, that year on the last night of Chanukah, my parents presented me with Veda The Magic Answer Man. I checked in with him often. Most of my questions were about Joe. I knew my brother would pass and get his wings, and unlike my parents, it didn't matter to me where he ended up. I believed in Veda, and he had already told me Joe would be coming home.

# 5

---

# 1968

I N 1949, A year before I left for college, there were about sixteen thousand people living in my hometown. A decade later, the population had more than quadrupled. The Huntsville I was now visiting, once a small insignificant cotton town, was now the center of the nation's aerospace industry. No longer was there simply a police station; it was now called the Public Safety Building. It was there where I found myself waiting, on an uncomfortable ladder-back steel chair, for the arrival of Chief of Police Cole Preston, who was finally going to let me know what was going on.

"Tommy Stern, you made it," he said. "I guess it took a phone call from me to finally get you back. How was the drive?"

He grabbed me in a fierce bear hug.

"Uneventful," I answered, breaking free of Cole's embrace. I was in no mood for small talk or bear hugs, but I knew I had to get through some of the pleasantries if I was going to hear about the witness that had suddenly surfaced.

"You look good. Haven't changed a bit."

"You look great too. I would have recognized you anywhere."

I lied. He was twice the size of the man I had known twenty years earlier, and his head, which had once sported a thick thatch of blond curly hair, was nearly bald. Cole had played football with my brother, but the gap-toothed grin was the only resemblance to the best defensive end our high school had ever seen.

"Would you like a smoke?"

Cole offered me the pack as he lit one of the unfiltered Camels for himself.

"No, no thanks. I gave it up several years back. Cole, you've been sort of mysterious. Is there any reason you wouldn't tell me the name of the witness over the phone? The person may not even be credible, and then I'll have driven all this way for nothing."

"Oh, she's credible."

He smiled, and I immediately felt a slight chill on the back of my neck.

"No sense beating around the bush any longer. It's Karin Angel."

He actually winked, like we were part of the same inside joke.

"She's the one that made me promise to keep her name a secret until you got here. She thought you might not come if you knew it was her."

My silence must have encouraged him to keep talking.

"Come on. You remember her, don't you? She had that twin brother, Erich. They moved here after the war with their parents and all those other German families who went to work at Redstone Arsenal on the space program. Hello, am I ringing any bells? I thought you two were good friends."

"Cole, I hope it's just my imagination working overtime, but you seem to be enjoying this."

"Well, I am a little. She's still a looker, and I knew you were divorced."

Was my brother's old buddy really playing matchmaker?

"Well, where is she? Is she here in the building?"

"I had an officer call her as soon as I heard you were here. She ought to be arrivin' any minute. She wanted to speak with you privately, so I arranged for one of our interrogation rooms to be available to y'all. She refused to say anything to me, at least not until she spoke to you. Anyway, I can't see what she might have to add to the case. That boy hung himself all on his own. You know that better than anyone, being best friends and all."

I didn't bother to answer.

"Cole, thanks for the offer of the room, but when Karin gets here, I think we'll take a walk over to that coffee shop I spotted on the corner. Hope you don't mind, but I skipped breakfast this morning."

"Say no more. You go on and get yourself something to eat and visit with your old friend. You just be sure to keep me in the loop, just in case I need to reopen the case."

He winked again.

"Absolutely," I answered. "I think I'll wait for her by the front door. Nice to see you, Cole."

"Yeah, Tommy. You too."

Food was actually the last thing on my mind, but I was tired of Cole finding amusement in my discomfort. By the time I left his office I had a pounding heart, a churning gut and a desperate need for fresh air. Karin was the last person I ever expected to want to see me, and I couldn't imagine what she had to tell me about the day Ben died. I had a lot of regrets when it came to Karin, but I hadn't seen or spoken to her in years. As I was mulling over this, I saw her walking from the parking lot toward the front door. She was far enough away that I could observe her without being noticed. Cole was right. She was still beautiful. She had the same straight blond hair, hanging loosely just above her shoulders and the same drop-dead gorgeous figure and purposeful stride. She was on a mission. She was definitely on a mission.

"Karin, wait," I yelled. She was staring straight ahead and was aiming to walk right past me.

She turned and stared, and for a few seconds neither one of us said a word. It had been eighteen years since we had last seen one another, and it seemed that, just like me, she was suddenly being bombarded by memories of our shared past. I smiled, resisting the urge to move a loose strand of hair back behind her ear.

"Come on," I said. "There's a little coffee shop nearby. We'll have more privacy there."

I waited, still hoping to see a smile on the face of the girl I'd once dreamt of marrying. I didn't. Instead she leaned against the brick wall of the building and took a deep breath.

"Okay," she finally answered.

# 6

# 1941

TWO WEEKS AFTER I celebrated my birthday Joe earned his wings. Once again, he had finished at the top of his class and was given the rank of second lieutenant. He was assigned to the First Air Division, Eighth Air Force, to fly B-17s and was shipping out to England in two short weeks. They let him come home to say his goodbyes.

We celebrated his arrival with a special dinner. Mama asked Selma to set the table with my grandmother's cutwork tablecloth and our best dishes, which were only pulled out of the dining room sideboard for special occasions. That day, the two of them prepared all of Joe's favorites. We had fried chicken, hush-puppies, mashed potatoes, corn on the cob, and pecan pie. It was fine by me. They were my favorites too.

In between bites, Joe told us what his training had been like.

"It was tough. I'll say that for it. Worked my tail off. A lot of boys didn't make it. They washed out and were sent to gunnery school."

I must have peppered him with a thousand questions. Finally, my father interrupted.

"Joe, I want you to promise me one thing."

"What's that?"

"If you get shot down and sent to a POW camp, I want you to toss your dog tags."

My mother gave Daddy one of those looks, the kind that said *not in front of Tommy. Talk about this later.* Of course, I immediately stared at both my brother and father.

"Why would Joe want to do that?"

Ignoring my mother, Joe answered.

"Because I'm Jewish, and Daddy's worried that I'll get treated differently from the other prisoners."

The look on my face must have signaled that I still didn't really get it. *Besides,* I thought, *Joe was too good a pilot to get shot down.*

"Tommy," Daddy continued, "you're getting older. It's time I talk to you about what's been happening to Jews over in Germany and in other parts of Europe. Remember when the Lowe family came here?"

"Yes," I said.

*Not Ben Lowe again,* I thought.

"The reason the Lowe family is here in Huntsville is because life became unbearable for them in Germany. When the Germans confiscated Mr. Lowe's business he couldn't find any other kind of work. Every day, there were new laws prohibiting Jews from all sorts of things. Even the simplest pleasures were denied to them.

"Ben was forced to leave the school he was attending, and then on one particular night, in November of 1938, Mr. Lowe was beaten, arrested, and sent to a concentration camp just north of their home in Berlin called Sachsenhausen."

"What's that?" I asked.

The only kind of camp I was familiar with was the Boy Scout camp in Biloxi that a couple of my friends went to each summer.

"Please, Tom. He doesn't need to know details," said my mother. "He's still a little boy."

My father rarely disagreed with Mama when it came to us kids, but this time he did.

"He's old enough. Tommy needs to understand why I asked Joe to throw away his dog tags if he's shot down and captured. He needs to understand who the Nazis are and what his brother is fighting for."

My mother shook her head but let Daddy continue.

"Tommy, concentration camps are places where the Germans send Jews and anyone else who speaks out against them. It's sort of like a prison and there are a lot of them springing up in countries that the Nazis have conquered. Conditions in the camps are very bad for the prisoners. Ben's father and thousands of other citizens are not criminals. They are people who are either politically opposed to the Nazis, or they are Jews."

He must have noticed my confusion.

"Tommy, try and understand. Every day, people just like you, me, Mama, and Joe are being arrested because they are Jewish, and for no other reason."

I was trying to picture a concentration camp in my mind. None of this made any sense.

Our festive homecoming for my brother had suddenly turned very somber. Joe reached across the table and tousled my hair. That seemed to break the tension. Selma, who had been standing by the door to the kitchen, left the room only to return a few minutes later with the promised pecan pie.

By the time we finished our dessert the conversation had returned to normal—telling stories and joking around with one another. I kept avoiding my mother's gaze, hoping she'd forget about sending me to bed. It was already late and since I had school the next day, I knew my time downstairs was limited. I was desperate for a few more moments with my brother. My mother must have known that too, because she excused us both and asked Joe if he wanted to go on upstairs with me. Once there, he picked me up over his head and tossed me onto my bed, just like he did when I was much younger.

"So, little brother, how's school? You still at the head of the class?"

I knew Ben Lowe was making better marks than me, but I didn't want to bring his name into the conversation yet again.

"I guess."

"And are you still reading all those classic tales Daddy's always ordering for you?"

"Nope. I'm done with those. I spend most of my time with those books over there."

That's when my brother noticed the pile of comic books on my nightstand, and the stacks of them on the floor, within easy reach of my bed. He started laughing.

"Well I guess one hero is as good as another."

"You're my real hero, Joe."

I had finally said it. It was my way of telling my brother how much I loved and needed him.

"Tommy, listen to me. I'm no hero. I'm doing a job, the same as all those other boys who enlisted along with me. I'm glad I'm not going to the Pacific, not that I wouldn't mind dropping a few bombs in Tojo's direction, but the Nazis are doing horrible things to our people, to Jews, and now that we're in the war they can't get out. They have nowhere to go.

"Before I left for training, I spent a couple of hours with Mr. Lowe. Did you know that he has traced his family's roots in Germany back to the 1600s? He showed me the family tree. That's much longer than our family has been in America. His grandfather was a clothing designer and founded one of the finest women's dress shops in Berlin. Before Hitler, he made clothing for some of the most important people in Berlin. In 1938, his store was Aryanized. Do you know what that means?"

When I shook my head, he continued.

"It means that the business he owned, the one that was in his family for over one hundred years, no longer belonged to him. It was taken away and given to a non-Jewish or Aryan owner. When they threw him out of the store, the only thing he was allowed to take was his umbrella. Can you understand what I'm saying? Think about Daddy's business, Stern's Department Store. Our family has owned that store for over a hundred years. How would you feel if it was just taken away?"

"But that's not right. No one can just go in and take someone else's business. Daddy would never allow that. He wouldn't. Besides, the police wouldn't let them. Daddy's good friends with most of the policemen and with the mayor too."

"But what if there was nothing Daddy could do about it? What if the police and the mayor were no longer interested in protecting us? What if they threatened to arrest our entire family if Daddy didn't give a non-Jewish family our business? What then? What do you think Daddy would do then?"

"I suppose he would give it to them," I answered quietly.

"And that, Tommy, is what Mr. Lowe was forced to do, and that is why he ended up getting his family out of Germany, and why a once very rich man is working as a tailor in Daddy's store."

We were both so consumed by our conversation that we didn't hear the quiet patter of our mother's footsteps as she entered the room.

"I think it's time for bed. What do you think, Tommy?"

"Okay," I said.

I don't know who was more shocked, my mother or Joe. I never agreed to go to bed without begging for another few minutes. But that night, I couldn't wait to crawl under the covers. I wanted Joe to stop talking about the Lowes and what had happened to them. The other kids were still making fun of Ben, and I had yet to stick up for him. I had not done the one thing I knew my brother expected of me. Joe was putting his life on the line to save families like the Lowes and even though I was not actually joining in, when my friends mocked Ben's accent or pushed him around on the playground, I never stopped them. Once, I even saw him looking at me, begging me, asking, *Why don't you help me?* I turned away.

For the rest of his stay Joe never said another word about the Lowe family. Over the next few days we had fun the way we used to. We tossed the football around in the yard and played checkers and Monopoly for hours on end. I tried to ignore the gnawing in my stomach that told me I had failed my big brother, that I was a disappointment. I promised myself that I would do better, that I would find a way to make him proud of me.

# 7

# 1968

THE LITTLE DINER was known for its deep-dish apple pie, and once we were seated we both ordered slices. I was nervous and kept fiddling with the tabletop jukebox while Karin was busy picking at her pie. I had yet to see her take a bite. I dropped in a quarter and waited for Nat King Cole's "Mona Lisa" to come on. The year we graduated it was at the top of the charts, and we both had loved that song. I wondered if she remembered.

"I like your choice in music."

She smiled when the juke came on, and seeing her dimples made me grin right back. I knew I was staring, but I couldn't help myself. Except for a few more laugh lines around her eyes and a small scar on her chin she looked exactly the same.

"You look good," I said. "You haven't changed at all."

"Thanks, you either—that is, except for the clothes. You look very professional. Work must be good. You're a lawyer, right?"

"Yes, a defense attorney. My first job after finishing law school was with the prosecutor's office, but after several years of barely making a living, I switched camps. At times my clients are a little unsavory, but whenever I feel guilty I remind myself that everyone is entitled to a proper defense."

That was awkward. *Why did I feel the need to explain myself?*

"You were wearing a suit the last time I saw you too."

"I was?"

"Yes, you were."

"My father's funeral?" I said.

She nodded.

"I went. Did you know that?"

I did know. I'd seen her seated in the back of the synagogue.

"I thought about speaking to you then, but we had already stopped writing to each other, and I didn't want to make the day any more complicated for you."

"You wouldn't have, and thank you for coming."

I had actually tried to get her attention, but she was gone before I could make it over to her.

"I don't see a ring. I heard you were married," she said.

"I was, but we divorced a couple of years ago."

"Oh, I'm sorry to hear that."

"Don't be. It was a good decision for both of us. We're still friends. How 'bout you? I don't see a ring on your finger either."

Was that relief I felt?

"No, almost once, but I came to my senses. I do not think I am cut out for marriage."

I didn't know what to make of that comment. The conversation was getting uncomfortable, and I still didn't know why she had asked me to come to Huntsville. I was feeling unnerved by all the small talk and was about to move the conversation in another direction when she started up with the questions again.

"And your mother? How is she?"

"Good. She has a lot of family in Atlanta. They keep her busy. Are your parents still here, in Huntsville?"

"No, Mama passed away about five years ago and Papa died two years later."

"I'm sorry to hear that. What kept you here then? I'm a little surprised you never moved away."

"I left for a while, did that big city thing up in Chicago, but I missed life where people actually said hello to me when I walked down the street. When my parents died, I used some of what they left me to open a small bookshop.

It's actually not far from here. If you have time you should stop by and give me a little business," she said smiling.

I took a large gulp of the now lukewarm coffee and broke into a froglike croak as the liquid began sloshing down the wrong pipe. Reacting to the tears dripping down my face and my inability to speak Karin jumped out of the booth and began pounding on my back with both fists.

"I'm okay." I finally managed to say. "Are you taking boxing lessons or something? I think you may have broken a rib."

Reseated, Karin looked more bemused than amused.

"I really was simply suggesting you might want to buy a book when I asked you to stop by," she said. "I hope you weren't imagining some other kind of offer."

"No of course not. The coffee was hotter than I expected."

"Hmmm, if you say so."

I could feel the flush and envisioned the redness creep up from my neck, ears and onto my face.

"You haven't asked about Erich," she said.

The change of subject startled me. My head was already spinning and now she was wondering why I hadn't inquired about her brother, the boy who made a career out of taunting and bullying my best friend.

Before I could summon up a response, Karin continued.

"Erich moved back to Germany after college. That was his dream. He was quickly disillusioned. Germany was looking toward the future, not the past. I suppose he was hoping to find some vestige of the glorious Third Reich he had romanticized. Instead, he found a city in ruins and discovered that his old Hitler Youth friends, as well as everyone else, were denying that they were ever Nazis at all. Imagine, within the entire postwar German population it was hard to find anyone who didn't say they were coerced to join the party. So once he realized that the old Germany was gone he immigrated to Argentina. Many diehards, like my brother, moved there after the war. Now he is back here."

I should have sounded more interested. I could tell Karin expected me to ask why he returned to the city he'd never considered home, but I didn't.

"Karin, it's been great catching up, but I don't live around the corner. You really need to clue me in. Why did you ask Cole to get me up here, and what is suddenly so important about something that happened eighteen years ago? Cole said there was a witness."

"Erich's ill. He has cancer."

That's not what I asked her, but I was surprised by the news. We were all only thirty-six. I had never liked Erich, but I didn't wish cancer on anyone. Karin was being evasive, and I still had no clue why I was sitting across from her. Now that we had reminisced, I was ready to hear what she had to say about Ben's suicide.

"Last year he was diagnosed with leukemia and for whatever reason he moved back to Huntsville. Is it not ironic that someone with pure Aryan blood is now suffering from a disease of the same? Amusing, no?"

At the time I thought it was a strange comment, but I let it go to keep the conversation moving.

"He rented a house not too far from me," she continued. I am the only family he has left, and I suppose he thought I would take pity on him."

"And have you? Do you see him?"

"Occasionally, I make him some dinner. I don't stay. We have nothing to talk about. Mostly, he relies on the kindness of my parents' old friends."

"How sick is he?"

"Not too bad yet, but according to him, he will not be getting better."

"I'm sorry to hear that."

Surprisingly, I really was. He was Karin's twin after all, and the only family she had left.

"Karin, I hate to keep pressing, but I need to start heading back. I'm up to my neck in work."

"I'm getting to that. It's hard."

I waited, perplexed by her indecision.

"Karin, what's going on?"

# 8

# 1942

TWO DAYS AFTER Joe left to rejoin his group, I walked over to the Lowes and knocked on their door. It was a Sunday afternoon, and once again Ben hadn't shown up at the synagogue for school. Mr. Arnstein had stopped calling his name, and no one even wondered where he was or asked what had happened to him. Ben only lived on the next block, but the house was nowhere as nice as ours. It was smaller and badly in need of some paint. The front yard, though, was well kept and there was a beautiful garden with roses creeping onto the front porch. Someone had definitely been putting some time into the yard. As I approached their door, I thought again about what the Lowe family had lost in Germany and I felt a renewed guilt for ignoring the new boy for so long.

The doorbell wasn't working so I knocked.

"*Wer ist da?*"

It was a female voice, and I assumed she was Ben's mother calling out from behind the still-closed door.

"It's Tommy Stern."

The door cracked open.

"*Ja, Tommy. Was ist falsch?*"

"Huh?"

When she saw the look on my face, she smiled.

"Please forgive. I forget and speak German. Is something wrong?"

"No, nothing's wrong. I'm wondering if Ben is home."

"*Ja,*" she answered.

Just then the door swung open wider, and Ben skirted around his mother to face me. His knobby knees peaked out from those ridiculous leather shorts that were held up with flowery suspenders. *At least he has stopped wearing them in public,* I thought.

"What do you want?" he asked in English almost as good as mine. Joe was right. He had already lost most of his accent.

"I thought maybe you might want to do something today?"

"Why? I've been living here for almost a year, and this is the first time you've bothered to say anything to me. Why today?"

I didn't know what to say. I couldn't tell him that my brother had made me feel ashamed of my past indifference to him, that I had finally tried to put myself in his shoes, so I just shrugged and stood there saying nothing at all.

"Okay, come on in."

I walked through a room filled with old-world paintings and porcelains— priceless objects I didn't appreciate at the time. Ben would later tell me that only one container holding some of the family's possessions, including the art, had made it out of the port of Bremerhaven before it was bombed. They had lost everything else. Ben's mother had held on to the keys, the ones that locked the drawers of the furniture that had never arrived. I imagined that the keys were another way to remember what the family had lost.

When I finally reached Ben's room I was surprised by its orderliness. It was a small space, but everything was in its proper place. There was a single bed, made up neatly, with a blue slightly-worn chenille bedspread. Next to the bed was a small nightstand piled high with some of the same comic books I was reading. Across from the bed, and in front of the room's only window, was a wooden desk covered in sketches. No, not just sketches but drawings of a strange and wonderful superhero, in my mind a figure even more amazing than those drawn by some of the comic book greats like Jack Kirby and Joe Simon, the creators of Captain America, my all-time favorite.

Ben was an artist, a good one. If he had lived past his eighteenth birthday, he would have probably become a great one.

"You drew these?" I asked.

He nodded.

"Can I look through them?"

He nodded again. I spent the next thirty minutes or so looking at the drawings. Ben had created a new superhero named Stark, who roamed the streets of German cities in the dark of night trying to help Jews escape to freedom. His alter ego was the blond-haired, blue-eyed Kurt Bahn who, as a member of the Nazi Party, secretly sabotaged and thwarted the evil plans of the Nazis. I later learned that *Stark* was the German word for strong. Unlike some of the most popular superheroes, Stark exuded not only strength but also compassion. While Batman hid behind a mask and Superman's stony expression never seemed to change, Stark's eyes revealed what he was feeling. His blue and white costume consisted of the requisite superhero tights, cape, and boots, but nothing else identified him as the protector of Jewish victims, other than the small metal Star of David on his belt. Whenever Stark touched the star he and all the people he was saving could disappear and be transported to safety. As Bahn, Ben's creation wore the high jackboots and black uniform of a member of the SS, its cuffs and collar covered in Death's Head insignia and swastikas.

The stories that accompanied the earliest illustrations were written in German, and over my next several visits to the Lowes' home Ben translated them for me. Stark was, of course, fighting the Nazis, but for me his exploits became far more realistic than those of Captain America. Ben wasn't writing and drawing for an American public who, in the late 1930s and early 1940s, were still, for the most part, unconcerned or unaware of the plight of the Jews. He was doing this for himself. I was the first person with whom he had ever shared his stories. Stark and his alter ego Kurt not only fought Hitler and his henchmen, they also tried to save their victims. In each episode Kurt/Stark barely escaped being discovered by the Gestapo or by a member of the SS as he spirited Jews to safety. Ben explained that the *Schutzstaffel* or SS was an elite paramilitary group. A recruit had to prove he had no Jewish ancestry. I quickly became immersed in the exciting escapades of this strange and new superhero. Somehow, Kurt always found ways to fool the Nazis and avoid being discovered. As the story developed, I learned that Kurt had two Jewish grandparents but was able to hide his background by forging his *Ariernachweis*, or Aryan certificate, to prove his racial purity.

Over the next several weeks I ended up in Ben's bedroom every day after school. He continued to draw, and I began to help him write and develop new and intricate storylines. We also talked about our lives. I spoke a lot about my brother, and he told me about his boyhood in Germany—his happy memories interspersed with the gruesome details of life under the Nazis.

"You were really kicked out of school?" I asked.

"Yes. One day the head of school came in and asked all the Jewish children to step to the front of the class. Months before, we had all been told to move to the back row, so I knew it was not for something good we had done. No one expected an award. He then announced that we would no longer be attending school with our Aryan classmates. We were compared to rats, vermin who were contaminating the purity of the air the other students were breathing in. We were then told to pick up our belongings and that was that. Kaput. It was over.

"In a matter of minutes, I was no longer welcome at the school I had attended since kindergarten. I didn't understand what was happening. I had what I thought was a special bond with my teacher that year. She knew that I liked to draw and often asked to see some of my artwork when she thought we were out of earshot of anyone who might report us. When we were told to leave, I tried to get her attention, but she had already turned away."

He shrugged, but I couldn't imagine how hurt he must have been.

"I was glad to leave. By 1938, no one paid any attention to me or to the other Jewish students anyway. There were only five of us in the classroom, and once we had been moved to the last row, we had become invisible. There, but not seen. I had stopped raising my hand. It was pointless."

"Didn't any of your friends say or do anything?"

After I asked the question, I could feel myself turning crimson red. I thought about the similarity of my own actions, of my prolonged reticence to stick up for Ben. Ben may have connected the dots, but he didn't say anything.

"No, not then, but later that same day, Friedrich, a boy I had known most of my life, came over. It was obvious he had been in a fight. When I asked him what had happened he wouldn't tell me, but I knew he had stood up for me, for all of us, with some of the other students, but all it got him was a black eye and a bloody nose. Most of the boys in the class were already members of the *Deutsches Jungvolk* and were glad to be rid of us. Friedrich had also been pressured to join and knew he would not be able to avoid membership for too much longer."

"*Deutsches* what?" I asked.

"Yes, a crazy sort of club for boys. Younger children joined the *Deutsches Jungvolk*. Later, once they turned thirteen, they moved on to a Hitler Youth chapter."

He must have noticed the blank look on my face.

"Hitler Youth, something like your Boy Scouts; only the members are taught to hate Jews and love Hitler while they are hiking and building campfires."

"What happened to Friedrich?"

"He stopped coming over. I told him to. What good would it have done? He would have kept being hit, and we were already making plans to get out. I never saw him again. Perhaps, someday, I will try and find him."

Two weeks later, after I started visiting Ben, he came back to Sunday school. At least at the synagogue, with a bunch of other Jewish kids, he stopped feeling like an outsider. I made sure I saved him a seat, and before too long the other boys were talking to him too. It wasn't quite as simple at our public school.

Even though Ben despised peanut butter and jelly sandwiches he started bringing them to lunch every day. I suppose it helped some. Ben's accent was now almost nonexistent, but whenever he chose the wrong word or happened to use a German expression some of the kids still made fun of him. They never understood that the Nazis were his enemy too. They thought of him as German, and since there were a lot of kids with brothers like mine, fighting over in Europe, they thought that they should fight the one German going to school with them.

I tried explaining that even though Ben was German he hated the Nazis more than they did. I started defending him, even to the point of giving and receiving a few bloody noses and black eyes. I repeated all the reasons why the Lowe family had left Germany and moved to the United States. By the end of that year, not all but enough of them got it.

# 9

# 1968

KARIN WAS NOW on her third cup of coffee, and she still hadn't said anything that I already didn't know.

"Tommy, remember when we first met?"

"Yes, of course I do.

She smiled.

"How old were we? Seventeen, eighteen?"

"Yeah," I answered. "That's about right. We were beginning our senior year in high school."

"And I was one of the new students and still could not speak English very well."

Now it was my turn to smile. I remembered how confused she looked when the bell rang at the end of the day, and I told her it was time to blow this popsicle stand. On the way out of class, I explained that it was just an expression, and no there really wasn't a popsicle-stand at school. I was still caught up in the sweet innocence of our shared past when she spoke again.

"You sat next to me in homeroom, and Ben, he sat on the other side of you," she continued. "For the longest time, neither one of you spoke to me."

"I remember."

"Ben wouldn't even look in my direction. His hatred was palpable; I could actually feel it."

"Well, in his defense, I think the appearance of five Germans marching into our class, kids whose fathers were either Nazis themselves or worked for the greater good of Germany, was slightly unsettling to a kid whose entire extended family was murdered."

Immediately, the tears began to well up in her eyes, and I was overcome by guilt.

"I'm sorry," I said. "I shouldn't have said that."

"And I'm sorry I asked you to drive up. It was a mistake—I can see that now."

"A mistake? Cole said there was a witness, that someone had some information about Ben's suicide. That's why I came. If you wanted to see me, you could have just called and asked."

Her smile was sorrowful, and I knew how absurd I sounded. I had walked away from her without so much as a goodbye, and we hadn't spoken in eighteen years.

"I didn't think you'd come and with Erich sick, I wanted to reach out to try and make things right. I always hated the way my brother treated Ben and I wanted to apologize for him."

"You have nothing to apologize for. You weren't anything like your brother."

"Perhaps, but Erich is my twin and his treatment of Ben has always weighed heavily on my conscience."

"How long does Erich have?"

I'm not really certain. He doesn't confide in me."

I thought about saying I was sorry. But I couldn't, because I wasn't.

I despised Erich Angel. He enjoyed taunting Ben and worked hard to sabotage the life he had forged for himself with the other guys in the class. To Erich's surprise they never took to him, and besides, by the time we were seniors, most of the kids sincerely liked Ben. Erich was an odd duck, and I doubted whether time had changed him for the better.

"Ben used to say that there was no way he was going to let that little Nazi get under his skin."

Karin paled. That was the second time in a matter of minutes that I had called her brother a Nazi.

I had a vivid memory of Erich, the angry boy whose hate-filled eyes and clenched fists said it all.

"I know how he acted. I was there too, remember," said Karin.

Neither of us moved. Minutes later when the waitress brought our check we were still sitting looking at our plates, at the counter, at the other customers anywhere but at each other.

"He detested both of you, but for some reason he really had it in for Ben," she said. "He was obsessed with his hatred for him. He'd been indoctrinated at such a young age."

"Karin, you don't need to defend him, at least not to me. I never blamed you for the way Erich behaved."

I suddenly had the urge to reach for her hand. I forced myself not to. I was afraid she'd get the wrong idea.

"Are you driving back to Atlanta this afternoon?"

"Probably. I have a couple stops to make first and then I guess I'll be on my way. And Karin, I'm glad I came. It's been nice catching up."

I really meant it. Truth be told, I could have sat there for the rest of the day. Later, I realized I should have. Instead I placed my hand on her shoulder, gave it a gentle squeeze and left her sitting in the booth. I wanted to look back, to see her once more, but I forced myself to keep walking. All these years later and she still had the same effect on me. I felt like I was back in high school. My heart was pounding and I felt stirrings for her that I thought were long gone. Seeing her reminded me of how much I had once loved her.

# 10

---

# 1945

NEW YEAR'S DAY came and went like all of the others before it. Mama served up her traditional platter of black-eyed peas, meant to bring our family luck, and Daddy raised his glass to ask for good health and happiness for our family and friends. Ever since the attack on Pearl Harbor, he also included prayers for Joe and all the American troops who we hoped would soon be coming home. I was thirteen, and I had finally accepted that I would never be old enough to get into the fight. Besides, by war's end, it had lost some of the glamour that I once attached to it.

After Joe left, I started reading the newspapers and listening to war updates on the radio. When your brother was risking his life each and every day, you grew up fast. Daddy subscribed to the *Southern Israelite*. It was published in Atlanta but covered Jewish life in the entire Southeast. If you looked deep enough and read the back pages, you could find articles hidden away between the advertisements and social columns about what was going on in cities with foreign-sounding names like Lodz, Warsaw, Vilna, and Bialystok. It wasn't hard to see that what was happening to the Jews of Europe was becoming more and more horrifying. I wondered if Ben was reading the same articles. Did he feel the same ominous forebodings of news that was yet to come as I did?

What I didn't know was where my brother was. We hadn't heard from Joe in over a month, but in my young mind I decided that if he had made it that far nothing would stop him from coming home. Besides, Veda was still assuring me that all was okay with my brother even though, several weeks earlier, we were all sobered by the news of German victories in their last major offensive in the densely-wooded Wallonia region in Belgium. The Battle of the Bulge was one of the fiercest battles of World War II and resulted in about seventy-five thousand American casualties, but by the end of January the Germans had been pushed back and the Allies were victorious.

The war and constant worry about Joe had aged my parents. There was a lot less laughter going on in my house and less at Ben's. They already knew that Ben's grandparents had died, but for a while, they had remained hopeful about some of the others, even though they hadn't heard from any other relatives in over three years. As news about the liberation of concentration camps began to filter in, Ben became more convinced that they were all gone.

"My parents can't accept that all our family is dead," Ben said. "They refuse to believe it, but I do."

It was an unusually warm Saturday in January, and Daddy said I should skip work at the store and play some ball. Ben and I were walking toward the field to meet up with friends from school. I wasn't expecting to talk about his family. It was a painful subject for him to discuss, and he rarely brought it up.

"Ben, maybe your parents are right. Just because your relatives haven't been heard from doesn't mean they're all dead. No one's been getting any mail from folks over there. You know that."

"No, they're dead. I know it. I can feel it. My father has a younger brother. He kept begging Bernhard to take his family and leave while there was still time, but he was a doctor and couldn't bring himself to abandon his patients. He and his wife had a little boy. His name was Walter. The last time I saw him he was only two-years-old."

"I'm sure he's okay. No one would kill a two-year-old."

Ben shook his head and just kept walking. I suspected he thought I just didn't know what was going on over there. He would have been surprised by how much I had read about Nazi atrocities, but I was trying to make him feel better. I already knew that the Nazis were indiscriminate killers. If you were wearing a yellow star on your clothing, it didn't matter what age you were.

I had nothing else to offer him, and it turned out he was right. One year after the war ended, Ben's father got a letter from the International Red Cross. Their tracing service helped families like the Lowes locate relatives. Most of Ben's relatives had been sent on a train east to a place called Auschwitz-Birkenau, an extermination camp in Poland, where they were murdered along with over one million others. They were still waiting to hear about the fate of Mr. Lowe's brother and his wife and son. They were not optimistic.

Years later, I often thought that maybe Ben had a premonition, that somehow he knew that I too was about to be pulled into the abyss. But on that morning, we continued on to the ball field and chose up sides like we always did. I made sure Ben was picked for my team. If I wasn't the captain, he was usually the last one standing, along with Lester Bubba Phelps, who was over two hundred and fifty pounds and could barely round the bases.

Even though I had managed to shove most of my childhood memories into the deepest crevices of my mind, there was nothing about that day I don't remember. I pitched great and only gave up one run. I also cracked a game-winning double in the bottom of the ninth. The excitement of the win left me feeling euphoric. Even Ben's earlier gloom-and-doom pronouncements could not bring me down. Besides, the war was winding down, Joe would soon be home, and my teammates were slapping me on my back and singing my praises. My house was closest to the park, and I asked Ben if he wanted to come in for a while. I'd been working on a new storyline for *Stark* and wanted to run it by him. When I walked in, I was surprised to see Daddy sitting on the couch staring into space. He was never home on a Saturday. We were in the room before he noticed that Ben had followed me in.

"Daddy, why are you home?"

"Tommy, come sit with me."

He patted the spot next to him on the sofa.

It was then that I saw the tears in Daddy's eyes. Before he even said the words, I knew. My brother was never coming back. I couldn't even ask what happened. I didn't care. I was thirteen-years-old, and I climbed onto my Daddy's lap and let him hold me while I cried for the brother I was never going to see again. He kept holding me until my sobs had quieted and I was finally able to speak.

"Where's Mama?" I asked.

"She's lying down. Mama's taking this very hard and we're going to have to be strong for her. We're going to have to try real hard to make her feel better. Do you think you can summon up the courage to do that, Tommy?"

I thought about lying. I knew what Daddy wanted to hear.

"I don't know, Daddy. I think I'm gonna miss Joe just as much as Mama will."

I could tell he understood my answer, because he hugged me even tighter.

Daddy and I both heard Mama calling out in her sleep, and Daddy said he needed to go to her. Once he left, I realized that Ben was still standing there. Tears were streaming down his face too. He took Daddy's vacated place on the sofa. For the next few minutes, we just sat there. Ben didn't need to say anything. I knew he understood.

"Do you want to work on the comic book?" he finally asked.

"Yeah, but first I need to do one other thing."

I walked over to my bed and pulled the box containing Veda The Magic Answer Man from beneath it. Ben watched as I ripped the contents to shreds, walked to the kitchen and threw the whole thing into the trash. He never said a word.

Stark would become my avenger. Ben would draw him, and I would create the words so Ben's superhero could kill every single Nazi remaining in Germany.

# 11

# 1968

MY ORIGINAL PLANS hadn't included a stop to see Alvin Stern, my cousin and my only family member still living in Huntsville. I didn't think he would find out I was in town, but after using a visit to him as an excuse to leave Karin, I felt obliged to see him. He was my first cousin and twenty years older than I. His mama and my daddy were brother and sister. We were never close.

After I called, I felt even guiltier. He sounded eager to see me. I didn't need directions. He still lived in the same old, blue-frame house in the middle of the downtown that he had grown up in. When I pulled into his driveway I spotted him sitting on the front porch swing waiting for me.

I hadn't seen him in years and I was startled by his appearance. His hair had thinned in all the wrong places, and what was left was mostly gray and combed over in an unsuccessful attempt to hide the bald spots. He was no longer the gangly older cousin of my youth, but then he smiled, suddenly revealing the man I remembered. Soon we were embracing, and he was slapping me on the back telling me how great it was to see me.

"Tommy, it's so good of you to come by. I heard you were visiting."

I had forgotten how quickly news traveled in a small town, not that Huntsville was that small anymore.

"I should have called, but it was a last-minute trip. I didn't know myself until yesterday."

"No worries. I'm retired now, and my schedule is wide open," he said.

He was chuckling, and I imagined him saying that line often.

"Come on in. I made us some lunch."

As soon as I stepped through the front door, I was thrown back into the 1950s. Al had not purchased a new piece of furniture in all that time. His mama's white club chairs were now more of a tawny shade of yellow, but they were still protected by zippered plastic slipcovers that were brittle to the touch. I took a seat on the sofa.

"Tommy, you look great. You haven't aged at all. You're still that good-looking kid that used to come over to play checkers with me."

Another memory resurfaced.

"I didn't know you retired."

"Yep, six months ago, and now I'm wondering why. I'm constantly looking for things to do. I'm thinking of taking up tennis or golf. What do you think?"

The table had been set, and I watched as he threw open the door of the fridge to reveal a mound of cold cuts and an enormous bowl of coleslaw. The bread was already on the platter and waiting for us on the table.

"Golf," I answered. "It takes up more time."

"Good idea."

I looked again at the table.

"How many people were you expecting?"

"I guess I overdid it. It's been a while since I had company. I'm out of practice."

Al had been married a short time and then divorced. I hoped I wasn't looking into a mirror and seeing my own future.

As soon as we sat down, he started giving me updates about some of the people with whom I had grown up, as well as some of Mama and Daddy's old friends. A few of them were now deceased.

"I suppose you know," I said, "that Ben's mama and daddy moved to New York after…"

"Yeah, I had heard that," he said.

I had a twinge of guilt. I hadn't called them in a while.

"Most of the German families are still here, although a few got jobs at NASA and moved to Florida or Houston."

"Karin's still here," I said.

"Yeah, I know. I see her around. She owns the Book Nook. It's a little shop on Franklin Street. I stop in every once in a while. She carries all the new stuff and some collectible first editions. I seem to remember that you were head over heels for that girl. Thought you might have even ended up getting married."

"You knew we were together? I thought we did a pretty good job at keeping our relationship a secret."

"Your mama told me after your daddy died. She knew you liked that girl. She never did tell your daddy. She was a tad more forgiving than him, and she knew he would have tried to put a stop to it."

"Yeah, I always knew he wouldn't have approved. You know, because of what happened to Joe."

"Elizabeth, she was never the same after that."

"No, none of us were. It was like our whole family went into the grave with him."

For the next several minutes we ate in silence.

"You staying the night?" he finally asked. "I made up the guest room."

"Sure."

I hadn't planned on it, but I suddenly realized I actually wanted to.

"I wasn't sure how long I would be here so I canceled tomorrow's appointments anyway."

"You still defending criminals?" Al said with a smile.

"Only the innocent ones."

I immediately thought back to my last case. The guy was guilty as sin, but I managed to get him off with a slap on the wrist.

"I think I'm going to drive over to the cemetery and spend some time with Daddy and Joe," I said. "I'd like to say a few words to Ben too. It's been a long while since I've been over there. Do you want to come along?"

"Nah, you go on. I'll see you later."
"Yep, see you later, and thanks for lunch."

§

The drive over to Maple Hill Cemetery took under ten minutes. I parked as close to the Jewish section as I could get. Maple Hill was Huntsville's community cemetery and everyone found a permanent home there eventually. The Jewish section had been consecrated in the 1870s, and I found a parking spot as near to my father's grave as possible. The sky was overcast and was a fitting setting for this mournful walk down memory lane. The path I took was akin to a macabre reunion of sorts. I recognized many of the names. Some of the earliest graves belonged to my forebears, and many of the later ones were friends of my grandparents or parents, whom I recalled from my youth. They all reminded me of the impact that the small, tightly-knit Jewish community had on Huntsville. I had forgotten how imbedded they were in the growth and development of my childhood home.

When I finally reached my father's grave, I noticed a small stone on the top of his marker. Someone else had been by to pay their respects and had left a memento of their visit. I assumed it was Al.

I stood before my father's grave for several minutes and found myself smiling at the memories of the person he was before Joe died, and not the diminished, mostly angry man he became in the years that followed. Daddy had a massive coronary two days after his fifty-second birthday. He died all alone in the stockroom of the store he loved. The doctor said it was sudden, but I knew differently. His heart problems started on the day the "*I regret to inform you*" telegram was delivered into his hands. My brother's grave was on a grassy hillock behind that of my father's, and I walked over to it next. There was a small stone on top of it as well. I still missed him. Some pain never goes away. It had lessened, but was always there, simmering, just below the surface. It never took much for the grief to come raging back. Anniversary days were especially hard. I always spent his birthdays with my mother. We would both have one too many cocktails in a futile attempt to ease each other's sadness. I often thought about the man Joe would have grown into if he had been given the chance. There was no doubt, at least in my mind, that he would have been accomplished in whatever field he chose. Standing by his grave I envisioned his dismay at finding out that his little brother was defending criminals, and I was ashamed that I probably hadn't lived up to the man he thought I would become. When the war ended his remains were interred in an American cemetery in Belgium. A few years later my folks arranged for him to come back home. They wanted him buried in southern soil.

As I stood in the cemetery, my mind wandered back to those days just after we got the news. My mother could barely stand up at the memorial service and had to be supported by Daddy. It was unusually hot, and someone held a big black umbrella over Mama's head to block out the sun. Our Atlanta relatives had arrived the morning of the funeral, and after the service, the house was filled to capacity with aunts, uncles, cousins, and neighbors. Ben and his parents were there too. Ben had been given permission to spend the next couple of nights at my house, and that helped to keep me occupied. I hated leaving the confines of my bedroom. Every time I emerged from its quiet I stood in the kitchen with Selma and peered out into the dining room watching as people stood around eating, talking to one another, or maybe even laughing at something someone had said. I couldn't imagine finding anything funny ever again.

§

The wind had picked up, and I sensed that the darkening skies were keeping pace with my mood. I scoured the ground, searching for just the right stone and placed it atop Joe's headstone next to the one that was already there. I was making my way over to Ben's grave, to apologize in person for not understanding his despair or sensing his depression, when I saw Karin sitting on a bench close by. Once again, my heart began to pound, and I chastised myself for my lack of self-control and my latent teenage hormones that seemed to be resurfacing. I was at a cemetery, for God's sake. I stood there for several minutes watching her and wishing we could roll back the clock.

"Karin, are you stalking me? Should I be worried?" I said, as I finally approached.

She smiled.

"Yes, I guess I am. I went over to Al's, and he told me you were on your way to the cemetery. I figured it would only be a matter of time before you made your way to Ben's grave. I come here often. I like the quiet. It allows me a chance to think."

She moved over to give me room to sit next to her.

"Ben was a special person. I want him to know that I still think about him," she said.

"You still haven't said why you're here, now, today."

"I needed to see you again. Yesterday, in the coffee shop, I lost my nerve."

"About what? I'm confused. You said your brother was dying and you wanted to make amends for the sins of his past. Was there something else? Something more about why Ben committed suicide? Because for the life of me, I've never really understood why."

"A couple of weeks ago I found something. I thought about calling you immediately, but then I couldn't decide if I had the right to pull you back, to make you relive the worst time of our lives. I was going to give it to you at the coffee shop, but like I said, I lost my nerve. Seeing you stirred up a lot of old emotions, ones that I thought I had dealt with long ago, but apparently, I haven't."

"I know, and I'm sorry. I haven't dealt with all my stuff about Ben either."

"Don't apologize. I get it."

It seemed that apologizing to each other was all we were doing. I was about to ask what she had found when she reached into her satchel and pulled out an old dog-eared spiral notebook. I hadn't seen one of those in years. It was the kind with the big blue horse on the front cover. I used to collect the coupons that were in the back. Kids could redeem them for prizes and I had always hoped to save enough for a bicycle. It never happened.

"What's that?" I asked.

"It belonged to Erich. I was going through some of our old trunks, up in the attic, and I found it. I thought about destroying it, but in the end I couldn't. That's when I asked Cole to help me get you up here. He did it as a favor to me. He thinks I just want to see you again, and he was happy to help play matchmaker."

I reached out to take the notebook, and she immediately pulled it back and clenched it against her chest.

"I assume you've read it."

She nodded and continued.

"There are one or two entries that have led me to believe that maybe Ben's death wasn't an accident. I've penciled in the translations wherever Erich couldn't express himself in English and reverted back to German."

I felt like I was going to be sick. I reached for the notebook again. This time she handed it to me and walked back to her car.

# 12

# 1949

IN THE FOUR years that had passed since the Enola Gay had dropped its payload on the city of Hiroshima, finally forcing the Japanese to surrender, I had come a long way from the unaware little boy who had clamored for a war he didn't understand. Losing Joe was akin to losing a limb. Our family was no longer complete, but sometimes I still felt his presence. My parents were alive but not really living, and their melancholy was contagious. After we were notified of Joe's death, I kept imagining his final moments. I had a hard time sleeping. It was not unusual for me to meet one or both of my parents in the kitchen in the middle of the night. We all needed a respite from the nightmares that were keeping us awake. Over time, our midnight meetings happened less often, and once in a while we managed to sit down for dinner as a family, like we used to. I dreaded those rare attempts by my parents to resurrect what we had, because it was during those times when I felt most adrift. Joe, not me, had been the linchpin that had held us all together. I missed the spontaneous laughter in our home, the banter that my brother used to generate, but at least my mother had stopped crying herself to sleep.

We had experienced a monumental loss, but somehow, we were quietly moving forward. I was still working at Stern's and I had finally left the safety of the stockroom for the sales floor. I still read often, played ball, and hung out with my friends, but I had matured into an observer of some of the inequities that existed in Huntsville, the hometown that I'd once considered perfect in every way. The war and the persecution and murder of so many innocents had changed me in ways I had not thought possible. I was no longer unmindful to the signs that dotted the landscape of our town, specifying where our Negro citizens could drink, eat, or even try on clothes. Even Stern's had separate dressing rooms marked "White" and "Colored," and I was ashamed that I had ignored the obvious affront to our Negro customers for so long. When I asked Daddy about it, he said it couldn't be helped. If everyone could use the same one, his white customers would stop coming in. He wished it were different, but that's just the way things were down south, and there was nothing he or anybody else could do about it. I doubted that, but I didn't want to question my own father's passivity. Every time I looked at Selma's kind, giving face or remembered the tender touch of her hands when she bandaged one of my skinned knees, I felt guilty. Integration was still years away, and even returning Negro soldiers, men who had fought for their country, my country, were not able to drink out of the same water fountain as I.

There was one standout case that made the papers. A Negro soldier, a sergeant who had returned to his native Birmingham, just a stone's throw from Huntsville, was arrested for accidentally touching a white woman when she stopped to ask him for directions. He had a trial, and, by some miracle, he even had a good attorney who fought hard in his defense, but the all-white jury convicted him for assault anyway. He was sent away to break rocks for the state of Alabama for five long hard years. He paid dearly for the unforgivable crime of black skin touching that of a white woman.

All this had occurred during the time of my life when I still believed that I could change the world. I was optimistic about my future, and Ben and I would often discuss the hopes and dreams we had for the rest of our lives. Ben, of course, wanted to continue drawing and envisioned himself working for one of the big comic book companies. I knew I wanted to study law and perhaps do work for the Justice Department. One day, I wanted to look Selma in the face and not be ashamed.

While I studied, hung out with friends, and pondered upon where I would be in the next few years, life in Huntsville continued to move at an unremarkable pace. Daddy assumed I would follow in the family tradition and go to the University of Alabama, but lately I'd been thinking of making a change, like maybe going up north to school to get out of the South and the segregated community I was living in. I had done well in school and felt I had the grades to go just about anywhere.

I knew Ben would not be staying in Alabama or anywhere else below the Mason-Dixon Line. He was destined to do great things with his artwork and was applying to multiple agencies and to universities for scholarships. Even with aid, he needed to supplement what his parents could provide, so my father offered him a job at Stern's. Ben and I were old enough to wait on customers, and we both worked alongside our longtime saleslady, Miss Ella Mae Hobbs, afterschool, on weekends, and during breaks.

I was in my junior year of high school when my life was upended once again by events over which I had no control. When Ben rushed into the store waving the local newspaper in front of me, in early November of 1949, I had no ominous premonition that once I read the one-column article held out to me the trajectory of my life would be dramatically altered and reset.

Ben was enraged.

"Here, read this," Ben demanded.

He shoved the paper into my hands.

*Fort Bliss, Texas Rocket Office to Be Moved to Redstone Arsenal: Involves about 900 Civilians and Soldiers; 100 German Scientists among Those Who Will be Transferred Here.*

"What the hell," I said. I stormed over to Daddy to show him.

He wasn't surprised.

"Daddy, you knew?"

Both Ben and I looked at him, waiting for an answer.

"Yes, boys, for a while now. Hadn't quite figured out how to tell either one of you."

"Does Mama know?"

"Yes, I told her this morning and she's sick about it. Couldn't get out of bed. The Simpsons and the Wilsons lost sons in the war too and they aren't too happy about it either."

"How can this be happening?" I asked.

He then told us that because he was on the Chamber of Commerce, he had known since the previous November that they were coming.

"I couldn't bring myself to tell you or your mother either. She's more than a little angry with me. Thinks I could have done something about it. Believe me, I tried, but Senator Sparkman has been lobbying Congress since the end of the war for a way to keep the Arsenal open and this is what we ended up with— Nazis. The town's gone mad. Some folks actually seem excited. They have short memories. Maybe some of them need to be reminded about what those bastards did to our boys."

Daddy slammed shut the ledger book he had been working on and walked off the sales floor, leaving Ben and me to consider the implications of what was about to happen to our town.

"Maybe they'll only be here for a while," I said.

Ben still hadn't said anything. His clenched fists and red ears were a sure sign that he was about to lose control. I could read Ben's emotions like they were my own.

"Those bastards killed my family and now they're going to be living and working in Huntsville. How's that even possible? Damn them," he said.

I didn't know what to say. I hated the Nazis as much as Ben did. They killed Joe. I worked hard at not thinking about the way my brother died. Whenever I did, the nightmare would resurface. I suppose, in retrospect, it was then that I first started to perfect my ability to selectively forget certain parts of my life. In the first months after the Army notified us about Joe, that's all I thought about. We had been told that my brother and several of his crew had parachuted safely from their plane. They were immediately caught by an SS unit of the soon-to-be- defeated German army. Taking prisoners was not part of their mindset. Joe and his crew were beaten, gunned down in a field, and left to rot. The area was soon retaken by our troops and the bodies were discovered. I didn't lose as many family members as Ben, but I lost the most important person in my young life. I would never forgive them, and now some of them would be living nearby and possibly sitting next to me at school. Their impending arrival was all we talked about.

That summer we finally had our first look at our new neighbors. A man with his wife and two young daughters came into Stern's to shop. Mama walked right out the back door and left Daddy and me behind the front counter.

"Daddy, no way. No way am I waiting on them," I whispered in his ear.

The man and his wife were staring at us. I supposed they were nervous and were hoping we would ask them what they needed. I stared back, savoring their discomfort, expecting them to leave.

"How can I help you?" asked Daddy.

I couldn't believe he was waiting on them.

"We need new clothing for the children," the man said.

The sound of his German-accented English made the hairs on my arms stand up on end. I was glad Ben wasn't working that day, but his father was. If they needed anything altered, Mr. Lowe would have to take the measurements. Thankfully, Daddy steered them over to Ella Mae, and she whisked them away to help them with their purchases.

I kept thinking that they had no right to be walking around enjoying the day, buying new clothes, while my brother was lying two blocks away and six feet under in Maple Hill Cemetery.

I never questioned my father's decisions. I had too much respect for him, but I wondered why he hadn't asked them to leave. He must have understood my confusion because he answered without my saying a word.

"Tommy, I can't throw them out. I'm not happy about them being here, but the Chamber of Commerce and the mayor have requested that we treat these newcomers with civility. Huntsville's struggling, and these Germans might end up changing all that. Tommy, son, don't look at me like that."

"Have you forgotten what they did to Joe?" I asked.

The look on my father's face frightened me. For a second I thought he might actually slap me. Seconds passed with each of us not saying anything. He then reached over and hugged me. My father hadn't shown that much emotion in years.

"Tommy, I will never forget what they did to your brother. When I look at them, all I see are the people responsible for Joe's death, but I will not treat those two innocent little girls over there as if they are criminals. That is what the Germans did to families like the Lowes. I'm not saying it's going to be easy, but we will wait on these customers and treat them just like everyone else. Now I have to go home and see after your mother. I'm counting on you, son."

Once he was gone, I did as he asked. I kept an eye on things, or to be more exact, an eye on them. I couldn't believe that they had come to our store. They had to know Stern's was Jewish owned. Everyone in town did. It wasn't a secret.

§

I quickly discovered that my father had been right about the citizenry of Huntsville. No one, it seemed, was voicing much concern about our newcomers. Maybe I hoped there was some dissent and I just hadn't heard about it. We all seemed to be keeping our feelings pretty close to the chest. I sensed, though, that among most people, the excitement was building up about what these Germans could do for our town. I couldn't believe how quickly they had forgotten that a short five years earlier these men had been our enemies. When the war was raging everyone hated the Nazis, and now they didn't. No one even called them that anymore, and in my book that's what they all still were—goose-stepping, Jew-hating, Hitler-loving Nazis. The welcome mat had been rolled out, and I felt as if I had been dropped into an alternate universe from the pages of one of my comic books.

Over the next couple of months, more and more Germans started coming into town, and most ended up shopping at Sterns. I guessed that my unfriendliness had not scared any of them away. By the end of that first summer they were in the store all the time, and I had finally stopped being chilled to the bone every time I heard the harsh foreignness of their accents.

# 13

# 1968

I WAS ANXIOUS TO look at the notebook, so as soon as Karin left I walked to my car and drove back to my cousin's. I had an hour or so before dinner and told Al I was going to lie down. Once I was cloistered in my room, I opened the journal and began to read.

*Diary of Erich Klaus Angel*

*April 15, 1950*

*Our trip from Fort Bliss in Texas to Huntsville, Alabama, took two days by private bus. The terrain was monotonous filled with cotton fields and not much of anything else. I spent most of my time reading, sleeping, or staring out the window. Papa sat with the other men and was occupied in conversation. Mama and Karin sat across from me, and I tried to block out our mother's endless chatter about what to expect in our new home. I wonder still if I am the only one who is homesick for the Fatherland. Papa refuses to discuss the past. I think he is afraid. Some of his friends and colleagues have already been tried and convicted. One of the accused was George Rickey, the general manager at Mittelwerk, the rocket factory where Papa worked. I suppose he is grateful that he is not in the same boat, and he made it clear that we were to forget our old lives. Now that we are in America he wants us to speak only in English. Karin and I were forced to spend much of our time in language class when we were still interned at Fort Bliss. "There is no going home," Papa said. Berlin is in ruins and partially controlled by the Russians, who Papa distrusts even* more than the Americans. My only hope is that once my father no longer proves useful they will send us back.

April 30, 1950

My father's compatriots, their nervous wives and children have now been at the Redstone Arsenal for one week. On arrival we were moved into buildings subdivided and converted into apartments in the northeast corner of the facility. Everyone is a bit on edge. All, perhaps with the exception of von Braun, are worried they will end up back in Germany. The Arsenal is about five miles from the downtown of Huntsville. Few have ventured there yet. I must admit that northern Alabama is prettier than Texas, hillier, and it reminds me a little of Germany. I sometimes fear I will never return home. It is not yet summer, and it is already very hot. I cannot bear to think how oppressive it will feel by August. Karin barely speaks to me or to Papa. Our father has yet to notice, and I don't care. We are nothing alike. It still baffles me that we shared the same space in our mother's womb for nine months. Karin is useless. If the war had ended differently, I would have suggested that she be sent to a Lebensborn center to produce Aryan children for the Reich. That, I truly believe, is all my lovely sister is good for. Ever since the United States military required us to watch the newsreel footage of the liberated camps, she has become even quieter and more boring, if that were possible. The reporter explained that Mittelwerk was one of the many factories within the Mittelbau complex, all of which were located in the Dora concentration camp near the city of Nordhausen. Like many of the engineers, Papa worked at Mittelwerk, where the V-1 and V-2 rockets were assembled. Karin, the dolt, was obviously unaware of Papa's activities until the day of the forced viewing. After, she went to her room and refused to come out for the rest of the day. I suppose she was making some sort of statement. Neither of my parents remarked about her absence, and since then she has rarely uttered a word to either one of them.

May 10, 1950

I have not written in quite some time because honestly, one day is very similar to the one before and the one after, and I have had little news to report. Earlier today, though, we went into town as a family. It was our first public outing. We all needed new clothing and some basic essentials. Papa had forewarned us about the large Negro population, but it was still a shock and a bit unsettling to see so many black faces. I find it amusing that here in the land of the free there is a class of Untermenschen, subhumans like the Jews, who must use separate public washrooms, drinking fountains, and restaurants. I will have to remember to mention this observation to Karin. My lovely twin sister does not share my viewpoint about racial mixing, but apparently many southern Americans do. At the fort and in the town, people stare at us. Papa says it is only because we are newcomers. Time will tell if he is right.

Our destination was Stern's, the largest department store in Huntsville. Unfortunately, it was owned by a Jewish family. When we walked in, I saw two boys close to my age, standing behind the front counter. Both were waiting on customers. Mama and Karin had already moved on to the women's section and were being helped by a saleslady. Papa was busy looking through the ties, and I was left on my own. The boy on the left was the taller of the two and was leaning on the counter and talking to a pretty blond girl who was deciding between two blouses. He seemed to know her. They were both laughing. The other boy, the fairer one, was also speaking to a customer. I moved closer. He intrigued me. His English was far better than my own but there was a subtle hint of a German accent. Who was he? A Juden perhaps?

I now remembered that day clearly. I closed the notebook. I couldn't read anymore. I needed some fresh air and told Al that I was going to take a short walk around the block before dinner. What I really wanted was to go home and forget that Cole had ever called me. The memories, suppressed for so long, were returning in a torrent. I didn't want to go back; it was all too fucking painful.

# 14

# 1950

ANOTHER FAMILY I didn't recognize had come in to shop. There was a time, not too long ago, when I knew everyone who crossed over our threshold, but no more. Times were definitely changing. I was speaking with Linda, a friend of mine from school, when I noticed them. They were one of the Arsenal families. They had that look and they seemed a little lost. I was hoping to snag Miss Ella to help them out, but she was in the back with Daddy. He was showing her how to use our new, shoe-fitting fluoroscope. Daddy said the new machines ensured a proper fit and were the wave of the future. Ben was busy helping Mrs. Pritchard decide between two hats, and since I was just about finished with Linda, I resigned myself to the task at hand.

"Bye, Tommy," Linda said. "Will I see y'all later?"

"Sure, we'll meet you at the drugstore in about an hour. My treat."

I had known Linda since our time together in Mrs. Howard's first-grade class. She was always a skinny little thing, but lately I'd been noticing how much better her clothes were fitting. I watched as she did that little thing with her hips and walked out. I liked her and thought about asking her out. My mother always told me I was a late bloomer, and I guess she was right. When I turned fifteen, something kicked in, and I was now six-foot-one and no longer a string bean, and even though I didn't love the game as much as my brother had, I made the high school football team and was pretty popular at school.

When I started walking toward the family, I saw the boy staring in Ben's direction. He wasn't hiding it.

"May I help you find something?" I asked.

"Yes, please," answered the woman. "We need the school dresses for *meine* daughter and the trousers and blouses for my son."

"Shirts, Mama. The boys' tops are called shirts," whispered the girl.

"Yes, then. Trousers and shirts for my son."

"You can find it all on the second floor. The elevator is in the back of the shoe area. I'll go and get my mother to give you a hand. She's in the back."

Girls' dresses were not my department. When I returned I saw that the boy hadn't moved at all and was still staring at Ben, who had just finished up with Mrs. Pritchard and was now staring back.

"Can I help you?" I said again, this time to him. He continued to stare with no expression at all on his pasty white face.

"No. I don't see anything that interests me," he finally said.

He then dismissed us with a wave, moved toward his parents and walked off with them toward the elevator.

"What was all that about?" I asked Ben.

"Not sure, but I'd like to get my hands around his neck. In fact I'd like to wrap my hands around the necks of each and every one of them."

I agreed, and I was more than a little annoyed with myself for noticing that the girl in the family was drop-dead gorgeous. I could tell they were brother and sister. They did share the same shade of golden-blond hair and both had green eyes, but that was where the similarity ended. The boy's skin looked washed out; there was something almost unhealthy about him. The girl was also fair-skinned, but her cheeks were full of color and her eyes seemed to dance with pleasure as she inspected all the merchandise.

Once my mother slowly walked off to wait on the Germans, Daddy offered to give Ben and me the rest of the day off. He didn't have to ask twice. We only had a few more weeks of summer vacation, and we both had been putting in a lot of hours at the store. Our early arrival at the drugstore had caught Linda off guard, and in turn, I caught her flirting with Clayton Dobson, one of my friends. Maybe I wouldn't be asking her out after all.

We bought a couple of sodas and joined the rest of our group before heading over to Ben's.

We were planning to put the finishing touches on a comic book—one we had finally decided was good enough to send off to D.C. and Atlas, two large comic book publishers. We weren't optimistic. No one cared about the war anymore. It was a new world with different heroes. Kids were immersed in the tales of the Lone Ranger and Hop-a-Long Cassidy, and for most readers, Nazi-fighting superheroes were no longer interesting. But Ben and I, for our own reasons, were still immersed in that dying genre of the comic book world. We read everything we could get our hands on about the different writers and illustrators and were proud that so many of the creators were Jewish. We idolized Jerry Siegel and Joe Shuster, the co-creators of Superman, and Jack Kirby and Joe Simon, who wrote and illustrated the Captain America stories, and Ben worshipped Jerry Robinson who illustrated many of the early Batman covers and who had created the Joker, America's first super-villain. But even those Jewish writers and artists were done with the Nazis. It was all about selling books, and everyone, with the exception of Ben and me, had obviously moved on. I'm not sure why we sent it in. What I do know is we never heard back.

When we got to Ben's, we were surprised to see my father's Buick in the driveway. We were even more shocked to see our parents huddled in the living room in deep conversation.

"Hey, y'all," I yelled. "What's going on? Why are y'all here?"

I saw that they were obviously deciding whether to confide in us or not. I wanted to remind my parents that Ben and I were both seventeen and no longer children, but I bit my tongue and waited.

"Franz, do you want to tell them or should I?"

No one except my daddy ever called Ben's father Franz anymore. He had changed his name to Frank years ago. He wanted to be more American. He wanted to fit in.

"Go ahead, Tom."

Both of our mothers sat quietly with pained expressions.

"What?" Ben finally asked. "What happened?"

"Did you see the German family in the store today?" asked Mr. Lowe.

We both nodded.

"The parents and the girl were nice enough, but the boy, he said he wanted his pants hemmed. When I was finished, he whispered something to me while the others were still trying on their clothing."

"Papa, what did he say?"

"*Juden*, how lucky for you that we missed a few."

# 15

## 1968

When I got to Al's the table was set and sitting before me was another mound of food. This time the platters held fried chicken, mashed potatoes, and greens. I could feel myself salivating. I rarely gave in to my craving for true southern cooking. I was only thirty-six years old but I already had high cholesterol.

"I had no idea you could cook like this."

"I can't, and I didn't. Selma comes over every day, and I pay her to cook and clean for me."

"You mean the Selma who used to work for Mama and Daddy?"

"Yep, one and the same."

"She must be eighty years old."

"Tommy, she was only in her forties when you moved to Atlanta. She must have seemed a lot older to you."

"I guess she did. What time tomorrow? I'd like to say hello."

"Around eleven, but I thought you were driving back to Atlanta in the morning."

I realized then that I had no intention of going back. Not yet anyway.

"No, I think I'll stay on a few days. That is if it's all right with you?"

"I've got nothing going on, and I'm enjoying your company," Al said with a smile.

Once we sat down, and I had taken a few bites of the best fried chicken I had tasted in years, I decided to see what my cousin remembered about the arrival of the Germans in Huntsville.

While Al gnawed on his drumstick, I asked him what it was like when they came.

"Tommy, do you remember what Huntsville's claim to fame was before 1950?"

I smiled.

"I seem to remember that it had something to do with watercress."

"Yep, before 1950, Huntsville was known as the Watercress Capital of America. The German scientists changed all that. I'm not telling you anything you don't already know. Within a few years of their arrival, we moved from watercress to rockets. Rocket City, that's what Huntsville is today.

"I think there were almost a hundred and thirty scientists with their families in that first group. At first, I didn't know who was more skittish, them or us. In the beginning we didn't see too many of them. They were all holed up at the Arsenal. We all thought the government was trying to keep them isolated until they could measure the reaction of us townsfolk to all our new neighbors. Of course the Army, as well as the Chamber of Commerce, were careful to never say the word Nazi. These scientists were sold to us as "good Germans," who had been coerced to join the Party and to do work for the Reich. That's the line they were promoting. It was a pretty slick advertising campaign by our government. Some of us, including your Daddy, knew it was a whole bunch of hogwash, but, and this is the God's honest truth, they accepted that the scientists would be good for the town.

"And honestly, they were. You and I both know that. Before 1950, we had about sixteen thousand people living here. By the mid-50s, our population had tripled. Before too long those scientists started to purchase homes and move out of the Arsenal. Fifteen families bought property on Mont Sano just east of downtown and built over there. Don't you remember, we called it Sauerkraut Hill because there were so many Germans in one area? Didn't Karin and her family live over there?"

I nodded in agreement.

"But you didn't come to town for a history lesson. You ready to talk about what's really troubling you?"

"No, I don't think so. Not yet anyway. I'm trying to sort a few things out. Tell me what you know about von Braun."

"Not too much, to tell you the truth. He was the big man in town and we didn't have many run-ins. It's a shame you can't ask your daddy some of these questions. Being in the Chamber of Commerce and all, your daddy was better acquainted with von Braun and the others. What I do know is that everyone in town loved him, and they still do. He's a good-looking man, handsome, even now. Looked almost like a movie star, especially when he was young. Anyway, von Braun seemed to fit right in. He was very civic-minded, you know. Did a lot for the community. We wouldn't have a symphony orchestra if it weren't for him and some of the others."

"Didn't anyone ever question what he and 'some of the others' did during the war?"

"No, not really. It's human nature, Tommy. People didn't want to know and by that time most folks didn't care. World War II was over, and the Cold War had begun. By 1947, Joseph Stalin, our one-time ally, had conquered most of Eastern Europe. Nations that had been suppressed and tyrannized by the Nazis were now being suppressed and tyrannized by the Soviets. They had exchanged one maniacal despot for another. The US and our Western allies were fearful that if the Russians were not reined in, communism would continue to spread. Honestly, there was nothing we feared more than communism. We wanted to beat the Russians at everything, including the race into outer space, and it was our very own Huntsville scientists who were going to get us there."

"You know, during all these years, I had never really spoken to anyone about all this," I said. "After Ben died, I just wanted to leave Huntsville and forget. Now, I want to know. I want to know what some of the scientists did do during the war."

"Why? It was an awfully long time ago."

"Because I owe it to Ben. I owe it to him to find out. Something's not right about the way he died. There should have been more of an investigation."

"Is that what this is all about? You think one of the folks from the Arsenal had something to do with Ben's death? Tommy, that boy committed suicide."

Al shook his head and started to clear the table.

"I'm not crazy," I said. "Ben was looking forward to graduating, to going to college; he was happy. Why would he have done something like that? It never made any sense, and I can't believe it's taken me this long to realize it."

"Okay, okay! I'm on your side, but one of the Germans, no way. They were busy proving their worth to the government. They kept to themselves. Besides, no one in that group would have done anything illegal. They were all too careful. They knew they could be deported if they stepped out of line. They wanted to be Americans and in 1955, a large group of them, including von Braun, became citizens. They weren't about to do anything to jeopardize their standing in the community."

"Maybe not—okay, probably not, and maybe Ben did commit suicide, but I need to be sure."

§

After a fitful night, I got up early the next morning and decided to walk over to the library. I was about halfway there when I realized I should have asked Al if it was still in the same location. It was cooler than I expected, but the crisp air and the fluttering crimson and yellow leaves helped to lighten my mood. I imagined my mother whispering in my ear the John Donne poem she used to recite, whenever the leaves began to change. "No spring, nor summer beauty hath such grace / As I have seen in one autumnal face." I would have to remind her of that when I returned to Atlanta.

When I got to the corner of Fountain Street and Williams Circle, I hoped to see the old Carnegie Library that had graced that spot since it was built in 1916. I didn't. At first, I thought I had made a wrong turn. I hadn't. The stately building had been razed and replaced by a new and modern-looking structure that only added to the sense of loss I had been feeling ever since coming back home.

Once I checked in, I took a seat by one of the microfilm readers and asked to see the reels from the *Huntsville Times* beginning in 1946. I wanted to understand when in the hell the citizens of this town, my town, first became aware of its postwar German invasion.

I hadn't used a microfilm reader in years, and it didn't take long for me to get frustrated with the tedium of scrolling through the reels. I searched for about an hour before I located a mention of the arrival of the first group to Huntsville. On November 4, 1949, the headline read, 'Army will Move Rocket Center.' It was short and to the point and announced that an 'Army rocket development center employing more than one hundred German scientists will be among the personnel to be transferred from Fort Bliss, Texas, to Huntsville, Ala., in an effort to save $4,500,000.'

Unlike Daddy, who couldn't quite figure out why these Germans had been given such special treatment, I had the benefit of eighteen years of news coverage to help me out. I spent the remainder of the morning pouring over the periodical index searching for any additional articles that mentioned the scientists' arrival. They were few and far between, but by lunchtime, I had a pretty good idea of how it happened. By then I had spent hours hovering over the microfilm reader and was rewarded with a crick in my neck, a sore butt, and a building rage.

I decided I needed some fresh air, and the walk back to Al's helped clear my head. Somehow he had sensed I would be joining him for lunch. I had barely said hello before a salami sandwich and a cold beer were placed in my hands. Cousin Al was growing on me.

"This looks good," I said. "Thanks."

"No problem. How did it go? Did you find what you were looking for?"

"Some. I think I've started to understand how and why they came here. Did you know that there was an actual name for the plan that brought all these Germans over to the States?"

"No, but I'm not surprised."

Over lunch, I pulled out my notes and began to fill Al in on what I had learned.

"The mission was named 'Operation Paperclip' because if the Army was interested in a particular German, they marked his folder with—can you believe?—an actual paperclip."

"Clever. The top brass can be real innovative when they want to be," he answered.

"I was surprised that the operation made it into the papers at all. I found a couple of articles from 1946. One was in the *New York Times* and the other appeared in *Newsweek*. They were short one-column stories, and I doubt if many people paid them much mind. What struck me was that when the operation was first disclosed, the reports were not the least bit obsequious about the project and identified this 'special' group of immigrants as Nazis. The *New York Times* went so far as to question whether some of those admitted into the United States should even be called scientists."

I picked up my notes.

"According to the article, there were 'misgivings at the liberal provisions of "Project Paperclip" in virtually promising United States citizenship to ardent Nazis or pro-Nazis and families in return for services that could be required in any event.' But by June 1947, the adjectives that described the new arrivals had changed and the scientists and doctors were being identified as Germans with tenuous connections to the Nazi regime. The more I read the more I realized their records were being whitewashed to convince us, the American public, that these particular Germans were vital to America's future."

"Maybe they were. Maybe they still are," said Al.

I ignored him and continued reading from my notes.

"There was some dissension and anger about the project. Not everyone was on the same page. A congressman, John D. Dingell, a Democrat from Detroit, denounced the operation on the floor of the House of Representatives. He said, 'I have never thought that we were so poor mentally in this country that we have to go and import those Nazi killers to help us prepare for the defense of our country. A German is a Nazi, and a Nazi is a German. The terms are synonymous.' Other notable Americans—including Albert Einstein and Rabbi Stephen S. Wise, the president of the American Jewish Congress, and Minister Norman Vincent Peale—also objected to the privilege they were receiving. The government was determined and the dissenters were few and far between. I just don't get it."

"Tommy, maybe you were too involved with your studies because you clearly don't remember what it was like back then. The United States was in an arms and space race with the Soviet Union. It wasn't a war with men dying on the battlefield, but it was nonetheless a war, and one that our government intended to win. The military convinced the powers in Washington that without the expertise of these so-called former Nazi scientists and engineers, the race would be lost before it was even begun. The Soviet Union was and still is a very real threat to our nation's security. I'm not sure they were wrong."

I pushed my plate away. The half-eaten sandwich felt heavy in my gut.

"What about the survivors of the Holocaust?" I asked. "I can't swallow it. While special provisions and exceptions were being made for the Paperclip Germans, the Jewish victims of the Nazis, also Germans by the way, but without the right academic credentials, were herded into displaced person's camps because they had nowhere else to go."

I could no longer stay seated. I was ready to end the conversation. I took my plate to the sink hoping Al would get the hint and stop speaking. He was talking about the space race, and I was trying to get him to understand how wrong it was for our country to give jobs to former Nazis.

"Tommy, are you okay?"

"No, actually I'm not. It was just dumb luck that Mr. Lowe was a tailor and my father happened to need one and was able to offer him a job. Just dumb luck. If that letter hadn't come to my father's attention, then Ben and his parents would have probably gone up in smoke like everyone else who couldn't get out. But even if, by some strange twist of fate, they made it through without being killed, then the old quota system—you know, the one that limited undesirable immigrants and kept them out before the war—was still in effect. Did you ever think that maybe one of those Jews, someone desperate to emigrate, had miraculously survived the slave-labor regimen at Dora-Mittelwerk where the V-2 rockets were manufactured? Maybe this person had barely escaped being worked to death by one of these same scientists, and now he couldn't leave because there was no room left for some nobody who couldn't provide a service to the military."

Al stood up and placed his two hands on my shoulders.

"Tommy, calm down. You're right. It wasn't fair or morally just. I'm just trying to explain why it happened. When I was discharged from the Navy and came back to Huntsville, I remember how horrified our neighbors and friends were by what had happened to the Jews of Europe. There were vivid descriptions in all the newspapers about what was discovered in those camps. You couldn't go to the movies without seeing newsreel footage from places like Dachau and Buchenwald. People sent money and care packages overseas, and President Truman loosened the immigration restrictions so more survivors could come in. But we are a fickle people with short memories, and within a few years heightened tensions with the Soviet Union overshadowed everything else. We were frightened of the Russians. I know it's hard to hear, but for most Americans, including some Jewish Americans, there was a new enemy and Nazis were old news."

I shook my head. Disbelief, disgust, I wasn't sure what I was feeling. Al went to the fridge and brought each of us another beer.

"You're upset," Al said. "Are you disappointed in me, your parents, American Jews in general?"

"I'm not sure. I guess I just don't get it."

"Get what?" Al asked. "That we were afraid to speak out. We prided ourselves on our loyalty, but a lot of us always felt as if we had so much more to prove. Everyone I knew, including yours truly, served during World War II. I knew a Jewish guy from Birmingham; he had flat feet. This guy went back four times until he finally found a doctor who didn't notice or care, and he was able to join up. He ended up being killed at Anzio. When we came home, not much had changed. Americans may have felt bad about the Holocaust, but there were still plenty of country clubs we couldn't join and neighborhoods where "our kind" couldn't live. Speaking out against something that was seen by the government as good for the country, even if it was the employment of ex-Nazis in scientific and medical fields, was not something most of us were willing to do. We worried that it could be interpreted as being un-American, or as sympathy for communists, and trust me, being labeled as a left-winger or a communist was not going to win you any popularity contests.

"I know it's not an excuse, but honestly, everyone was ready to leave the war behind. Maybe American Jews were grateful and thankful that, by the luck of the draw, we had escaped the carnage. Maybe we felt a little ashamed that we hadn't done more to help. Your daddy was one of the few who actually did more than talk when he brought the Lowe family over here. Not many people did that. And you know why?"

I shook my head.

"Because the Depression was still raging, and folks right here in Huntsville needed work. I'm sure some of them were resentful that a good job at Stern's was given to a foreigner."

"I vaguely remember Joe telling me the same thing."

"Joe was a smart kid. I don't know, there are times when I believe we've gotten past all the fear, but then something happens and anti-Jewish feeling rears up again. I think it was a couple years after you left for college when Julius and Ethel Rosenberg were found guilty of espionage for giving classified information about the atomic bomb to the Russians. Do you remember how you felt when that was front-page news?"

It must have registered with me at some level but to be brutally honest I was too wrapped up in socializing and studying to be too concerned about current events.

"I'm embarrassed to say, I didn't feel much of anything."

It was slowly dawning on me that I wasn't that different from the people I was disparaging.

Al ignored my comment and continued.

"I was a lot older than you and I do remember how I felt. I cringed and was ashamed every time their names were mentioned at a public gathering. We worried that people would think we had communist sympathies too. I was furious that two Jewish Americans would have spied for the Soviets, and I am not ashamed to say that I was not the least bit troubled when they both received the death penalty. They had jeopardized the security of my country as well as that of every other patriotic Jewish American.

"And then, of course, there was Senator Joe McCarthy and his House Committee on Un-American Activities."

I finally sat back down. Maybe I did have blinders on. I needed to shut up and listen. Al's face was flushed, and he was gripping his beer a little too tightly.

"Al, look, I'm sorry. You're right. I probably don't get it."

He kept talking. I could sense his desperation. He wanted me to understand.

"Those times were frightening. The House Un-American Activities Committee investigated thousands of individuals and destroyed lives and careers in the process. The hearings convinced a fearful American public that communists were infiltrating all levels of society—including our own government—with the intention of destroying the very essence of what it meant to be American. Down here, in some circles the words *Jew, communist,* and *integrationist* became interchangeable. It gave white supremacists another reason to hate. John Crommelin, do you remember that name? You were living up north when he ran as an independent candidate against Lister Hill for the United States Senate."

"Vaguely," I answered.

"Crommelin was from Montgomery. He had a distinguished career as a Navy combat pilot during the war. Anyway, when he came back to Alabama he entered politics and campaigned throughout the state that there was a communist-Jewish conspiracy to mongrelize the white race through integration. Thank God he never won, but he had a lot of supporters."

"Look, I overstepped. I've upset you, and that was not my intention."

He ignored me again.

"Weren't you living in Atlanta when all those synagogues and churches were being bombed?"

"Yes."

"The only reason that Temple Beth El in Birmingham wasn't blown to bits was because of rain. The fuse got wet and failed to ignite. Then six months later, The Temple in Atlanta, the same one your mother's grandparents helped to found, was bombed. That time there was no rain. The Confederate Underground took credit for the attack. Jews were scared. For the most part, with the exception of a few courageous individuals, they kept their heads down and tried not to make waves."

"I remember the investigation," I said.

"Yeah, nothing came of it. Five men, all members of the National States' Rights Party were arrested, but only one, George Bright, was indicted and then the jury found him not guilty."

For the next several minutes we sat there in silence.

"Tommy, I'm sorry too," he said.

"What for? Like I said, I get it."

"Well, I'm glad you do, because sometimes I'm still not sure I understand all the motivations that drive people to act one way or another."

"Self-preservation," I answered. "It's human nature to want to save ourselves."

*On the other hand*, I thought, *why do some people stick their necks out for total strangers while most of us, myself included, don't?* I felt like a jerk.

"I've sat on the sidelines for all of my life," I said.

"Don't be so hard on yourself. Most of us have," answered Al.

I was seeing myself with greater clarity and I didn't like the view. What had happened to the altruistic young man who wanted to work for civil rights? I was no superhero. I had no right to judge.

"I'm sorry I didn't understand, and I should have."

"And I'm sorry that we didn't speak out more. I'm sorry that we were all too afraid."

"Al, please don't apologize. It's complicated. I'm going to head on back to the library."

"Do you mind some company? I could use the exercise."

Al walked me to the front door of the building and surprisingly pulled me into a protective embrace.

"You're a good man," he said. "Don't be too hard on yourself."

§

Sitting in the quiet of the library, I began to think about what I had said about self-preservation and how easy it had been for my community to accept over one hundred German scientists, some of whom were certainly Nazis, while still holding fast to Jim Crow. What did that actually say about us? As long as you were white, your past crimes would be forgiven. Even the murder of innocents could be quietly erased from your resume, but if your skin was a darker shade you could be arrested for drinking out of a whites-only fountain or for sitting at a whites-only restaurant counter. In retrospect, I suppose, I needed to thank the German scientists for ensuring that, at least in Huntsville, there wasn't the kind of trouble that took place in Selma or Birmingham. Our little synagogue was not targeted by white supremacists, and there weren't any marches or black heads being bashed in. Public facilities, like lunch counters, were peacefully integrated in 1962. NASA had made it clear: They could and would move their operations out of Redstone if Huntsville mirrored the actions taken in other Alabama cities. Money was the motivating factor. White people moved away from black neighborhoods, and the schools remained segregated, only this time it was legal.

While synagogues and black churches were being bombed and civil rights workers were killed in other cities, Huntsville remained relatively calm. Our Germans had buried their pasts and were now being promoted as our best chance to keep up with the Russians.

I had about an hour left till closing and couldn't look at one more reel of film. Instead, I pulled out Erich's diary from my briefcase.

I skimmed through the next six months of entries. There wasn't much of any interest. Erich spent a lot of time disparaging his fellow students, describing everyone, with the exception of Ben, as country hicks not worthy of his association. That was not anything I didn't already know. Erich always thought he was better than the rest of us and for the most part he kept to himself. His tiresome meanderings were starting to put me to sleep.

I was starting on the final couple of entries when something slightly more ominous caught my attention.

*May 15, 1951*

*Tonight, we graduate from high school. Soon I will be on my way to university. Father was pleased with my acceptance at Emory in Atlanta. I had hoped to move back to Germany, but my parents persuaded me to stay in America to complete my education. Over there, everything is still in chaos. My sister had her own plans, but I've managed to change her mind. She will also be attending Emory. The boy is going north to school. She thinks I don't know she is involved with him, but I have known for some time.*

*June 4, 1951*

*There is a barbecue tonight for the senior class. I would rather stay home, but I will go to keep a watch on Karin. She is in love. I am sure of it. Sacrifices must be made for the good of the family.*

That was the last entry in the diary.

What in the hell were Karin's "other plans," and how did Erich find out about Karin and me? What would any of that have to do with Ben? I had more questions than answers.

The morning after the barbecue, Ben was discovered hanging from a tree in the little, wooded area in the back of the school parking area by a neighborhood woman walking her dog. The medical examiner said there was no sign of any struggle, aside from the few bruises on Ben's face that I had helped to explain away. I was the one who told the police that Erich and Ben had gotten into a fight the night before, and explained that, after a few punches, my friends and I had stepped in to break it up. Later, when Erich was asked about the fight, he claimed that once he and Karin left the barbecue for home, he never went out again. His parents backed him up. Two and a half months later, Erich and Karin started at Emory, and I left for the University of Pennsylvania.

"Tommy, Tommy Stern." My reverie was suddenly cut short. It tickled me that everyone in Huntsville still thought of me as Tommy.

I knew that voice. The slightly stooped older woman walking toward me looked familiar. Her dark hair was now streaked with gray, but the pencil hovering over her ear and the bun perched on the top of her head were the final giveaways. There in the flesh was Miss Alma Jones, the same librarian I had known as a kid. Most of the buildings had changed, but it seemed as if the people inside had all stayed put.

"Miss Jones, good to see you. It's been years."

The library was closing in a few minutes, and I suppose she wanted me to finish up.

"I'm just about done," I said.

Where had she been hiding all day? I had been sitting in the same spot for hours.

"Come here and give me a hug," she said.

I got up and gently embraced her. I was afraid to hug her too hard. Miss Jones always looked a bit frail, but now there seemed to be even less of her. I must have only been thirteen or fourteen when she handed me a copy of *The Heart is a Lonely Hunter* by Carson McCullers. That book changed me. After I read it, I began to pay more attention to my surroundings. I began to notice both the literal and figurative signs of Jim Crow, and I began to understand that for a large segment of my community, life was exceedingly unfair.

"Tommy, it's so good to see you. What brings you back to Huntsville, and how's your mother doing?"

"It's good to see you too. Mother's well; she'll be glad to know that you asked about her."

Nothing ever got by Miss Jones, and I was sure she noted that I avoided answering her first question. I then made a point of looking up at the clock and started to gather up my papers.

"I'll be back in the morning," I said.

"Good, we open at nine. We'll catch up then."

"I'd like that," I said. I wasn't sure how much of my research I would share with Miss Jones, but regardless, I needed more time at the library. I couldn't shake the feeling that Erich and the Germans had something to do with the way Ben died. I wondered how much Ben might have known or discovered about von Braun and the other scientists' Nazi connections. Maybe he found something incriminating. Could he have uncovered something that could have gotten him killed? I hoped my imagination was not working overtime. I was suddenly overwhelmed by the need to fly up to New York and see his parents. It was a visit that was long overdue.

# 16

## 1949

Except for the once-in-a-while encounter with Huntsville's newest inhabitants, the summer of 1949, the one before the start of my senior year, was more of the same ole, same ole. I worked at the store, played ball, hung out with friends, and read. The German families kept coming into the store, and I was becoming more accustomed to seeing them. It wasn't like I hated them any less. It was just that I had other things, seventeen-year-old boy things, with which to occupy myself.

After that incident at the store involving Ben's dad and the German boy, Ben was even more anxious to get out of Huntsville. He talked about it nonstop. He was moving up north, away from our colony of Germans scientists and their families and as far from the Jim Crow south as he could get. That summer also marked the end of our comic book collaboration. We were starting our senior year of high school and between extracurricular activities and our studies we had little time left for anything else.

I expected that the first day of school in September to start out like all my other first days since I began my school career twelve years earlier. No one seemed to ever move away, and the few changes in my classmates were barely discernable. As I looked around and took in the scene, I noticed that Petey Nolan had started to sprout a few hairs on his chin and that Peggy Sue Perkins had put on a few pounds, but other than that everything was boringly the same. Ben was in his usual seat, the one next to mine, and we were horsing around with some of the other kids while we waited for Mr. Warner, our homeroom teacher, to arrive. The bell had already rung and he was uncharacteristically late.

"Maybe he's sick or something," I said to no one in particular. One could always hope.

"Thank you for your concern Mr. Stern, but no, I'm not sick, just detained," he said.

I could feel the blush creeping up from my neck to my scalp, and as he walked in, I saw that five new students were trailing behind him, like little ducks waddling behind their mama or, in this case, their teacher. Three were new to me, but two I immediately recognized. One was the German boy, the one who had intimidated Mr. Lowe, followed in by his sister.

"Good morning. Welcome back to school. I hope y'all had an enjoyable summer."

There were a few muttered responses, but we were all too intent on staring at the faces of the five new students who were standing before us.

"Class, I'd like to introduce the newest members of East Clinton High School."

I had stopped listening. I was looking at Ben, whose face was turned toward the window. He wasn't about to acknowledge their presence. There were four boys and just one girl. Three of the four boys had brown hair and dark eyes and were not exactly model Aryan prototypes. The other two were introduced as the twins, Karin and Erich Angel. If I recognized Erich as the boy who had taunted Mr. Lowe, I was sure Ben had too. Either one of those two could have been poster children for Nazi purity. I couldn't believe I was now going to be in the same homeroom with kids whose parents fought for the country that killed my brother. One by one, Mr. Warner asked them to tell us a little about themselves and where they were from. I barely heard the first three recitations. I had already decided that I wouldn't have anything to do with them. I tried not to listen, but there was something about Erich's tone that drew me in. He was being too careful. Trying too hard to say the right thing. His sister waved to the class and smiled but never said a word. It was obvious that he took it upon himself to speak for both of them.

"We, my sister and I, are from Berlin. Our father is Dr. Hermann Angel. Like the others, we have moved here from Fort Bliss in Texas. Thank you for all the kindness you have shown us since we arrived in your beautiful city."

When he thanked the class, I saw him looking directly at Ben and me. Had anyone else noticed the smug expression, the slight curl of the left corner of his mouth as he tried to suppress his smile? Ben had still not turned away from the window. I felt a chill on the back of my neck and wondered if Ben felt a similar one on his own.

When the seats were assigned, Ben and I were asked to move apart to make room for Karin, who would be sitting between the two of us from now until we all graduated in June.

At the end of that first day, Ben and I decided to not speak to any of our new classmates and agreed to pretend that they didn't exist. Even though we were on the verge of manhood, we were still boys holding on to the belief that we could simply will something away that we didn't like.

As the weeks wore on, we realized how childish our pact was. Ben had always been the smartest boy in class, and I had been his only competition in his quest to be our valedictorian. That was until Erich Angel decided to make it known that he was also in the running. It was an undeclared war, but everyone knew that the two were competing.

Ben was pushing himself, and I was beginning to get worried. He studied constantly. On the rare occasion when Erich made a better grade, Ben would sulk. Erich never said a word, but his expression said it all. Ben, of course, wanted to show Erich and every other German in our class that he was one Jew who couldn't be beaten. I could only assume that Erich was as driven to prove the superiority of the Master Race. I thought, maybe if I said something, I could help clear the air between them. We were outside of class, ready to leave for the day, when I caught up to him and his sister.

"Erich, wait a minute," I said.

He was shocked. This was the first time I had said a word to him since that day at the store.

"What?"

Karin stood to the side, struggling to hold the pile of books she was carrying home. Once I said his name I didn't know what to say. I couldn't come up with anything that could possibly ameliorate their deep-seated hatred toward one another.

"Oh, nothing. I just wanted to see how y'all were adjusting to the new school and all."

Erich shook his head and grabbed his sister's hand to pull her away. It surprised me when she pulled it back and smiled. She had dimples.

"It is good. I like the school very much. Thank you for asking."

"You're welcome."

Erich reached for her again and yanked her along. I kept watching as they turned the corner.

That was the beginning, the moment I started to fall in love with Karin Angel. It was the first time I had really looked at her. She was incredibly beautiful. She and Erich shared the same coloring, but looked nothing alike. Erich's features were hard. His skin was cratered and his nose was slightly off-center making me believe that he had been in one too many fights. Karin had escaped the teenage acne that had maliciously scarred her brother, and, unlike Erich, she had one of those cute little button noses. The best part was the radiance that lit up her face the moment she smiled and showed her dimples. I couldn't help but smile back.

I felt guilty. I was betraying my pact with Ben and consorting with the enemy.

*Hell*, I thought. *A few words just to be nice didn't make me her friend.* I vowed to myself, that would be the first and last time I spoke to either one of them. I owed that to my brother and to Ben and his family.

By the following morning my vow had already been broken.

§

The next day I was up and dressed by seven-thirty even though the school didn't start until nine.

"Tommy, where are you going?" asked my mother. "You haven't touched your breakfast."

"I'm having trouble with calculus and there's an early morning study session."

I rarely lied to my parents, but I knew my mother wouldn't approve of my latest crush. I also knew that Karin was always there early to work with the English teacher. I hoped to have a few minutes alone with her before the rest of the class arrived for homeroom.

We were four weeks into the school year and it didn't seem as if Ben had even taken notice of the girl who started each day of school seated between us. I had been discreet and felt confident that he hadn't noticed my furtive glances in her direction. I was wrong. We were walking home from school when he looked at me with one of those typical Ben Lowe bemused expressions.

"Tommy, you like her, don't you?"

"Hell, Ben. What are you talking about?"

He shook his head and started to laugh.

"I'm talking about the fact that you keep looking at the beautiful little *fräulein* in our class."

"You're crazy."

And then Ben got serious.

"Look, it's okay. I get it. She's gorgeous, and shockingly, she doesn't seem to be at all like her asshole brother. I've done a lot of thinking since I first noticed your lovesick face mooning over her. Without you, my life in this town would have been hell. Once you accepted me as your friend, everyone else did too. I may not be the most popular kid in school, but I'm not picked on either. You told me to stop bringing sauerkraut for lunch and to have my mother buy peanut butter and jelly. That alone saved my ass from being kicked. Besides, if she likes you as much as you like her, it will drive her brother crazy. What more could I ask for?"

"You mean it?"

"Yeah, I mean it. Besides, I can't blame her for who she's related to. What kind of person would that make me?"

Everything changed after that. The next day when I saw Karin at school, I reached for her hand and she didn't pull back. We started slipping notes to each other when we passed in the hall, and met up between classes and during our free periods. Within weeks she was my girl and Ben—kind, caring Ben—opened up to a friendship with a German girl. Before too long, the three of us started hanging out together—that is, whenever we could get away from the prying eyes of her brother, which wasn't often. He watched over Karin like a hawk. It was unnerving. Karin and I were also worried about how our parents would react to us dating. We were sure neither set would be too happy about it. In our adolescent naivety, we thought we had fooled them all.

# 17

# 1968

AFTER SPENDING ANOTHER hour at the library, I called my office to check in and to tell my still slightly angry secretary to clear my schedule for the remainder of the week. I then booked a flight to New York City, where Ben's parents had been living for the last eighteen years.

"I'll be back tomorrow evening," I said to Al.

"Tommy, I don't get it. I haven't seen you since your Daddy's funeral, and now I can't get rid of you."

Thankfully, he was grinning.

My flight was leaving from Birmingham, and I was driving well over the speed limit in my effort to make it on time. I hadn't flown in years. If I couldn't get somewhere by car, I usually didn't go. Flying terrified me. I had already started to sweat just thinking about being in that winged, oversized tube with no avenue of escape. I had a first-class seat and hoped for a traveling companion who didn't mind my obsessive need to make conversation during the takeoff and landing.

I was up in the air before I realized that I hadn't picked up the telephone to warn Frank and Helen of my impending arrival. They might not even be there. Worse yet, I knew I would be dredging up the past. We had never talked about the last day of Ben's life. We had all gone to the funeral and accepted that Ben had committed suicide. I was his best friend and had never questioned why. Did anyone ever look at the medical examiner's report? Ben was excited about his future. He had already been accepted at the Art Institute of Chicago. They had seen his work and his grades and had offered him a full scholarship. He was anxious to move away from the South. He was not in a hurry to die.

Over the years, I had tried to keep in touch with Ben's parents, but lately I had dropped the ball. I was sure I was the only one of Ben's old friends who kept in touch. I had to do better. Whenever I did call, it was to check in to see how they were getting along. I never asked them how they were feeling, or if they wanted to speak about what had happened to their only child. I told myself that it was to protect them from any more pain. I finally realized I was protecting myself from the same.

When I got to LaGuardia I found a pay phone and made the call. It was Helen who answered. Unlike her husband and son, she had never lost her heavy German accent.

"Mrs. Lowe, it's Tom Stern. Tommy."

"*Ja*, Tommy. It is so gut to hear your voice. How are you?"

"Good, I'm good."

"You are old enough. Call me Helen," she said.

Like her husband, Mrs. Lowe had Americanized her name changing it from Herta to Helen when they were still living in Huntsville.

"Helen, I know this is unexpected, but I'm actually in New York, and I was hoping I could come by and see you today."

"*Ja*, Tommy, of course. This is such a nice surprise. Frank is at work, but I will call him and have him come home. Have you eaten?"

"No, actually, I haven't."

As soon as she mentioned eating my stomach started grumbling, and I realized I hadn't had anything since breakfast.

"Come now, and I will prepare a late lunch."

"Great. I should be there shortly."

The ride from the airport to their apartment in Manhattan took about thirty minutes, and I found myself paying the driver before I had a chance to collect my thoughts.

The Lowes lived in one of those upscale buildings on New York City's West Side near Central Park. The doorman must have been expecting me, because when I told him my name, he directed me to the elevator. As soon as I knocked, the door swung open, and there were Ben's parents smiling from ear to ear, welcoming me with open arms. I reached down to hug them. Mrs. Lowe was barely five feet and Mr. Low wasn't much taller. The last time I saw them was about six years earlier, when I was up in New York taking a deposition. Amazingly, Mrs. Lowe looked younger than the last time I saw her. For a second I was taken aback by the darkness of her hair. The Mrs. Lowe I remembered had brown hair peppered with gray. On the other hand, Mr. Lowe had aged more naturally and there was little left of his once thick head of red hair. All that remained was a wispy band encircling his neck and a few slicked down strays on the top.

"Come in," they both said in unison.

"Something smells terrific," I said.

"Your favorites. I remembered from when you were a little boy. I prepared the noodle kugel and the schnitzel as soon as you called to say you were coming. Come sit at the table. We will have a little snack while the kugel finishes baking."

For the next several minutes, we caught up on what we had been doing. Helen asked if I was dating anyone. They both looked disappointed when I answered no, and I almost apologized for letting them down.

"Tommy, you need to find a good wife. You would make a fine husband and a father. You are still a young man. I am sure your mother would like a grandchild."

I would be thirty-seven in a few months, and I wasn't sure I would ever meet either of the goals they thought were important for me to attain, but why burst their bubble?

"I'm still looking," I answered.

"When are you going to retire?" I asked. I was trying to be subtle, but the last thing I wanted to discuss was my divorce or my love life.

I knew Frank was in his mid-sixties and still working full-time. He had done well once he and Helen left Huntsville. Frank had opened up a small fashion design shop on New York's Lower East Side and within a few years had managed to snag some very good up-and-coming graduates in the field. Five years later, the Lowe label was being stitched into collars of clothing worn by well-dressed women everywhere.

"I don't think moving to Florida is right for us. Helen doesn't like sitting in the sun or playing canasta, and I don't golf. Right, Helen?"

She nodded in agreement.

I took a minute to look around their apartment. It was spacious and tastefully decorated. It was a far cry from the rundown little house they had lived in while in Huntsville. So many of the antiques I had first became acquainted with during my childhood had found a new home in Manhattan. I wondered if the Lowes still had all the old keys from the prewar furniture that had never arrived.

There were beautifully framed photographs of Ben on the mantel and on the piano. There was even one of Ben and me together. I remembered that day. We were out in the Lowes' backyard horsing around, and Helen brought out her little Brownie camera and snapped away. My friendship with Ben was unique. I missed him more now than I had in a very long time. Yes, I had people with whom I spent time. I even participated in a weekly poker game, where I smoked cigars and bullshitted with my fellow card players, but they were not men with whom I would ever share a confidence.

It was Frank who finally asked if I had business in New York. They were obviously a little perplexed about my out-of-the-blue phone call and unexpected visit.

"No, actually this isn't a business trip."

They looked confused.

"I got a call. I'm not sure if you remember Karin Angel?

"*Ja*, of course, the pretty German girl with the twin brother. She was in homeroom with you and Ben," said Helen.

I thought I detected a slight hesitation in Helen's answer. I was also surprised they remembered her. I had no idea that Ben ever mentioned any of the German kids to his parents.

"Yes, right, Karin. She, indirectly, asked me to drive to Huntsville. She said she had some information about the night Ben died."

All the color drained from Helen's face. This was the first time in all these years that any of us, let alone me, had brought up the subject of his death.

"Yes, I also remember her," added Frank. "I can't imagine she could add anything of importance after all these years."

I was surprised by his lack of curiosity.

"Honestly, not much," I answered. "But she gave me her brother's journal, and the last couple of entries were unsettling. Erich found out that Karin was secretly seeing someone. He may have realized it was me or maybe he thought it was Ben. I'm just not sure. Regardless, Erich was in a horrible mood when he got to the senior class barbecue and, for whatever reason, Ben and he got into a fight. Did you know they had a fight that night?"

No response. I kept going, digging myself in deeper and deeper. This was not going well.

"I hope I'm making some sense. I'm trying to explain why it's taken me this long to see the truth, to understand that Ben, my friend who couldn't wait to go off to Chicago, would never have taken his own life."

They still hadn't said anything. I understood their silence. I tried not to think about that morning. My mother was the one who woke me up with the news. She sat down on my bed and tried to explain the unexplainable. I pushed her away and accused her of lying. When she reached over again and embraced me in a fierce bear hug, I understood it was true. My initial shock gave way to unbearable grief and then, I'm ashamed to say, to all-consuming anger. I was furious. What right did Ben have to take his life and leave the rest of us to suffer the consequences? All I wanted to do was to get away and forget. I never took the time to really consider the facts.

"I know it's been years but my gut is telling me that something about that night is just not right. I think Ben had been looking into the backgrounds of some of the engineers and scientists who were living in Huntsville. That's really why I came. I was hoping you might know what he was into those last few weeks before we graduated. Maybe he discovered something incriminating about Erich and Karin's father. He could have confronted Erich and then who knows what could have happened. I'm sure you know that Erich and Ben despised each other. I guess I have a lot of unanswered questions."

I was unnerved by their silence. I was a fairly intuitive observer of body language and I could feel the tension radiating off of them. They were now holding hands tightly. I was missing something.

Did they know that Karin and I were dating? I didn't think anyone suspected, but it was only the day before that I found out from my cousin that my mother thought something was going on. Karin and I thought we had done a pretty good job at keeping our relationship a secret, but apparently we hadn't. We hadn't wanted to upset my parents or hers. She was even more concerned that Erich would find out. Even then, I knew how skittish he made her. At the time, I hadn't known what I felt more guiltier about—deceiving my parents or actually being in love with someone whose father may have been a member of the Nazi Party.

Mrs. Lowe's composure looked like it was about to crumble, and I had no idea what to say or do next. They were still holding hands and seemed to be sinking into their own memories from that long-ago morning.

"Look," I said, "I'm sorry. I shouldn't have come. This was a mistake. I can see that. I don't know what I was thinking."

I started to get up to say goodbye, and suddenly Helen could no longer hold back her tears. They were now running down her face, and Frank had moved over to take his wife in his arms.

"Tommy, no, do not leave," Helen said.

Frank offered Helen the handkerchief from his pocket, but instead of wiping away her tears she buried her face in the cloth.

Finally, Frank spoke.

"We have held on to our own complicity in this for so many years. It is very difficult for us to speak about that time. After losing so many relatives and friends in the Holocaust, to lose our son in that way—for him to have taken his own life."

He could barely finish.

"Frank, that's why I'm here. I think there's a possibility that Ben may have been murdered. I never thought Ben committed suicide. Not really. I should have said something when it first happened."

"STOP!"

I was shaken by the outburst. In all my years of knowing Frank Lowe I had never heard him raise his voice.

"Tommy, no more. What you are saying is nonsense. Ben was not murdered. He took his life, and it is our fault. We should have told you long ago, but we could never bring ourselves to talk about what happened the night before he was found. We betrayed our son. He came to us for support, for understanding and we denied him that one simple request. That is why we never questioned the report from the medical examiner. We knew why our son took his own life."

"Please," I said. "I don't understand."

He looked at Helen. He was asking her for permission to go on. She nodded toward him and he continued.

"We never wanted to hurt you," Frank continued. "More importantly, neither did Ben. We're so sorry, but on that last night he finally told us that he and Karin were in love and were hoping to someday be married. He was riddled with guilt. He had betrayed your friendship and he was planning to come clean the next morning. All that time they spent together. He said they had so much in common. He told us that he could barely look at you any longer, because he was so overcome by guilt. You were like a brother to him. He wanted to tell you, but Karin kept telling him to wait. She was terrified of the reaction she would get from her father and from her brother, and, like Ben, she didn't want to hurt you. Our son had finally convinced her that they had to tell the truth to their parents and to you. The night of the barbecue, Ben came home to speak with us, and Karin, I always assumed, went home to talk to her parents."

What do you do when everything you believed is suddenly upended? *Was I that much of an idiot? I was eighteen and in love, but come on, was I that blind?*

"I never suspected. Not ever. Are you sure? I mean, of course you're sure. She always acted like my girl. We would meet up at the movies and hold hands when no one else was around."

I tried to think of all the times we had been alone together. It wasn't often. Karin was never very amorous with me. She'd kiss me a few times on the lips and then would tell me that she wasn't ready for anything else. I respected her. I never pushed for something more. We were young, and the era of free love was years away. I suddenly realized that I was on the brink of losing it too. I was not only sad, but I was also pissed. The two people I trusted most had lied to me. Maybe I didn't owe Ben anything after all.

"That night, Ben came home late," Frank continued. "We always stayed awake to make sure he was safely home. He was our only child. When he came in he was angry. He was swearing, muttering something about Erich. We didn't know what to think. We saw the cut above his left eye, but when we asked him what happened he refused to tell us. We now think Erich may have learned the truth about his relationship with Karin, and they fought. We did not know what to make of it. We had never seen Ben act that way before. We were frightened. We kept asking him what was wrong. At first, he would not tell us. He must have known how we would react. He was as frightened as we were. He told us then about Karin, that they were in love and about his plan to tell you the truth. We overreacted; there were words. I threatened to disown him, my own son. I told him that if he brought that shame upon our house he would be dead to me and to his mother. When he said they had so much in common I could no longer control my rage and I slapped him. I hit my child across the face, and for what? For being a teenager in love with a girl? I will never forget the silence that followed. Ben, my beautiful boy looked at me with what I then thought was comprehension. That he understood the pain his relationship with *Herr* Angel's daughter was causing us. I was wrong. Ben left the house and that is the last time we saw our son alive."

"So you really don't know what happened after that?" I said.

"Yes, yes we do. It is obvious, is it not? Don't you see? Ben came to us for understanding, for acceptance, and we denied him the only thing he'd ever asked of us."

My own emotions were whirling. I was still working it through. I had been played and was feeling like a fool. My game was really not my game at all. It was Ben's. For a second, I thought about making up some excuse and just leaving, but when I looked at the Lowes all I saw were their pained expressions. They were the real victims in all this. I knew I would stay and hear the rest of the story.

Frank left Helen's side and walked over to the cabinet on the far side of the room. He was obviously looking for something. I hoped he was bringing over a couple of glasses from the bottle of scotch that was sitting on the nearby bar. I was in desperate need of a drink. Helen and I sat there waiting. After several minutes of searching he found what he was looking for and motioned for me to come closer. They made room, and I took the seat between the two of them on the sofa. Once I was wedged in he gently opened a worn leather-bound photograph album, its black pages brittle from age. I remembered seeing something similar in my own home. The pictures had been carefully arranged and were held in place by black paper corners, some of which were unsuccessfully reinforced with stiff, yellowed tape that floated to the ground as soon as the book was opened.

"This album came with us when we emigrated from Germany in 1939," said Frank. "At the time we could not imagine that it would become a family memorial book. All of our relatives, the faces on these pages, are no more. No one survived. Only us—Helen, myself, and of course, for a time, our Ben."

It was hard to take in. Set before me were photographs of men, women and children engaged in all sorts of activities. There were dozens of images of a much younger Frank and Helen posing with Ben as a toddler and then as an eight or nine-year-old. In one, they were enjoying the beach with several other families. In another, I saw Ben posed with a stuffed teddy bear sitting on a tricycle. I viewed countless pictures of aunts, uncles and cousins. They were snapshots in time. Photographs of people who wanted to capture their memories on film, hoping that one day they would be able to look back and admire their younger selves. In some, Frank was proudly standing in uniform. Ben had never mentioned that his father had served the Kaiser during the First World War. I couldn't turn away from the image of a five-year-old Ben in lederhosen and knee socks. *So that was when the affinity for those shorts started,* I thought. I couldn't help but smile. In the photograph, he was carrying a paper-wrapped cone full of candy. Helen told me that all German children were presented with a *Schultüte* on the first day they started school. She explained that it was a tradition that could be traced back to the early 1800s. I could barely continue looking, but if they could then I had to. It was hard to reconcile these fun-filled images with the horror that I knew awaited those smiling faces. Frank now turned to the back of the album to show me a very professional looking portrait of an extremely handsome man—someone who reminded me of how Ben might have looked if he had lived past his eighteenth birthday.

"This is my younger brother, Ben's uncle. His name was Bernhard. He was twenty-seven when this photograph was taken, and he had just completed his medical training. He had no interest in the family business. Even as a boy we all knew he wanted to be a doctor. He couldn't wait for me to scrape my knee or to skin an elbow so he could clean the wound and make a bandage for it."

Frank's fingers were lovingly touching the photograph of his younger brother.

"If you have more time, I have a story I'd like to share," he said.

"My flight isn't until this evening; I have plenty of time."

§

"I am not sure how much you know or remember about how and why my family ended up in Huntsville," Frank said.

"I know you were arrested and sent to a concentration camp. Ben never wanted to talk about it. I learned a little of your story from Joe. He wanted me to have an understanding of what he was fighting for."

"Ah, your brother," added Helen. "He was a very courageous young man. We both liked him very much."

"Thank you. He liked the two of you as well."

My emotions were getting the better of me. I could feel myself beginning to choke up again. I prided myself on controlling myself in front of other people. I had developed a technique in the courtroom, and in my personal life, of hiding behind a mask of indifference. Nothing was working. Helen got up and handed me a tissue and Frank continued.

"After the night that they now call *Kristallnacht*, I was sent to Sachsenhausen, a concentration camp about twenty miles north of Berlin. Even now, after all these years, I find it hard to grasp how honest and productive citizens were so easily stripped of all their rights and criminalized. I was a loyal German, wounded in the Ardennes during the First World War. I loved my country and served proudly. It counted for nothing. I was sent to hell for the crime of being a Jew. The food at the camp was meager and I along with most of my fellow inmates were regularly beaten. We worked for ten hours a day without any rest. Many died from the horrible treatment. I was one of the lucky ones. I was let go after several weeks because my documents were in order. Your father had offered to sponsor me, and we promised to leave Germany, to comply with the Nazi plan to make the country *Judenrein*, free of Jews. Of course this was all before the final solution, when emigration was still an option.

"Being able to leave was one thing; finding a place to go was quite another. Unfortunately, most of our other relatives waited too long, or went to what they thought were safe havens in other parts of Europe. Bernhard and his young wife, Lizbet, stayed. Her parents were in denial and would not consider emigrating. They were fools. She did not want to leave them, but could have been persuaded if Bernhard had insisted. He didn't. He felt a responsibility toward his Jewish patients. He didn't want to abandon them and believed they could weather the storm. They had a child, a beautiful little boy with brown, curly hair and bright blue eyes. His name was Walter. Helen and I adored him and so did Ben. The two of them looked so much alike, even down to the freckles scattered across their noses and cheeks. I begged them to leave, if not for themselves then for their child. When Austria and the Sudetenland were annexed, I was sure their time was running out.

"Once Poland was invaded, Bernhard and Lizbet finally accepted the inevitable. Your father signed an affidavit for them, but it was too late. Like so many others, they had nowhere to go, and since miracles were in short supply, they were doomed."

I looked at my watch and realized another hour had flown by. My flight was due to take off in ninety minutes. I would never make it. I no longer wanted to. I needed to hear the rest of the story.

"Tommy, we have kept you too long," said Helen.

She had seen me checking the time.

"You have a flight to catch, no?"

"No. I mean yes, but I need to know about the part of Ben's life he never talked about. I thought he told me everything. I didn't think we had any secrets."

"We are so sorry. You are hurt, no?"

"I'm fine. I'm the one who should be apologizing. I'm the one who arrived on your doorstep unannounced, and I'm the one who dredged all of this up. I was a kid. I thought Karin was in love with me. Trust me, I've moved on. No worries on that score."

They looked so relieved. As my mama used to tell me, some lies are okay if they're for the greater good.

"Let me use your telephone. I'm sure there's a flight in the morning. Do you mind having a houseguest overnight?"

Helen got up from her chair and came over to hug me.

"Thank you," she whispered into my ear.

Frank then walked over to the cabinet, where earlier he had retrieved the photograph album, and finally poured each of us a drink from that bottle of scotch I had been eying. Once we were all resettled into our respective seats, he continued with his story.

"By 1939, the situation for our remaining relatives in Germany was urgent. We received desperate letters asking for our help. Life had become intolerable. No one could work, and food was getting scarce. We sent money and parcels but could do little else to improve their lot. We waited, praying that they would move up on the quota register for individuals allowed to emigrate from Germany, but by then the list was so long, and we had little hope."

Once again, Frank got up and returned to the cabinet. This time he came back with a tattered shoebox tied with a dingy string that he struggled to unknot. When he finally removed the lid I could see small piles of correspondence, held neatly together and bound with a ribbon. I watched as he tenderly untied one of the packets and took out the last letter in the stack. The blue onionskin paper was fragile, and Frank took his time to unfold it. He began to translate.

*10 September 1941*

*Dearest Franz,*

*It is with great sadness that I write to you that our beloved parents decided to end their lives in the same way they had chosen to live for the last fifty years, as a couple. They refused to submit to any more indignities and Lizbet found them lying in bed this morning still holding hands. Please know, that in the conditions under which we are now living, it was the right and only choice for them to make. They are finally at peace.*

*Lizbet and I are young, and for the sake of our son, will continue to try to emigrate. Recently, we heard that Cuba is once again an option. Until then, our hope is that we can somehow find a way to survive the madness that has overtaken our country.*

*The conditions we are living in are beyond my capabilities to describe. As you are well aware we have been denied all of our rights. I fear that soon we will be denied even the right to exist.*

*As of last week we were required to wear a yellow star on our clothing. Thank God that Walter, who is only five, does not understand what is going on all around him. He was too young to be sent on one of the Kindertransports, and of course they have long been discontinued. Lizbet and I are tireless in our efforts to save our son. It occupies our thoughts day and night.*

*I hope this letter reaches you. I pray for your good health and for that of Herta and Benjamin.*

*Your beloved brother,*

*Bernhard*

"This was the last letter I ever received. Once the war was over I contacted the Red Cross. It took some time, but they were finally able to tell us the fate of our loved ones. In February of 1942, Bernhard and Lizbet were deported to Auschwitz-Birkenau. According to the Red Cross, Lizbet was gassed to death on the same day that she arrived. Bernhard survived the selection process and was put to work in the camp. I have no record of his time there. I do not want to know what he must have endured. They could not find any information about Walter. It's as if he disappeared. He must have been hidden before they were deported."

"*Du nehmen zu lang,*" whispered Helen under her breath.

Frank smiled.

"Helen says I'm taking too long and that I should get to the end already. She still lapses into that dreadful language whenever she is upset."

"No, please. I want to know what happened."

Helen got up and walked into the kitchen.

"It is hard for her. She does not like to be reminded of the war. She rarely speaks about it. Walter was like a second son to her, and for a long time we both hoped he was still alive and would somehow find his way back to us. We searched survivor registries and contacted tracing services throughout Germany. Once in a while we would hear a story of a child being found in an orphanage or living with a family. So many children had been lost. Organizations in Israel and America tried to find them all."

When it became obvious that Helen had decided to stay in the kitchen Frank continued.

"Bernhard was not in Auschwitz too long, perhaps a few weeks. According to the records he was then sent to several other labor camps, and finally, he ended up near the city of Nordhausen at a sub-camp of Buchenwald called Dora. The conditions were unbearable. The Nazis were losing the war, and Hitler was convinced that the V-2 rockets would turn the tide in his favor. Production was at a frenzied pace, and Bernhard, like thousands of others, was worked to death. He was expendable. They all were."

I had now come full circle. The pieces were coming together. Dora was the camp where Karin's father, along with von Braun and many of the other Huntsville scientists, had worked to create Hitler's Vengeance Weapons. The V-1s and V-2s were pilotless, subsonic, and supersonic missiles that were responsible for the deaths of several thousand individuals in 1944 and 1945 in England and in Belgium.

"Is that where Bernhard died?" I asked.

"Yes, although we did not find out for another two years. The Red Cross tracing service told us he had been at Dora, but that was where the trail ended. We did not know if he died there or if he had been sent elsewhere. We still fantasized that he would somehow reappear, but in 1947 we received a letter from a man we all knew from our days in Germany. An acquaintance really, but he recognized Bernhard when he arrived at Dora and was there with him at the end. The Red Cross had also helped him to locate us. I've saved the letter. It's in here with all the others."

After searching for a few minutes, Frank pulled out another letter still neatly folded inside of its envelope. It was in German and Frank translated as he read.

*Dear Mr. and Mrs. Lowe,*

*Your brother Bernhard and I enjoyed a short reunion of sorts when he arrived at Dora. We knew many of the same people from our days in Berlin. Speaking with him about our respective lives before the war provided a short respite from the horror surrounding us. I only wish I had better news to share. I am deeply saddened to tell you that he was already in a very weakened state when I first recognized him. It was February and extremely cold. We worked nonstop in inhumane conditions. We had little food and no clothing to protect us from the elements. Bernhard knew his days on this earth were coming to an end and asked me to try and locate you if I survived. He wanted to let you know how hard he had tried to live and that his son was in safe hands. He said you would know how to find him.*

"But I didn't. God forgive me, I didn't."

Tears were now steadily streaming down Frank's face.

"I got in touch with the letter writer, hoping he had more information about Walter's whereabouts, but he had nothing else to add. Helen and I have wracked our brains. So few of our old friends survived the war. We contacted everyone possible and wrote countless letters, but no one had any information. It made no sense. All we needed was a name. Why didn't my brother just give us a name?"

"The war was still raging," I said. "He was probably still worried about Walter's safety."

"Perhaps, but we were left with nothing to go on."

Helen must have noticed the silence that now pervaded the living room. She reappeared and once again took the seat next to her husband.

"So you see," she continued.

She acted as if she had never left and knew everything Frank had just told me.

"What happened at Nordhausen, or Dora, whatever you want to call that dreadful place never leaves us. When I used to see von Braun and the others driving around town, shaking hands, being patted on their backs for their contributions to the space program, I wanted to shout out 'MURDERERS!' Sometimes I would tremble, unable to contain my rage. Thousands of people, not just Jews, were killed at Dora. In fact most of the slave laborers at Dora were not Jewish. Those who had somehow managed to still be alive when the Nazis ceased production were sent on a death march, where thousands more perished.

The Germans didn't want their crimes discovered by the liberating American troops. *Ach*, but the scientists and engineers were in hiding. They had already been evacuated to relative safety in the Bavarian Alps."

"And then they surrendered to the Americans and were eventually brought to Huntsville," I muttered quietly.

"Yes," Helen said.

"I remember how awful it was for my parents when the Germans first arrived. They never forgave them for Joe's death. He was killed for nothing. The war was almost over. I can't even begin to imagine how it was for all of you."

"We felt as if our world had been turned upside down," Helen said. "Once again, we were living amongst the same men who had either committed heinous acts at the camp or at least were culpable because they turned a blind eye to what went on there. We began to question our own sanity. How could the perpetrators suddenly be living next door? Why hadn't they been punished?"

"My father never felt as if he could say anything," I said. "It seemed like everyone was taken with the new folks in town. Daddy kept saying that his friends and neighbors had short memories. It was a hard pill for him to swallow."

I thought about my recent conversation with Al. I couldn't bring myself to tell them that even my father chose to keep quiet about the newcomers.

"We began to feel isolated in the town that had once been so welcoming," said Frank. "The arrival of the Germans changed how we felt about Huntsville, how we felt about our neighbors. Before they came, we felt safe. Everyone was nice. During the war there was even an article about our family in the local paper. I still have the clipping. It was all about how your father helped to save us from the clutches of the Nazi beasts. They even sent out a photographer to take a photograph of us for the article. For a short time we were celebrities, but in all honesty we never really fit in.

"After the war I think we seemed more foreign to the local population than the newcomers. They were Christian, and on Sundays they all attended church and began to socialize with their neighbors. And most importantly, because of them, jobs were created and Huntsville became the center of the space program. No one remembered or cared about what happened during the war, let alone the feelings of one insignificant family. We understood that, as Jews, we were still considered the outsiders."

*Had I been fooling myself all these years?* I was Jewish, but my personal history was different. I had been raised as a Southerner, albeit a Jewish Southerner, but nevertheless, I considered myself part of the fabric of my community. It was my heritage. I still identified myself as such. My Jewishness was always secondary. I had lived in Atlanta for almost twenty years and I still hadn't joined a synagogue. My mother had to remind me about the High Holy Days. She would buy me a ticket so I could accompany her a couple of times a year. When Joe was killed there was an outpouring of support from the entire community. The town even raised money for a scholarship fund in Joe's memory at the University of Alabama. The scholarship is awarded each and every year to a worthy student from East Clinton High School's football team.

For really the first time, I was thinking about what Al had said about not wanting to make waves, because some Jews in the South, maybe even in Huntsville, didn't want to stand out. Is that what my father did when he accepted the Germans in our town? Is that what we all did when we put up our Christmas trees and hunted for Easter eggs? When Frank and Helen moved to Huntsville they were still afraid, but rather than trying to fit in, they voluntarily excluded themselves from civic and social organizations and made no friends other than my parents and a couple of other Jewish families in town. In retrospect, I'm sure they wished they had moved away from Huntsville sooner, to a larger city where there was a community of survivors, people with whom they could connect. The German scientists came as a group, and even though they initially found comfort among themselves, they quickly adapted. Their leader, Wernher von Braun, was a charismatic self-promoter. If I found it difficult to imagine him in the uniform of the SS, I imagine most other people felt the same way.

"Did you ever think about moving to Israel?" I asked.

"Once," Helen said. "We talked about it, but decided no. America is our home. It is the place that took us in when we had nowhere else to go. And here, in New York, we no longer felt so alone."

"Did Ben know that his uncle died at Dora?"

"Yes, we kept nothing from him. He also knew that his grandparents had committed suicide. He wanted to know what happened to his family. We waited until the war was almost over to tell him."

I remembered the day when Ben told me his grandparents were dead. We had been walking to the ballpark. It was the same day I found out about Joe. I didn't understand why Ben was so convinced his grandparents were gone. Now I knew. Bernhard had let his parents know in a letter written two years earlier, and the Lowes must have just told Ben.

"But I still don't understand why you're so sure you had anything to do with Ben's death. He may have been confused. He may even have been angry, but the Ben I knew would have never hurt you like that."

*The Ben I knew. Maybe I hadn't known him that well after all*, I thought.

"You must face the facts," said Frank. "Ben saw no other way out. We gave him no choice. I told him he was dishonoring the memory of all our relatives who were murdered during the war. We refused to accept Karin. We told him to give her up. He was probably dreading telling you the truth. Eighteen-year-old boys sometimes act irrationally. He must have felt he had no other option."

I didn't say anything. It was obvious; I was on the verge of antagonizing Frank. I was more convinced than ever that my friend did not kill himself. Ben, just like his parents, was a survivor. Something else had happened and for all of our sakes, I was going to find out what it was.

# 18

## 1968

I SAID MY goodbyes to Helen and Frank before heading up to bed. I had an early-morning flight and after the day's revelations I suspected they needed their rest. By the end of the evening they had relaxed a little, and we spoke about other, more pleasant memories. They were relieved to have finally told me about Karin and Ben's secret relationship and about their guilt over the events of that last night. They thanked me for coming. Then they handed me a large art portfolio. I immediately knew what was inside.

"These are for you," said Helen. "Ben would have wanted you to have them. We should have given them to you years ago. We know you will take good care of them."

I decided to wait until I was back in Huntsville to look at the drawings and stories from the comic book Ben had created, and I had worked on. My emotions were in turmoil, and I couldn't trust myself to revisit *Stark* in front of the Lowes.

I was glad Helen and Frank felt that my visit was healing. I, on the other hand, felt worse. Not only was I now firmly convinced that something other than suicide was the cause of Ben's death, but I was also dealing with the realization that Karin never loved me, and that my best friend had duped me. I was startled by how much that bothered me. My so-called relationship with Karin had happened eighteen years earlier. I had been married and divorced in the ensuing years. Why in the hell was I was taking it so hard? I already knew the answer. I still had feelings for Karin.

The flight back to Birmingham went off without a hitch, and within two hours' time, I was searching for my car in the airport parking lot. I was back in Huntsville by eleven o'clock. The plane ride had given me a chance to think. My anger toward Karin and Ben had ebbed. We were kids. We did dumb things. If anything, my visit added to my conviction. Ben didn't commit suicide, and the Lowes deserved to know the truth and finally find some peace.

The urge to call Karin the moment I landed was hard to tamp down. Thankfully, the more measured side of me won out. Anything I thought we had was not only long over, it had never existed in the first place.

Still, I wondered if she had left any messages for me with Al, or if he had told her where I was; then I wanted to kick myself for wondering. I was getting another headache and popped a couple of Excedrins. I needed to focus on something other than Karin so I headed over to the library where Miss Jones welcomed me back with a broad smile and an outstretched hand.

"I expected you yesterday," she said.

"I know. Something came up, but I'm here now."

"I'm wondering if you have any resources relating to Dora-Mittelbau and the manufacturing of the V-2 rockets," I asked.

"There's not much," she said. "I'll see what I can get my hands on."

She returned several minutes later.

"That didn't take long."

She was smiling.

"It's sort of been a pet project of mine."

Alma handed me a file.

"Is that it?" I asked.

"I'm afraid so. If you were interested in Auschwitz-Birkenau or Treblinka, extermination centers created for the sole purpose of killing, I could bring you several well-researched histories. Unfortunately, there's been little to no scholarship completed on the lesser-known camps and almost nothing about Dora. Do you mind me asking why you're interested in that particular camp?"

I kind of did mind, but I couldn't bring myself to be rude to Miss Jones.

"I'm doing a little research for a friend. His uncle died at Dora."

"Oh, I see."

I had no idea what she saw, but noticed a slightly upward tilt to her lips as she handed me the file and walked back to her office.

The documents were mostly copies of clippings from various papers and were arranged in chronological order. I started with the first, a *New York Times* article published on May 4, 1945. It was written by Clare Boothe Luce, the wife of Henry Luce, the publisher of *Time*, *Life*, and *Fortune* magazines, and a congresswoman from Connecticut. She was reporting back from a recent two-month tour of war-torn Europe that included a visit to Nordhausen and the Dora-Mittelbau complex of camps.

In the article, Luce described what she saw. "When the Third Armored Division came to Nordhausen, they liberated the prisoners of that camp. There were some 50,000 of them. They were dying at a rate of 900 daily when our troops arrived. Indeed, the dead and the dying were difficult to tell apart in the hideous barracks of Nordhausen. Nevertheless, numbers of them were still capable of working, and had, they said, been laboring for the Nazis. The Nazis forced the prisoners to work in what appeared from the air to be an abandoned salt mine."

She then went on to write: "Deep in the green mountains our troops found a vast underground network of tunnels, well lighted, air conditioned, full of the finest modern machine tools. And on its mile-long assembly belts they found in various stages of completeness thousands of V-1s and V-2s—the great secret weapons that might have destroyed Britain, but for D-Day." Luce had accused the Nazis of deliberately starving and torturing slave laborers to death to protect the secrecy of the weapons they worked on.

The original production facility for V-1 and V-2 rockets was at Peenemünde, on the coast of the Baltic Sea. Allied bombing forced the Nazis to move to a yet-to-be-built, underground location in the Harz Mountains north of the German city of Nordhausen. Slave labor, and a lot of it, was used to dig the massive complex out of the rock. The work began in 1943, and because the prisoners were kept underground the mortality rate was higher than at most other slave labor camps. Once a prisoner was too weak to work they were sent to Auschwitz-Birkenau to be gassed to death. *How efficient*, I thought.

Throughout the morning I kept thinking about Bernhard. He was probably about my age when he died. I imagined each new indignity that he and Lizbet must have suffered, the multitude of restrictions and pronouncements that methodically closed off all avenues for him and his little family to escape. And how, even at the end, when he and wife were loaded on the train, how hard it must have been to fully comprehend that something so outrageously preposterous could actually be happening to them. I also wondered if they had really found a sanctuary for their son, and if they did, where in the hell was he? I thought Frank mentioned that Walter was five when they left Germany. That would have meant that he was at least eight or nine when he went into hiding. Certainly, a boy that age would have remembered his real parents and want to be returned. Wouldn't the people who had sheltered him have been searching for his relatives? I didn't like the answers I was coming up with and thought that Walter was very likely dead.

I had closed the file and was thinking about all the horrors that the Lowe family had endured, when Mrs. Jones quietly appeared by my table to ask if she could bring me anything else. Were all librarians inherently quiet? She was like an elderly sprite—there one minute and gone the next. It must have been the sensible soft-soled shoes she was wearing. I had already exhausted all the articles I could find about the camp, so I asked her to bring me whatever she had on the scientists who came to Redstone in 1950.

"Why?" she asked. "Perhaps if I knew the nature of your research, I could be of more help."

I hadn't studied in a library setting since law school, but Miss Jones seemed nosier than the librarians I remembered. I wasn't sure how to answer. Should I tell her that I was trying to prove that my best friend, the boy who had spent so much time in this building as a child, did not commit suicide? I looked around, not wanting anyone within earshot. There was one older man at the table next to mine with a pile of old *National Geographic* magazines in front of him and two senior women on his other side immersed in their own whispered conversation. No one was paying attention to Miss Jones and me.

"Thomas Stern, I've known you your entire life. Tell me what you're up to and maybe I can help."

I decided to trust her. She loved Ben too. All those suppressed memories were flooding my brain. I hoped I wouldn't stroke out from the onslaught. Many of the children who had made use of this library were reluctant students at best. We were still a farming community back then, and a lot of the kids didn't have much interest in furthering their education. Once high school was over, they were heading back to the family farm. If Ben and I weren't playing ball or working on *Stark* we were usually found at the library. We both loved to read, and we both loved to learn. I suppose Miss Jones remembered all that.

"I'm trying to figure out some things about the last couple of days of Ben's life. I should have tried harder years ago. Ben wasn't the kind of kid who would have taken his own life. I'm not even sure what I'm looking for, but I went up to New York yesterday and spent some time with Ben's parents. They blame themselves for his suicide. I need to prove them wrong. I need to find out what happened to him, for their sake and maybe for mine too."

Miss Jones pulled out the chair next to mine and sat down. It offered me the chance to really look at her. When she placed her hands on the table, I saw that her fingers were gnarled and misshapen. She had to have been suffering from arthritis for years, and I had never noticed. Miss Jones caught me staring and pulled her hands back onto her lap. She was a proud woman. She had always been thin, but now she seemed frailer. She had to be over seventy. The Huntsville Library must not have had a retirement age. We sat for a few minutes in silence. Was Miss Jones thinking about the boy who read every single book in the section on art?

Finally, she spoke.

"It's about time someone looked into this. I never thought Ben Lowe committed suicide. That boy loved life and he was looking forward to his future. When his body was discovered in the schoolyard, no one really bothered to investigate. His parents were in shock and for whatever reason they didn't question the police or the medical examiner. It was easier for everyone in this town to believe that a smart, good-natured kid with a great future killed himself rather than imagining that something as nefarious as murder might have happened."

She rose from her chair with a determined look on her face.

"Now what do you need?"

I had a renewed respect for my local librarian.

"I want to learn as much as I can about the scientists that came here in 1950. More specifically, I'd like to find out what some of those guys did during the war."

"You know, Tommy, this town is very protective of those fellows. They put Huntsville on the map, and some folks aren't going to take too kindly to you asking a lot of questions."

"I know. So for now, let's just keep it our little secret."

I couldn't believe I had just made a pact with Miss Jones, but before I could offer her my thanks she was off again, only to return five minutes later with a thick file labeled "Wernher von Braun."

"You should start here," she said. "Von Braun was the star of the program. He still is. Did you know he's living in Washington now?"

"No, I thought he was still the director of the center here in town."

"He was, but he was just appointed as NASA's deputy associate administrator for planning."

"Did the town go into mourning when he moved away?"

This time her smile went from ear to ear. She then put her hand on my shoulder and left me to the task at hand.

Von Braun was a media magnet, and the file was filled with news articles about his arrival, his marriage to a cousin from Germany, the births of his children, and most importantly, his work as the director of NASA's George C. Marshall Space Flight Center here in Huntsville. This was where the Saturn rockets were developed that would eventually launch men to the moon. Some of the articles jogged my own memory of the man, and I remembered watching our local hero standing next to the creator of Mickey Mouse when he appeared on *Walt Disney's Wonderful World of Color* in a three-part series about space. What I didn't know was that he also became the technical advisor for Disney's Tomorrow Land, the futuristic section of America's most beloved theme park. No one could have possibly entertained any lingering doubts about von Braun's past once Mr. Disney introduced him on national TV. I know I didn't.

I finished the entire folder and still didn't have any insight into what von Braun and some of his associates might have known, or possibly been complicit in, at Nordhausen/Dora. Were they culpable for the atrocities carried out there? How much did they know?

I had spent over two hours poring over the material, and thus far all of my reading had only supported what everyone in Huntsville already felt. Von Braun was a great guy who had managed to outwit and outrace the Russians and had become a national hero in the process. He was on Disney for gosh darn sakes.

I thought about leaving for a while—maybe taking a drive to clear my head—when Miss Jones reappeared at my table. This time she had a much thinner folder in her hand.

"What's this?" I asked.

"My secret stash. It hasn't been easy, but I've managed to put together a more complete dossier on our leading scientist. I've also gathered some information on some of the others, if you care to take a look."

I was now observing Miss Jones with renewed interest. Perhaps I had never before really looked at her with any interest at all. She had been the librarian ever since I could remember, and even though she must have only been in her fifties when I first knew her, she'd always seemed old. There was a twinkle in her eye and a kind of "I gotcha" smile.

"Why?" I asked. "Why did you do all this?"

"Because I never felt like we were getting the whole picture. Those fellows were brought here because of what they knew, and because they could get us to the moon before the Russian cosmonauts got there. I lost a brother on the beaches of Normandy, and I, for one, never forgot what they did to all those innocent people. After the war, so many Germans claimed that they hadn't known, heard, or seen anything. They reminded me of those three little monkeys. Evil was all around them and they chose to ignore it."

"That's pretty much what my daddy used to say."

"Well your daddy was a smart man. I always liked him, and, by the way, I miss Stern's. It was a great department store. I still have a hat I bought there right before it closed up. Everyone was treated fair and square by your daddy."

Once Mrs. Jones walked away I opened the file. I couldn't believe it. She had put together a dossier that would have made the CIA proud.

Von Braun was born in Wirsitz, Germany, in 1912, to a military and aristo-cratic family. As a boy, he developed a love for astronomy that led to a passionate belief in the possibility of space travel. In 1932, he transferred from a technical school to the University of Berlin where he received his PhD in physics. While attending the university, he joined a cavalry unit within the *Schutzstaffel,* or SS that was founded in 1925 as Hitler's personal bodyguards and whose members would later be responsible for much of the genocide of millions of innocent people. One year later, von Braun dropped out, only to rejoin at a later date. By 1935, he led a group of eighty scientists and caught the attention of the *Luftwaffe,* the German air force, for whom he and his team were commissioned to de-velop a rocket-powered fighter plane. With the Nazis in power all non-military rocket research was strictly forbidden, which limited von Braun's options. In November 1937, he officially joined the Nationalist Socialist Party. A little over two years later, he received an officer's commission in the SS. He remained in the German military until the end of World War II and was eventually pro-moted to *Sturmbannführer,* a rank equivalent to that of a major in the United States military. The only dark spot in his exemplary resume happened in 1943 when he was arrested by *Reichsführer* Heinrich Himmler, the SS leader and chief of the German police, on the pretext that von Braun was overheard saying that rockets could be used for space travel after the war. He was released two weeks later, but Himmler had made his point and von Braun accepted his role in the manufacturing of weaponry and the use of slave labor to accomplish the task.

I read on through the morning, and two hours later I was even more con-fused about the man who had become the adored denizen of Huntsville. In an official government document dated April 23, 1947, von Braun stated that he was already the technical director of the Army Rocket Center at Peenemünde when he was officially asked to join the Nazi Party. He added that his refusal to join would have meant abandoning his life's work. Was that it? Would that have been his only punishment? How complicit was von Braun in the deaths of thousands of slave laborers? He visited the plant at Mittelwerk on numerous oc-casions. He was a witness to the conditions. Was he a perpetrator or a reluctant participant?

Von Braun and his team, including Hermann Angel, Karin and Erich's father, surrendered to US troops on May 2, 1945. The engineers were desperate to stay out of the hands of the Russians who, like the Americans, were dogged in their determination to capture and then exploit their knowledge. Under Operation Paperclip, the government-sanctioned program, deals would be made, personnel files cleansed, and pasts whitewashed in an effort to make the war records of these former members of the SS palatable to the American public. Simply put, the war was over and the United States was ready to move on. There was a new adversary to turn our attention toward. Within a few short years, the Third Reich was no longer Public Enemy Number One. Stalin, the Soviet threat, and the fear of a worldwide communist conspiracy to take over the world had displaced the Nazis. The Cold War was on its way.

By lunchtime my neck was aching, my eyes were burning, and I was yawning—surefire signals that a migraine headache was brewing. I knew I needed to take a break or I'd be lying in bed for the next two days. I got up and quickly located Alma (we were now on a first-name basis) behind her desk.

She had another file in her hands. It had the name of Hermann Angel on the tab. This one was thinner than the one on von Braun and held only a few pages. Good sense told me I should call it a day, but my curiosity got the better of me. I sat back down and started to read. There was nothing about his formative years, those that may have given me insight into the man's psyche. I did discover that in 1933, he joined the Nazi Party and started at the Technical College of Berlin, from where he later graduated with a degree in mechanical engineering. He joined the team at Peenemünde in 1936 and later, like von Braun, accepted an honorary rank in the SS. It was Angel who was responsible for establishing and maintaining the V-1 and V-2 production schedule at Dora and for making sure there were enough slave laborers to meet it. Again, I was unsettled by what it all meant in terms of complicity. The pressure must have been enormous and failure was not an option.

I must have looked miserable because as soon as I closed the file Alma appeared by my side and placed a hand on my shoulder.

"Are you okay?" she asked.

"I'm exhausted and my head is pounding. Is there any way you'd let me take these home?"

"These are copies. You can keep them. Besides, this is my own research. It's not a part of the catalogued library. Call me if you have any questions.

"You can count on it."

The pain in my head was getting to the stage of no return. I managed to drive the few short blocks back to Al's, where I swallowed a couple of pills and hoped I could sleep away the symptoms.

# 19

## 1968

I STAYED IN bed for the rest of that day and well into the next. I vaguely remembered Al checking on me. By noon, the pain in my head had subsided, and I felt well enough to get dressed and maybe eat a little something. I went into the kitchen expecting to see Al. He wasn't home, but he'd left two cornbread muffins on the table and a prepared pot of coffee, ready to turn on. I was becoming very fond of my cousin. Once I sat down I noticed the art portfolio that I had left on the dining room table in my haste to get up to bed. I carefully untied the ribbon that held the package together.

I hadn't seen these drawings and stories for over twenty years. By the time we were seniors in high school, Ben and I rarely discussed the comic book creation that was my boyhood obsession. In seconds, I was once again immersed in the stories of Kurt Bahn and his alter ego Stark. I had to admit that even though the plots were written by teenage boys, they still drew me in and took me back to the war years and Stark's battle against the Nazis. When I looked up at Al's kitchen cat clock, whose eyes and tail kept time with the passing seconds, I realized I had been sitting there for over an hour.

I was surprised by how many stories and drawings there were; I didn't remember working on that many. Then I understood that there were a number of stories I had never seen—artworks and storylines that Ben must have completed without me. The illustrations were better and the writing more sophisticated than that of the earlier books I had collaborated on. I could tell they were the work of an older more mature Ben.

I started to read. The cover depicted an anguished and tearful Stark standing over a tangled mass of bodies. All of the faces were purposely blurred except for one—that of a soulful-looking teenage girl whose eyes were open who begged me to look at her and remember. I forced myself to move on and turned my attention to Ben's depiction of his superhero creation. The Kurt/Stark character bore a striking resemblance to Ben's handsome uncle. Had he always looked like him? Probably. I just hadn't known until I saw the photograph of Bernhard in the Lowe family album. Ben never shared that he was recreating his father's murdered brother.

Unlike the earlier renditions of our superhero, this Stark looked tired and defeated. The speech balloon above his head read, "I couldn't save them." I turned the cover over to the splash page. This was the part of the comic book that prepared the reader for the rest of the book, similar in a way to the coming attraction trailers at the movies. In one scene, Stark was seen revealing his true identity to the world. His mission was complete. In another, Stark was shown leading American troops into an underground world, where more dead and near-dead victims were discovered in numbers that astounded the liberating soldiers. The bodies were piled high, stacked like distorted cords of wood. The illustrations could rival the work of some of the greats of the comic book world. I found myself pulled into the story and anxious to turn the pages, ready to find out what kind of nefarious and sinister projects were being carried out in the shadowy labyrinth, the secret underground city of evil created to carry out Hitler's plan to be master of the universe. Of course, I knew the end of the story. I knew that this was where the V-1 and V-2 rockets had been manufactured and was the place where Ben's uncle Bernhard, along with thousands of others, had perished.

In all comic books, the superhero's foil is the super-villain. Batman's nemesis was the Joker. Superman contended with Lex Luthor and his diabolical schemes. Ben and I created a few super-villains in those early years, but no one stood out. My favorite was the one who bore a strong resemblance to Hitler's minister of propaganda, Joseph Goebbels. Ben didn't have to do much to make Goebbels into a comic book villain. He already had a cadaverous look about him and was often seen in newsreel footage yelling and screaming with spittle flying out of his mouth. In this book, there was a new creation, someone who shared a shocking similarity to a person I had seen around Huntsville, but had never met. This villain's name was Dr. Angela, a mad Nazi scientist, who was head of production at the secret facility in the Harz Mountains. The likeness was unmistakable, and I wondered if Ben had ever shared this particular book with Karin.

According to Ben's parents, Ben and Karin were in love, so maybe he decided to confide in her. But confide what? What was he trying to say by making his super-villain look like one of NASA's most preeminent aeronautical engineers? What did Ben know about Dr. Angel's past? What, if anything, did Karin know? I reopened the file Alma gave me on Dr. Angel.

In 1933, Angel joined the Nazi Party. That was the same year Hitler became chancellor, and that fact alone made me question whether he should have been allowed to immigrate as part of the Paperclip group. There was no pressure to become a National Socialist back in '33. The people who joined then believed in the racist and nationalist ideology. In other words, Karin's father wanted to be a Nazi. I wondered if she knew.

It was now almost six in the evening, and I decided to call Karin to see if she was up to meeting me for dinner. Maybe not the best decision since I was still processing the fact that her father was a full-fledged Nazi, a true believer. Regardless, it was a conversation that needed to happen if Karin and I were ever to discover what really happened to Ben.

§

After Ben's funeral all I could think about was getting away from Huntsville and starting a new life. Even Karin was part of my old one. We hardly saw each other the rest of the summer. I stayed hidden at Stern's, working every day, including Saturdays. With Ben gone, I stopped hanging out with the old crowd. My friends tried, but eventually they gave up calling and coming over. Whenever Karin and I did get together our conversations never scratched the surface of what either of us was feeling. I was eighteen and in pain. I never considered that she was mourning her loss as much as I was mourning mine. I should have.

When I finally went over to say goodbye, I knew I had nothing left to give her. Part of me still loved her, and I supposed a part of me always would, but seeing her kept reminding me of Ben. I promised to write once I got to college, but after a few letters back and forth I just stopped, and she never wrote to ask why. At the time I knew I was being an ass, but I just couldn't rise to the occasion. It was time to tell her I was sorry.

When I called she picked up the phone on the first ring and we agreed to meet. I made a reservation at the Carriage Inn Motel Restaurant, one of Huntsville's finest. It was my parents' favorite restaurant when I was a kid, and I looked forward to seeing the old place again.

I made a reservation for seven. I got there early, hoping that a few sips of scotch would still my nerves and fortify my courage, but when I walked in Karin was already sitting at the bar. She was chatting with the bartender and nursing a drink. The man sitting a few stools down from Karin had just gotten up and had moved to the seat next to hers. I shouldn't have cared, but I did. He was about to make his play when she turned around.

She caught me staring and smiled. I walked over, and Karin moved a stool over to make room for me. Her would-be suitor shrugged his shoulders and smiled and then moved back to his seat at the other end.

"What are you having?" I asked.

"A vodka martini with olives."

I motioned to the bartender and told him to bring me one of the same.

"I thought you left town without saying goodbye," she said.

She probably wanted to add—*just like the last time when you went off the college.*

"Nope, still here. I did fly up to New York the day before yesterday."

"New York? And now you're back here. What's going on? Did you read Erich's journal? Did your trip have anything to do with him?"

"Whoa, slow down. Let's see if our table's ready, and then I promise I'll answer all of your questions."

Besides, I had a few questions of my own.

"Do you mind if we order first?" I asked once we sat down. "I really haven't had a decent meal since I've been back. I've been nursing a migraine and had to lay low for a while."

"You still get those? I remember you used to have to stay home from school."

"Not as often, but yes. Stress usually brings one on."

"I'm sorry. I suppose I'm the one responsible for the surge in your level of stress."

I didn't answer and changed the subject.

"I used to come here with my parents. I hope the food is still good."

"Are you trying to make small talk?" she asked. "Aren't we a little past that?"

She was right again, but I didn't know how to begin.

Once our orders were taken, we sat in silence finishing our drinks. I motioned to the waiter to bring us another round.

"Okay, spill it," she finally said. "If you're trying to protect me, don't. I can handle it."

I hoped so.

"After I read Erich's journal, I decided to fly up to New York to see Ben's parents. I had a few questions I wanted to ask them."

She paled. That was not what she was expecting to hear.

"How could you have bothered them? Don't you think they've suffered enough?"

"You're kidding me, right? Are you saying that I should have left well enough alone? Damn it, Karin. You're the one who started all this. You called me, remember?"

Silence.

"I'm sorry," she said. "I shouldn't have said that. It's just that I didn't think you would act so quickly. You should have told me."

"Why? You didn't even know them, or did you? Did Ben introduce you and tell them you were just friends?"

She looked puzzled.

"We were just friends."

I couldn't believe she was still being so evasive. What did it matter, after so many years?

"I never met them," she added. "Ben always spoke so lovingly about his parents. Are they well?"

"They're fine. Helen stays busy socializing with friends in the survivor community. They tend to stick together. They always felt so isolated living in Huntsville. Mr. Lowe, Frank, is a very successful clothing manufacturer and is still working."

"That's wonderful. I think I would even feel worse for them if I knew they were struggling financially."

"No, I suppose they're more than comfortable, but I wouldn't describe them as happy or even content. I doubt whether Ben's parents will ever again feel real joy. I think, maybe over time, it's become less of an effort to get through each day, but I'm not really sure. They lost every relative during the war and then they lost their only child."

"Can I ask you something?"

"Sure," I said.

"Do you blame me?"

"Blame you? For what?"

"For Ben's death of course and for the millions of Jews, Roma, Communists, Catholics, homosexuals, disabled and God knows how many other innocents who were killed during the war, or maybe for your brother who was mowed down, for no reason at all, in some farmer's field in Belgium."

"That's crazy. Of course not."

"Really? I don't think it's crazy at all. I think people like my brother, who can sleep at night, are the crazy ones. I've blamed myself for a long time. I have blamed myself ever since I saw that first newsreel footage from the camps after the war. My father and brother said it wasn't true, but I knew they were lying. I have blamed myself because I know my father was in the SS and that he worked at a slave labor factory. Do you know I've never said that to anyone before? I especially blame myself for every single member of Ben's family who died in some hellhole designed and operated by someone from my country. Do you know that Erich doesn't blame himself at all? Not one ounce of guilt. He's only sorry we didn't finish the job. I can barely look at him. I worry that some of his evil is inside of me too."

She already knew about her father. She had been holding onto that burden since we were kids. I handed her my napkin and she dabbed at the tears welling up in her eyes. We sat in silence for the next few minutes.

"You want to know the real reason I haven't moved away from Huntsville?" Karin asked.

She didn't wait for my reply.

"It's because I don't want to leave Ben," she said. "He was the kindest person I have ever met. I owe him that much. Don't I?"

"Why? Why do you think you owe Ben anything at all? It was a high school romance. The Lowes told me that the two of you were in love. And by the way, I had no clue until they told me. That's what a dope I was."

"Oh, Tommy. Deep down you are still the naive little boy you were back in high school. You think you understand, but really you don't understand anything at all."

I took another swallow of my drink.

"I owe it to Ben because I killed him. I may not have tied the knot or put the noose around his neck, but I'm still responsible."

"Karin, what in the hell are you trying to say?"

"Tell me what Ben's parents told you."

"They said that Erich was furious with Ben and with you on the night of the barbecue. They think he figured out that you and Ben were involved, and that's what led to the fight at the barbecue. When your brother left to take you home, Ben went to tell his parents the truth. They were furious. From what Frank told me, their argument got out of hand, and he ended up slapping his son. Ben stormed out of the house, and that's the last time they saw him. They blame themselves for his suicide. They think they pushed him into taking his life because they were so against your relationship."

Karin shook her head and reached for her drink.

"I need to go see them. I need to tell them. I'm the reason why Ben is dead. I should have told them years ago."

"You're not making any sense."

"I'm trying. I need to go back to the beginning. Remember when you first started to be a little friendlier to me at school?"

I found myself smiling at the memory.

"I couldn't understand why you had reached out. By the time we immigrated to America I knew about the war crimes of my countrymen, what we had done to the

Jewish people and to so many others. How could I have been anything other than ashamed? Then I was assigned to sit between the only two Jewish students in the homeroom. I was terrified. And of course, there was my brother to contend with. He had been fully indoctrinated in school by a fanatical Nazi teacher. He joined the German Young People when he was only ten and then, by the end of the war, he had matriculated into the Hitler Youth. He never changed his mind or felt the least bit of guilt for the crimes committed by our country."

"Karin, don't you see how strong you are? Most of us, myself included, imitate our parents. More often than not, Republicans beget Republican children and the same usually goes for Democrats. I don't know if I would have had the strength to resist the tug of my family's beliefs. That's an incredibly hard thing to do. You get that, don't you?"

The tears that Karin had managed to control were now streaming down her face, and once again I handed her my napkin. Even then, she looked beautiful and I had to suppress the urge to put my arms around her.

"I didn't. I couldn't really. My father forced me to join the *Bund Deutscher Mädel*, the girls equivalent to the Hitler Youth. I begged my mother to talk him out of it, but she had little say in those matters. She had little say about anything. My father ruled the home. He was an officer in the SS. Appearance was everything. He told me I would jeopardize his career, his standing, if I didn't join. Erich was no better. Pushing, always pushing me to become a good little Nazi. So, I signed up and wore my hair in braided pigtails and dressed up in my navy-blue skirt, white blouse, and brown jacket. We girls were carbon copies of one another. I doubted if our own parents could have told us apart from the back of our uniforms. We went on camping trips, exercised, and readied ourselves to one day serve the Reich by having as many purely bred Aryan children as possible."

"But you were different. Even with all that pressure you somehow managed to not believe. That's what separates you from your brother and people like him."

No reaction. I wasn't sure she had even heard me.

"We had a Jewish neighbor, Mrs. Weiss, a woman who lived one floor up in our apartment building. When I was very little she asked if I would like to call her *Tante* Anna, and that was how I came to think of her—as a beloved aunt who also happened to be a neighbor. She was probably no more than sixty when I first came to know her, but because of her thinning white hair, pulled into a tight braid atop her head, I always thought of her as old. *Tante* enjoyed baking and often brought my mother plates of warm streusel for our family to share. She also possessed a magnificent piano. It was a dark mahogany Bösendorfer, a gift from her parents in celebration of her tenth birthday. She had been classically trained, and we all benefited from her playing as the blissful melodies drifted up and down to the other apartments through the floorboards and grates. I was one of her students, and grew to love music because of her.

"At first, when Hitler came to power, the changes to everyday life had little effect on me. After all, I was shielded from all the new restrictions because of my privileged status as an Aryan. I've tried to retrieve my memories from those days. Did I think about the signs on the park benches or in restaurant windows that said No Jews? Did I notice if *Tante's* playing had taken on a more somber tone or if fewer children were showing up for piano lessons? I hope so, but I do not think I did."

I thought about my own acceptance of Jim Crow and shuddered at the realization that I was no less a bystander to all the inequities that surrounded my daily life. I didn't say anything and let Karin continue uninterrupted.

"Finally, on the same day that my Jewish classmates were expelled from school, I was also told that I could no longer visit *Tante* Anna or continue my piano lessons. I still wonder what affected me more—the expulsion of my friends or my own disappointment. I screamed and stomped at the injustice and was rewarded with a slap across my face from my mother. I suppose, in retrospect, that was probably my first inkling of the willingness of my parents to acquiesce, to go along regardless of their sense of right or wrong. Or perhaps I am giving them too much credit and they were true believers in *der Führer* and had few scruples to begin with. Honestly, I'm not sure.

"From that day on, whenever my parents and Erich went out I would sneak upstairs to her flat, and she would continue to quietly teach me. By then I was fully aware of her suffering and worried about her wellbeing. The ration allotments for Jews had been cut, and she was often too afraid to go out to purchase the few essentials of life she was allowed. Whenever possible, I brought her what I could, but it was never enough. Except for me, my *Tante* was alone in the world. Her husband had died in the trenches during the First World War, before they had the chance to have any children, and I don't think she ever thought about emigrating. She had nowhere to go, having lived in Berlin all of her life.

"One day, I snuck upstairs and found an open apartment emptied of its only occupant. All of her possessions were still there, but not her. When I ran downstairs to tell my mother, she told me that Mrs. Weiss had decided to move, that I should forget about her. My mother looked straight into my eyes and lied. By the resolve in her expression, I knew not to question her. In two days' time another family, a proper Aryan one, had slipped into her home, taking over her possessions. I used to hear their children banging away on her cherished piano.

"I never forgave my parents and never spoke her name again in their presence. They could have tried to help her, but they did nothing. I wondered if they ever thought about our kindly neighbor, but I doubted they did. She was that unimportant to them. When the war ended, and I saw the newsreel footage and read some of the newspaper articles about the camps, I kept picturing her there, alone, helpless, and terrified. I still dream of her."

I didn't know what to say. I finally reached out for her hand and she clasped my fingers. It felt good to touch her after so many years.

"Do you know you are the first person I have ever told that story to?"

"You never told Ben?"

"Oh no, I couldn't. I was too ashamed that I did nothing to save her."

"You couldn't have. You were a child. You didn't have the power to save her, and even if your parents had interceded on her behalf, they would have only postponed the inevitable."

"Don't you see? That has always been the problem. They didn't want to save her. They didn't care at all. There one day and gone the next. There were times I worried that I was going crazy and had imagined her very existence. People are only supposed to disappear in fairy tales, not in real life.

"Then finally, when the war was almost over, it was my family who needed saving. It was the ultimate irony, no? The perpetrators were the ones who were asking for help. Why were our lives more important than the millions of others who perished? We had all seen the writing on the wall, and my father had arranged for my mother, Eric, and me to be moved out of Berlin to the relative safety of the countryside. Even though we were only thirteen, Erich wanted to stay in Berlin and fight to the bitter end alongside his Hitler Youth friends, but my father insisted he leave with us. I often think it would have been better if he had stayed. For a time we didn't know where Papa was. We knew he had been with von Braun and the rest of the team, but we weren't sure if they had made it to safety, but they had. He and the others surrendered to the Allies on May 2, 1945. I never questioned what my father did at the Mittelwerk factory at Dora. I think he was involved with the production. I should have had that conversation with him. I suppose I was afraid to discover the answer and now, of course, it is too late."

She was about to say more when the waiter arrived to ask if we were ready to order. I didn't feel like eating and I didn't think Karin did either.

"Give us a minute," I said.

"We should get something. Should I order us both a burger? They were always pretty good."

"Sure," she answered.

"How about another martini?" I asked.

I knew I could use one.

"Yes, please. Maybe it will give me the courage to tell you the rest of the story."

I motioned the waiter back over and ordered the burgers and drinks. We waited for the drinks to come and then Karin continued.

"Remember the first time you brought Ben along to spend some time with us after school?"

"Sort of. I remember being nervous."

"Yes, so was I. I knew he was trying to be a good friend to you, but that he really didn't have any interest in getting to know me, or any of the other German students. For whatever reason, I was desperate to get him to like me, to understand why his best friend had fallen for me. I wanted him to see past my family. I needed him to believe that I wasn't anything at all like Erich.

"That first day we hardly said a word to one another. You were so happy he came along. I didn't think you noticed, but over the next several weeks we started finding out that we had a lot in common. You were busy with football practice, and Ben and I started meeting up without you. It wasn't easy with Erich always hovering, but I became involved in so many after-school activities that he finally became bored with keeping track of my whereabouts.

"It was fun for Ben and me to compare our pre-Hitler memories of Berlin. We were both born there. We were excited to learn that we had even lived in the same area, near the Grunewald, the city's park. We had probably passed each other on the street, or played on the same swing set. Before long, we realized we were not so different. His father always wanted him to speak English and so did mine, so when we were alone together we always practiced our German. He told me that his father had grown to loathe the German language and wanted his son to be as American as possible. He laughed when he told me how his mother still slipped up and how it drove his father crazy. I understood, even though my parents' aversion to speaking German was for different reasons. They did not want to remind their new American neighbors of the war or have their own personal histories questioned.

"As for my brother, he despised Ben from the moment he met him. He disliked you too, but with Ben, it was something else, something more primitive. He envied your popularity and your athleticism. He couldn't understand how a Jew could possibly be one of the better players on the football team. You were supposed to be inferior, and he couldn't reconcile that with what he'd been taught. It unnerved him.

"Ben, though, got under Erich's skin in a different way. Maybe he reminded him of all the Jewish boys he academically competed with in Germany. You didn't seem to threaten his sense of self as much as Ben did. You have no idea how he would rant and carry on when Ben scored higher than him on a paper or exam. I avoided walking home with him on those days. Erich still believed in Aryan superiority and could not accept his own limitations. At first Ben was caught up in the competition for grades. After a while, once we became friends, I don't think he really cared or paid Erich much attention at all and that seemed to anger my brother even more."

Once again, I smiled at the memory.

"Erich became obsessed with his hatred of Ben, and he was furious that the three of us spent so much time together. He told my father, expecting him to put a stop to our friendship. I told him we were all just casual friends, and he decided to not make it an issue. My father was not about to jeopardize his work at the Arsenal by stopping my friendship with a couple of Jews, which included the son of one of the town's leading citizens."

"You mean me."

"Yes, of course you. Your father was an important man in town. Everyone loved your father and everyone, including my family, shopped at Sterns."

"So is that when you and Ben started falling for each other, while I was sweating and straining away at football practice?"

Karin pushed her half-eaten burger away and took a large swig from her martini glass.

"Yes, that is when Ben starting acting differently toward me. At first it was gradual, but the more time we spent together, the more he began to confide in me. Believe it or not, we talked about you a lot. He admired you so much. He told me about the first time you came over to his house and how you became his protector and helped him be accepted by the other kids at school. He even told me about the comic book the two of you had created, and he showed me some of the early issues you had worked on."

"He actually said he admired me?"

"Yes, you didn't know?"

"No, I didn't. I mean, why would he? He was the one with all the talent. If anything I admired him. He was strong. He had a tough beginning here in town, and after what he endured in Germany, he still managed to be optimistic about his future. I know what everyone thinks, but they're wrong. Ben did not kill himself, and I'm ashamed that it's taken me this long to try and prove it."

Karin shook her head. I was tired of that look that shouted pity. *Oh poor, poor Tommy, you just don't want to face the facts.*

"Then finally, one day, we took a walk and ended up at that park at the edge of town. It was then that he told me that his feelings for me had changed, that he felt more than friendship for me. I wasn't surprised. I could tell by the way he had been acting. By the way his hand would accidently brush up against my own, or how he held on to my waist as we crossed a busy street. So I just let it happen. I let him believe that I felt the same way."

"What did you just say?"

At first I wasn't sure I had heard her correctly.

She took another sip of the martini.

"I said that I let him believe that I felt that same way."

"But you didn't?"

"No, I was in love with you. I was from the very first day we met."

Her chin was trembling.

"Did you even question what Ben's parents told you? Did you think I was that shallow, that I could exchange my feelings from one boy to the next so easily?"

"The Lowes," I stammered. "They were so sure."

"You should have had more trust in me, who I was, and still am. Even then I knew you didn't love me in the same way that I loved you," she said. "You made that perfectly clear as soon as you went off to Penn. But that night, I thought you did, and I was torn between hurting you and hurting him. In the end, I decided to tell Ben the truth—that I had let him believe I loved him because I didn't have the heart to tell him differently. He and his family had been through so much. They had been victimized and persecuted by a nation they loved, and I felt responsible. I didn't want him to be hurt by one more German."

I wanted to tell her she was wrong. I should have said that I loved her more than she could possibly imagine, and that I probably still did. Instead, I ignored that part of her confession and asked her more about Ben.

"But when did you tell him?"

"I finally made up my mind to be honest with him on the night of the barbecue. I wanted to tell him in person, but Erich was with me every second. It was the end of the year, and we were all getting ready to go off to our respective colleges. I couldn't keep up the charade one minute longer, so I wrote a note, stuck it in Ben's pocket and told him to read it when he got home. I realize now what a cowardly act that was."

"What did you say?"

"I told him how important our friendship was, but that I didn't love him the same way he loved me. Minutes later, he and Erich got in that fight, and then Erich grabbed my arm and forced me to go with him. Ben must have read the note when he got home."

"I don't think he saw the note till much later," I said. "He may never have seen it. That's the only thing that makes any sense. He told his parents that the two of you were in love, and that was after the barbecue, so he still didn't know. Do you see what I'm saying? You didn't have anything to do with Ben's death. He thought the two of you were going to be together."

"You really don't think he saw it?"

"No, I don't."

I wasn't certain, I couldn't be. Ben could have read the note after he left his parents, but regardless, I didn't believe that Karin's admission caused him to take his own life. Karin had carried that heavy burden of guilt for far too long. It was time to let it go.

"But then what made Ben want to take his own life?"

"That's what I've been trying to tell you. I think it was either an accident and someone made it look like a suicide or he was murdered."

"No, you're wrong. He must have looked at it later and that was the reason. I'm sure of it."

*Why wouldn't she believe me?*

"Stop! This isn't about you," I said.

Noticing a few accusatory looks from nearby patrons I lowered my voice.

"Listen to me. I'm trying to tell you."

She shook her head.

She didn't hear me. She had already grabbed her bag and was almost at the door before I thought of stopping her. I could have, but instead, I sat there paralyzed, trying to understand, hoping for clarity about my feelings and about the events of that evening that were still eluding me.

# 20

# 1968

THE NEXT MORNING, I packed my suitcase and told Al I was heading home.

"I'm sorry to see you go, Tommy. It's been nice getting to know one another again."

Surprisingly, it had been, and I said so.

"I'm going to miss Selma's cooking. Please tell her goodbye for me."

"I will. She'll be sorry to have missed you. Was the trip worth it? Did you get the answers you were looking for?"

"No, just more questions. I need to figure some things out."

"Are you planning a return trip any time soon?"

"I'm not sure. I don't think so."

§

On the road back to Atlanta, I put the top down and turned the radio volume up. I hoped the wind and the music would drown out the voice in my head—the one that kept telling me to turn around. Eighteen years had quietly slipped by since high school graduation, and I was still the same old, scared little boy who ran away when life got too tough. My MO had not changed. I'd listened as Karin revealed her secrets about her neighbor, about Ben, and even about me, but instead of understanding, I assaulted her with innuendo. *What a guy.*

The Beatles had just released "Hey Jude," and the station had not stopped playing it. Over and over again, I kept hearing the refrain, "You have found her, now go and get her." A better man might have done just that, but not me. Instead, I changed the station to country, turned the volume up another notch, and kept on driving.

It was twelve o'clock when I passed the Atlanta airport, and all I had eaten thus far was a stale pack of Ding Dongs that I had found in Al's cupboard. I stopped at a McDonalds for a little fortification and headed over to my office to contend with my irate clients and the wrath of my secretary.

I expected to be greeted with one of Helen's typical tirades admonishing me for not staying in touch. It would have been better than the cold stare she greeted me with. She was angry. I didn't blame her.

"Your messages are on your desk. Mrs. Kilpatrick keeps calling and has threatened to get another attorney if you don't get back to her today, and Judge Watson will not agree to one more continuance in the Williams case."

"Okay, I'm back. I'll call Kilpatrick and the judge. Is there anything else that's pressing?"

"Yes, actually. Your poor mother has called every hour since you've been gone. She's worried about you. I told her what you said, that you went home. She keeps calling back and saying you're not there. What's going on? You may not care about my feelings or leaving me to make up excuses for you, but I've never known you to be inconsiderate to your mother."

"Please, Helen, give me a break. I've got a lot on my mind."

Her right eyebrow was raised. It was her tell. It only happened when she was near her breaking point.

"I'm sorry," I said.

I walked into my office and shut the door.

It was all I could come up with at the moment. I would eventually tell her, but now I just wanted to dive into the piles on my desk and forget. But first, I did have to make a few more apologies.

The call to Kilpatrick and the judge were easy. The call to my mother not so much.

"Where have you been? I must have telephoned you twenty times over the last two days. I was driving Helen crazy and was about to send out the state police to start looking for you."

Helen was right. I had been inconsiderate and I was guilty as sin. I should have called to tell her I was going to Huntsville.

"Seriously, Tommy, I've been so worried. I called your house and no one answered. Then I called your office and Helen said you were at home. So where in the world were you?"

"I did go home in a manner of speaking. I went to Huntsville."

"You were in Huntsville? What in heavens name for?"

"It's a long story. I'm sorry. I should have told you I'd be going out of town for a few days."

"Yes, you should have. It only takes a minute to pick up the phone, and you know how I worry."

"I know, and I am really sorry."

"You're forgiven. Now, why don't you come over this afternoon and give your mama a hug? I'll cancel my bridge game."

"I can't. Not today. I'm bogged down at work right now. Leaving for a few days without giving much notice was probably not such a great idea."

"Work can wait. I can't."

I had a hard time saying no to my mother.

"Okay, you win," I said.

"Don't cancel your game. I'll be over around six. Do you have anything to eat?"

"I'll manage to scrounge something up."

Work took me longer than I expected, and I didn't get to my mother's until almost seven. Mama's house was about a ten-minute drive from my own and had the nicest yard on the street. My mother was a master gardener and spent hours pruning, planting, and tending her prized bushes and camellias. Mama had fallen in love with the grounds and the large front porch and decided to buy the brick 1920s bungalow even before she stepped inside. When I walked in, I could smell the familiar scents of Murphy's Oil Soap and Pine-Sol. I had been breathing in those aromas for as long as I could remember and they always conjured up warm memories of my boyhood in Huntsville.

I was thankful when Mama ignored my late arrival and even more appreciative of the bear hug and the tumbler of Jack on the rocks that she handed me as soon as I walked in. I don't know what I needed more, the whiskey or the hug from my mother.

"Okay, spill it," she said. "What in the world were you doing in Huntsville? You know you're not supposed to keep secrets from your mama."

I sat down on the sofa and buried my head in my hands. I could feel my mother's presence next to me.

"Tommy," she whispered as she wrapped her arms around me. "Talk to me."

"I think I've made a real mess of things."

My mother had canceled her bridge game and for the next hour, we dined on beef bourguignon and shared a bottle of outstanding French Bordeaux. In between bites, I talked.

I told her everything—about the call from Cole, about meeting up with Karin, my research at the library, the trip to New York, and my now unwavering conviction that Ben did not commit suicide.

I spoke a lot about Karin.

"When did you guess that I was interested in Karin?" I asked.

"A mother knows these things," she answered.

"Oh, really."

She smiled.

"One day I saw you walking her home. Even though you were trying not to draw any attention to yourselves, I could see the two of you touching hands and leaning in toward one another."

"And that was enough?"

"Yes, that was enough. As I said, a mother knows."

"I didn't have any idea that Ben was in love with Karin. When the Lowes told me I felt betrayed by both of them. I know we were just kids, but for whatever reason, it still hurts."

"That's because you still have feelings for her. If you didn't you wouldn't care about a long-ago high school romance."

"You're wrong," I answered. "We're friends, long-time friends. Nothing more."

"The gentleman doth protest too much," she said with a smile. "Don't you dare roll your eyes at me."

I rolled them again.

"Besides," I said.

I continued as if she hadn't commented on my feelings for Karin at all.

"If I had known how Ben felt, I would have stepped aside. He deserved her more than I did."

"That's ridiculous. Why? Because of Ben's past? Nothing would have made up for what happened to the Lowe family during the war. You weren't responsible for the crimes of the Nazis and neither was Karin. The two of you are more alike than you think. Both of you are still trying to pay for something you had no control over. You loved Karin and she loved you. You shouldn't be guilty about your feelings."

"That's just it. I am."

"Why?"

"Because Ben suffered so much more than me. His entire family was murdered. He deserved to be happy."

"And you lost your brother, and Daddy and I lost my son. Didn't we all deserve to be happy? There is no scoreboard out there keeping track of who suffered more and who should end up happier. Life does not work that way."

"It should."

"Yes, perhaps it should, but it never does."

"When did you get to be so wise?" I asked.

"Aging has its upside. I've had a lot of years to think about Joe and the effect his death had on our family. I've wanted to talk to you about this for a long time, and now is as good a time as any. I let you down after Joe was killed."

"No, you didn't."

"Yes, I did, and I've already told you, don't argue with your mother. You were only thirteen years old, and I should have been there for you, but I wasn't. I could hardly move. I had to force myself out of bed in the mornings. Daddy had to come home early every day from work, and Selma made you breakfast, lunch and dinner. I was barely there. Even a couple of years later, I was still just going through the motions of living. I felt as if one of my limbs had been amputated. If I'd been more available, maybe you would have talked to me about your feelings. Maybe I could have helped you sort things out. I'm sorry, Tommy. Do you forgive me?"

I nodded and hugged her, even though I still didn't think she had done anything wrong. I was never resentful. I understood her pain, but she needed me to forgive her, and that is what I did.

"Daddy was never the same either," I said.

"No, he was angry. The war was almost over and Joe died because the Nazis couldn't be bothered taking prisoners. Then, when that bunch moved into town he had to pretend, for the sake of the business and for the town that he was over it. But he never was. He started drinking way too much those last years of his life. It was the only way he could fall asleep at night."

"I didn't know," I said. "It's been a strange couple of days. The Lowes and Karin have both confessed to being responsible for Ben's suicide, and I'm more convinced than ever that he was killed. They all feel so guilty, and I did nothing to help any of them."

"Well then, I think you have to drive yourself back up to Huntsville and convince her otherwise, and then fly back up to New York and do the same for Frank and Helen. I also think you owe it to Ben to try and prove what happened to him. To tell you the truth, Daddy and I were always a bit suspicious about how quickly the police labeled his death a suicide."

"Really? You never said."

"I know. I suppose we were trying to protect you, and honestly, it wasn't our place to question the police if the Lowes agreed with their findings. You were a different boy after Ben died. You ran away from Huntsville, and as long as we're being honest, I think you're still running."

I had come to the same conclusion. She was right, and we both knew it. The moment Ben died, I cut all ties with my past. I didn't even come home that first Thanksgiving. Instead, I spent it in Philadelphia with my roommate and his family. Besides disappointing my parents, I knew Karin was expecting me. She was probably hurting as much as I was, and I ignored her pain, being too consumed with my own. She wrote to me often when I first left for school. She was trying to maintain a connection. She needed a friend. I now think she was trying to find a way to tell me her version of Ben's last night and about her relationship with him, but I never gave her the chance. My letters back then were mechanical. I wrote about my classes and my new friends. I never mentioned our relationship.

Now it was my turn.

"I'm sorry too," I said.

"For what?"

"For leaving you and Daddy to celebrate Thanksgiving alone that first year I was away at school."

"Oh, Tommy, that was so long ago, and we understood. We knew how heartbroken you were. Besides, we weren't alone. My sister came in from Atlanta, and we had Ben's parents. We hadn't seen them socially since Ben's death, but I managed to talk them into coming. It was a nice evening. So mark that one item off of your guilty list."

She hugged me again. It felt good to be with her.

"I thought Ben's family moved up to New York around that time," I said.

"They did. They left a week later. They couldn't stay in Huntsville. They had become so reclusive. I encouraged them to go. That town had nothing to offer them anymore, and every time Frank went to work he had to drive by that damn school parking lot. At first, I suggested they move to Atlanta. There was and still is a fairly large Holocaust survivor community here, and, of course our family would have welcomed them."

"So why'd they go all the way to New York?"

"I suppose the rise of the Columbians, a neo-Nazi hate group in Atlanta, right after the war, was enough for them to be done with the South."

"The Columbians? I never heard of them."

"They didn't last long, but for about a year they terrorized the Jewish and Negro communities. There were articles about them in all the newspapers. They even wore uniforms with little lightning bolt patches on the sleeves that looked an awful lot like the old SS insignias of the Nazis."

"Does nothing ever change?"

"Sometimes it does. The City of Atlanta revoked their charter and their leaders were arrested for inciting a riot, so yes, if enough people work for change it can happen."

I decided then that once I had figured out some things about Ben, I would do a little soul searching about what kind of attorney I wanted to be for the remainder of my career.

"Do Frank and Helen seem well?" asked my mother.

"They were well enough, I suppose. My visit was tough on them, but regardless, they seemed genuinely glad to see me. They gave me Ben's art portfolio."

"Did they? I would love to see it. Do you have it with you?"

"Yes, it's in the trunk of my car. I'll go out and get it."

My mother had cleared a space on the dining room table, and for the second time in eighteen years, I opened the folder.

"My goodness," she said. "I never knew. I mean, I knew you and Ben were creating comic books, but I had no idea he was this talented an artist."

It took her the next hour or so to go through all the original art and mock-ups of the finished books. It was obvious that long after I had stopped collaborating with Ben, he had continued to work on his comic book creation and to grow as an artist.

"What was your part in all this?" she asked.

"The stories. I helped write most of the early stories."

While she was perusing the last few illustrations, I pulled out a book, one that I had never seen, that depicted Kurt Bahn—whom I now recognized as Bernhard—on the witness stand. He was pointing a finger and shouting, "MURDERERS." I would never have known that Kurt and Bernhard were one and the same if I hadn't visited the Lowes in New York. Even though I had discovered Kurt's identity, I felt like I was still missing something. I kept going back through the pages of Ben's final comic book. *What wasn't I seeing?* It was my mother who finally figured it out. I was so intent on my reading, and analyzing Ben's creation that I didn't sense that my mother had been reading the book alongside of me.

Inside, on the splash page, I found myself looking at twenty defendants seated in a courtroom with numbered identification tags hanging from their necks. Those Nazis once dressed in pristine uniforms and adorned with medals, insignia, and armbands had been stripped bare by Ben's pen. Without their uniforms, they were just worn-out-looking men.

"Doesn't this one defendant look an awful lot like Dr. Angel, Karin's father?" she asked.

I looked closer. It was true. One of the disheveled soldiers sitting in the docket was definitely Karin's father. I had missed it, but my mother recognized him almost immediately. I had only seen Hermann Angel once, on the singular occasion when he came to a program at school, whereas my mother often ran into him at civic events.

The remainder of the comic book was more of a lesson than a story. Through the testimony of Bahn, Ben traced the history of the Mittelwerk factory at the Nordhausen-Dora-Mittlelbau complex. The trial of the defendants was held before the General Military Government Court at the United States Army Dachau Internment Camp located within the walls of the former concentration camp. The year was 1947, and the defendants were accused of *Vernichtung durch Arbeit*, or extermination through labor. As each accused was named, the crimes attributed to each of them were enumerated. Karin's father held the position of operations director at the Mittelwerk factory at Nordhausen. He was the one who oversaw the slave labor allocations to the different areas for the production of the V-2s. At some point, Ben had figured out that Karin's father had done more than design the rockets that had inflicted such heavy casualties on the citizenry of London. He had been involved in the inner workings of the camp. In Ben's eyes, and now in mine as well, Hermann Angel's actions killed Ben's uncle Bernhard

"Do you think Ben ever told Karin what he suspected about her father?" asked my mother.

"I don't think so."

"She deserves to know," said my mother. "It's late. Stay over. Tomorrow's Saturday, so you can't use work as an excuse. You need to go back, Tommy."

"I know."

# PART TWO

---

# RECONCILIATION

# 21

---

# 1968

MY MOTHER CALLED Al to let him know I would be driving back, and once again he was sitting on the front porch swing waiting for me. As soon as I approached, he handed me a slightly warm glass of sweet tea and motioned for me to take the seat next to him.

"How long have you been sitting out here?"

"Couple of hours. I read the newspaper and paid some bills. Like I said, retirement's not all it's cracked up to be. Your mama sounded good when she called. It was nice catching up. Is she happy?"

"She is. Moving down to Atlanta after Daddy died was the best thing she could have done. You know her sister's there and a lot of her old friends."

"So here you are, back so soon. If you don't mind me asking, why in the hell did you leave in the first place? That's a lot of driving to do in two days."

"It's a long story."

"Tommy boy, I've got nothing but time."

And so, for the next two hours, I once again spilled my guts. I told Al about Erich's journal, my trip up to New York, about the newly discovered comic books in Ben's portfolio that pointed a finger at Hermann Angel, and finally about Karin and what she had said about the night of the barbecue. The only part I didn't share was what Karin had said about her feelings toward me. She had thrown me a lifeline, and I held on to those words with a tight grasp. On the ride back to Huntsville, I realized that more than anything I wanted them to be true.

Al listened, interrupting only once or twice with a question.

"Go see Karin," he said. "Tell her everything you just told me. It's the only way you're going to get to the bottom of this. You need to work together or you're never going to figure out what happened. Now get going."

Twenty minutes later I was sitting in Karin's driveway, working up the courage to go inside. Al wasn't sure where Karin lived, so before leaving I looked up her address and was surprised to see that she was still in the same house her parents had built on Sauerkraut Hill way back in the '50s. I had only been there once—the one and only time she got permission from her father for me to pick her up. Back then, when I knocked on the door, it was Erich who answered and reluctantly called his sister to come down the stairs. I knew they weren't living together now, so at least I was safe on that score.

When I got out of the car, I quietly closed the door, just in case, I decided to cut and run at the last minute. I owed her an apology for what I had said in the coffee shop. I kept rehearsing the words in my head and hoped she would listen long enough for me to actually say them.

*Come on, Tommy, suck it up.* I walked up the stairs and onto her stoop.

Before I had a chance to knock, the door flew open, and there she stood looking as beautiful as the day I met her. She was wearing blue jeans and a tight-fitting pink sweater. Her hair was pulled back into a ponytail and she looked exactly like the eighteen-year-old I had once fallen so hard for.

"I recognized your car in the driveway. How long have you been sitting out there?" she asked.

"Too long. I was afraid you wouldn't want to see me."

"I've forgiven you. You were angry, and I did get you up here on false pretenses. You had a lot to take in, and I'm sorry too."

My speech was forgotten as I leaned in to kiss her. At first, she seemed startled, but within seconds we were both overcome by the intensity of our embrace.

"Come," she said, as she took me by the hand and led me to her upstairs bedroom. I knew what we were about to do would complicate everything even more, but I no longer cared. I was no longer in charge. Karin could have taken me anywhere. I just stood there as she removed my belt, slowly unzipped my pants, and then slipped her sweater over her head.

I pulled the band off her ponytail and watched her hair cascade over her shoulders. When I took her in my arms, nothing in my life had ever felt so right.

"I love you," I whispered as I picked her up and carried her to the bed.

Afterward, I was afraid to look at her, worried that I would see regret on her face.

"Are you okay?" I asked.

"I'm no longer that little school girl who used to kiss you under the bleachers, and yes, I'm fine," she said as she stroked my cheek.

"Are you making fun of me?" I asked. "I know how old we are. It's just that I don't regret what just happened, not for one minute, and I'm hoping you don't either. You are okay? Aren't you?"

"Hmm, I don't know. I just slept with my high school boyfriend, my brother is dying of cancer, and I'm convinced that he had something to do with our best friend's death."

"Okay, then. It sounds like everything is just fine."

She started to giggle and suddenly neither one of us could control ourselves.

"My stomach hurts," she said. "I can't believe we're laughing about this."

"I can. If you told anyone else this story they'd think we had the makings of a good mystery novel."

"Yes, except in our case, it's all too real."

"You're right," I answered. "It is all too real."

I paused and asked her, "do you really think your brother had something to do with Ben's death?"

I waited. I knew this was hard for her.

"Yes," she finally answered. "I do."

"Come here; you look like you need to be held," I said.

She snuggled closer and I kissed the top of her head.

"Why? Why do you think?" I said.

"That my brother could possibly be capable of something as awful as murder? Erich is capable of many things."

"Karin, tell me. Please. I want to know."

"I'm not sure you do. Sometimes it is better not to know."

"Whatever it is, I don't care. Let me help you."

"My brother is a brute," she finally said. "If Erich had been older, he would have made a perfect member of the SS. Perhaps that is why he is always so angry. He missed the war. He missed the chance to hone his skills. It is terrible to be afraid of your own brother, but it is hard to remember a time when I wasn't."

I had to ask the next question.

"Did he ever hurt you?"

By her silence, I knew the answer.

"I'll kill him."

"God is taking care of that for you. He will not be getting a last-minute reprieve. And no, I don't hate him."

"You don't. How could you not?"

"Erich wasn't always this way. The regime, the war, it changed him. You have no idea the demands that were put on children to conform, to be perfect little Nazis. I know you will find this hard to believe, but once upon a time, Erich played house with me. We fabricated an entire game where he was the father, I was the mother, and my dolls were our children."

"You're right. I find it hard to believe."

"He started to change after he joined the German Young People. When Erich turned ten, my father insisted he join. Even though I was told to join the *Bund Deutscher Mädel*, the girl's equivalent, I managed to keep putting it off. Papa didn't seem to notice. My father never seemed to notice much about me. When it came to Erich, he was different. He thought my brother was too soft, too much of a mama's boy. Papa decided the organization would cure him, so to speak, and toughen him up. You could not be soft and survive in a Hitler Youth organization. It was not tolerated.

"Within months of his joining, he began to change. His chapter leader was the son of one of Papa's friends, and he seemed to take a particular interest in Erich. My playmate disappeared and was replaced by a sullen and angry boy. Erich kept after me to join up too. I suppose he hoped I would share in his misery. I kept resisting, and he reported me to the organization. The area leader paid my parents a visit. They were irate. I had embarrassed them. My father forced me to join the next day. That same year, he discovered that I was still sneaking upstairs to spend time with Mrs. Weiss. By then, any fraternization with a Jew was strictly forbidden. He followed me. When I came back to our apartment, my brother struck me for the first time."

I took her hand and held it against my chest.

"Did you tell your mother or father about Erich, that he terrorized you?"

"Tommy, that's one of the many things I have always loved about you—your innocence. You defend the most hardened criminals, and yet you still believe all parents protect their children from evil. Your mother and father may have looked under the bed and opened the closet door to assure you that there were no monsters, but in my home there was a real monster and no one to protect me from his reach."

"But they must have known what was happening."

"My father was rarely home, and once Germany went to war, not home at all. My mother doted on Erich. He was her golden child. I was a surprise, a second baby born a few moments later. Once, I tried to tell her that Erich frightened me. She didn't believe me. Erich had recently received a commendation from his youth leader, and my mother actually told me I was jealous of my brother's success. After that, I remained quiet."

"Why didn't you tell me when we were in high school?"

"I couldn't. I knew how you would react. I was trying to protect you. Erich was and still is unpredictable."

"Did Ben know?"

"Toward the end of the school year, he may have figured it out. There was one brutally hot day in May, and I wore a long-sleeve blouse to school. I was hiding the finger impressions that Erich had left on my arm. Ben asked me why I was dressed for winter. I knew I looked ridiculous. When I told him I was too sensitive to the sun, I think he suspected, but he never said anything, so I'm not sure."

"When in May was that?" I asked.

"Probably a week or so before the barbecue."

"Are you sure?"

"Yes. It was on the same day the letter of acceptance came from the University of Pennsylvania."

"You applied to Penn?"

"Yes, I wanted to surprise you. I was desperate to get away from Erich and to be with you, so I secretly applied. Every day, I listened for the sound of the mail falling through the front door slot and onto the floor. When the letter came I couldn't wait to tell you, but first I had to build up the courage to tell my parents and, of course, Ben. I thought I had hidden the letter in a safe place. I should have known better. Erich was always going through my things. When he found the acceptance from Penn, he was furious. It wasn't because he wanted to spend the next four years with me. He was angry that I had done something behind his back.

"At that point, I no longer cared about what he said. I had a chance to get away, and I was going to take it. I was planning to tell my parents that evening and hoped they would agree to give me this opportunity. I had finally stood up to him. It was then that he grabbed me by my arm and held on until I almost passed out from the pain. When I didn't give in, when I told him I was still leaving, he threatened to hurt either you or Ben. By the look on his face, I knew he meant it. So I agreed to give up my plans. Instead, I spent the next four years at Emory trying to avoid him. When he left for Germany, it was one of the happiest days of my life."

"You should have told me."

"Which part?"

"All of it. Any of it."

"I already told you why I couldn't tell you about Erich. The other, the fact that I was going to surprise you about Penn, it was no longer important after Ben died. Besides, you couldn't wait to get away from Huntsville, away from me."

I reached for her hand.

"You're right, and I'm sorry. I hope, someday, I'll be able to make it up to you."

"I think you've already started."

I stroked her face and touched a little scar running across the bottom of her chin.

"How'd you get this?" I asked. I didn't remember the scar.

"Another gift from my brother. It happened right after you left for school. He pushed me and I fell against a table. It's the one and only tangible reminder I have of Erich's cruelty. Most of the time, he was much more creative. My punishments for perceived transgressions varied, and I was never sure if he would hurt me or destroy something I cherished. The worst of it happened on the one day he saw me alone with Ben. I tried to explain that it was because you were at football practice. He didn't believe me and told me to stay away from him. When I refused, he beat me. The next day, I stayed home from school. I told my mother I had menstrual cramps, and she left me alone."

"I'm so sorry," I said. "I should have been more aware of what was going on around me."

I had let Karin down in more ways than I could have ever imagined.

"You already apologized, and besides, you were no more than a child yourself. There was nothing you could have done. Erich had brutalized me for so long, I truly believed he would hurt you or Ben if I left."

"I should have protected you. I should have stayed. I ran away, and I left you as soon as Ben died."

"And I could have told you the truth. I should have had the courage to tell someone at school what Erich was doing to me, but I didn't. Besides, I understood what Ben's dying did to you."

"Where's Erich living these days?"

"Don't even think about it. Do not go over there."

"It's not what you think. I mean it is, but I can control myself. I want some answers. I promise I'm just going to talk."

I had a niggling feeling about something.

"I'm curious, did Erich ever marry or have a long-term relationship with anyone?"

"Not that I know of. Why do you ask?"

"It's just a thought I'm having. Your brother holds the key to a lot of unanswered questions."

"You're wasting your time. He'll enjoy playing with you, but he won't help. Why would he? He has nothing to gain and, regardless, he'll be dead by this time next year."

# 22

# 1968

KARIN FINALLY GAVE in and told me where Erich lived. She insisted on coming with me. I didn't have a prayer of talking her out of it.

"Don't tell him about the journal. I don't want him to know that I found it and gave it to you."

"I agree. Do you think he remembers that he kept a diary?"

"I'm not sure. He hasn't asked for it, so probably not."

The ride over to Erich's took less than five minutes. The location made me uneasy. He had chosen a rental close to the home they had grown up in and to where Karin was now living.

"I'm surprised Erich didn't try to move in with you when he came back to Huntsville."

"He couldn't. I am the sole owner of the house. In my father's eyes, unmarried women over thirty were old maids. He worried that I would never be able to support myself with what he called my quaint little bookshop, so he left me the house. Besides, Erich was still in Argentina and Papa never thought he'd return. I wish I could have seen my brother's face when he got the letter from the attorney."

"I hope he's home. Maybe we should have called first," I said.

"That would have given him the chance to tell you not to come. No, it's better this way. You're probably the last person he expects to see. Besides, he rarely goes out."

By the time we neared his street I could feel that little vein by my left eye starting its pulsating march, and I hoped Karin didn't notice the beads of perspiration collecting on my forehead. I hadn't seen Erich in eighteen years, and my dislike for him had only intensified over the last few days.

We knocked and waited. The yard was overgrown with weeds and the few remaining garden bushes were screaming for water. I gave the front porch swing a push and cringed when the rusty chains cried out as it slowing moved back and forth. We knocked again. A few moments passed, and we finally heard the sound of footsteps and the click of the lock. There he was, a much older version of my boyhood nemesis, peering through the opening of the slightly opened door.

"Ah, my lovely sister. Have you come to see how the disease is progressing or are you dropping off another pot of soup?"

"Erich, stop. I've brought an old friend over to see you, someone from high school."

I suppose his curiosity got the better of him, and he unhooked the chain to see his sister's mystery guest. He recognized me immediately.

"Tommy Stern? He is the mystery guest you've brought to see me? Well, this is a surprise. Come in, come in."

From the entryway, I could see into the living area. Erich must have rented the house furnished. It had a worn-shabby look to it and smelled of stale air, cigarette smoke and garbage.

"Would you care to sit down? Excuse the mess," he said as he pushed a pile of old newspapers off the sofa. "I must tell you, you've piqued my curiosity. I am interested in why, after all these years, you're paying me a visit. Are you taking up with my sister again, just like in the old days?"

His toothy grin, made even more menacing by the ravages of disease, did little to hide his contempt for me and for Karin. Any similarity to Karin was long gone. I didn't bother to answer.

"I hear you have cancer," I said.

It was evident by his appearance that he was suffering. His clothing hung loosely on his bony frame, and he walked with the gait of an old man.

"I see my sister has filled you in. Yes, I was told I have six months to a year and to not wait to put my affairs in order. I think the doctor was a bit too optimistic. It is ironic, no? I am only thirty-six years old and have exercised daily since I was a small child, and yet I am told there is nothing to be done."

"You should stop smoking," said Karin.

The ashtray was full, and Erich was in the process of lighting up.

Erich let out a strangled laugh.

"Thank you for your concern, dear sister, but I have leukemia, not lung cancer."

Karin didn't bother to respond.

"Why did you come back here?" I asked. "It couldn't have been for Karin."

"She is the only family I have left. Of course, it was to be near my sister."

"Stop," said Karin. "You came here because you had nowhere else to go, and you hoped that I and some of the other German families would take pity on you and visit with you once in a while. Have any of them actually come by?" She turned to me. "Erich was never very popular, even amongst the other German children."

"My, my, but you have changed, Sister."

"Yes Erich, I have. Does it bother you that you no longer scare me?"

His nicotine-stained teeth were peeking out of what I assumed was Erich's attempt at a smile. If skin could actually crawl, mine would have been inching across the room. He dismissed Karin with a wave of his hand and turned his attention toward me.

"Tommy, or do you prefer Tom?"

"Tom is fine."

"So, Tom, why are you here?"

"I have some questions for you. I'm curious about a few things relating to Ben Lowe's death. I was hoping you'd have a little insight into the night of the senior class barbecue."

"I don't know what I can possibly add."

He took a seat and motioned for me to do likewise. Karin was still standing close to the door and I could tell she already tired of participating in whatever game Erich was playing.

"I'd offer you something to eat, but unfortunately the cupboard is almost bare. I have little appetite these days."

I ignored him.

"Tell me about the fight," I said.

"Oh, that little scuffle? I'm not sure if I remember what it was all about."

"You bumped into Ben on purpose and said, 'Get out of my way, Jew,'" said Karin.

"My, my. What a memory you possess."

"I also remember that Ben was not on the bottom when Tommy and his friends broke up the fight."

The look he gave Karin sent a chill down my spine.

"Erich, stop. You honestly don't frighten me anymore. Don't you get that?"

He didn't bother to answer her.

"He killed himself because my sister broke his poor little heart."

I heard the door slam.

"Karin, wait," I said.

It was too late. She had already walked on to the porch, and I could see her through the blinds pacing back and forth. When I turned back, Erich was grinning ear to ear, and I wanted nothing more than to reach out and wipe that smug look of satisfaction from his face.

"It's all her fault, you know," said Erich. "My sister finally told him that she was in love with you, and that was the last time anyone saw him."

I was trying, but I was beginning to hedge on the promise I had made to Karin to stay in control.

"Earlier, you asked if I had taken up with your sister again. What I don't understand is how you could have possibly known that she was my girl. Didn't you actually suspect that she and Ben were dating? They were always together. I can't imagine Karin confided her true feelings to you. That night after the fight but before you dragged Karin home, she shoved a note into his pocket. That's when she told him that she was still in love with me. The only way you could have known whether or not he read the note was if you met up with him again."

Erich's face revealed nothing.

"You did, didn't you? Tell me, damn it. I need to know the truth."

"You want the truth. Your friend was weak. Yes, I saw him later. I snuck out for a smoke after I brought my sister home. I drove over to the school and

I found him sitting on a bench. He was blubbering, crying his eyes out. For a minute, I took pity on him and asked him what was wrong. He told me then that Karin didn't love him. It was embarrassing for him and for me, so I continued on my way. That is all I know. Now I'd like you to leave. I'm feeling tired, and I've have had enough of our little reunion."

He was lying. I didn't believe a word he said, and he knew it.

"This is not over. You're dying. Can't you find it within yourself to give Ben's parents some peace? They blame themselves."

"You want more truth, is that what you want? Tell his parents that I watched from the bushes. I saw their son move that little bench over—you know the one, the gift to the school from our senior class—and place it beneath the tree. Then he swung a rope over the thickest branch and put the noose around his neck. I waited. I thought the little coward did not have the nerve. Ah, but you know as well as I that apparently, he did."

"Ben just needed more time to sort things through. He would have been okay. You could have stopped him. You could have saved his life."

"Why would I have done that?"

I didn't remember pushing his chair over, nor did I remember Karin coming in and pulling me off of him. I think she may have hit me or grabbed me from behind to get me to stop. Erich was on the floor coughing and Karin was sitting next to me holding onto my hands as if at any moment I might lunge for him again.

"We need to go," she finally said.

When we left, Erich was still massaging his neck and sitting on the floor. Holding my hand, Karin led me to the car, where I was finally able to take a deep breath.

"What happened to *I only want to ask him a few questions?*" she asked.

"I'm sorry, I lost it. He was there. He saw the whole thing."

"What are you talking about?"

"I'm serious. He was there, hiding in the bushes. He snuck out for a smoke and drove over to the school after he brought you home."

"Oh my God. What did he tell you? Did he hurt Ben?"

"He said no, but he could have stopped him. He just sat there waiting for him to step off the bench. He acted like he enjoyed the show. He's lying. I've sat with enough defendants to know when someone's telling the truth or not. He may have been there, but he knows more than he's telling us."

"You think he did more than just watch, don't you?" she asked.

"Yes, actually, I do."

Karin lowered her head into her hands and started to sob. We were still parked in front of Erich's house, and I reached over to hold her. It took her several minutes to calm down, and when she finally looked up, there was a new resolve in her eyes.

"How are we ever going to prove what Erich did?" she asked.

"I'm not sure, but I think it has something to do with your father."

"My father?"

I had yet to show her Ben's *Stark* illustrations of the Dora defendants.

"Let's go over to Al's. I have something you need to see."

As we were about to pull away from the curb, we heard the sound of a siren. The police car was heading straight toward us and quickly blocked our exit.

"What the hell?" I said.

It was Cole.

"Erich," Karin said. "He must have called them."

"Hey, Tommy, Karin."

I didn't bother to answer.

"Tommy, would you please step out of the car."

"Why?"

"I think you know why. We got a call from Erich Angel. He said you assaulted him. He claims you nearly killed him. Damn it, Tommy. The poor man is dying of cancer. What's come over you? He wants to file charges. Now get out of the car, please."

I did, and so did Karin.

"Let me go in and speak to my brother. I'm sure this whole thing can be resolved."

"I'm going with you," I said.

"No, you are not going anywhere near that man," answered Cole.

"Karin, don't do it. I don't want you going in there alone."

"He's my brother; I know what I'm doing."

And before Cole or I had a chance to say another word, she was running up the front steps and going in.

Karin was only in the house a few minutes when she came out to tell Cole that her brother had agreed to not press charges.

"You can go in and speak with him now. He was angry at Tommy and he got carried away."

"Okay," answered Cole. "You two wait right here and don't go anywhere." We watched as he walked into the house.

"What did you say to him?" I asked.

"I told him that I had no problem revealing our family secrets to the good people of Huntsville."

"What secrets?"

"I really don't know, but apparently I struck a nerve. Our family's reputation is all Erich has left. Once I confronted him I knew he would withdraw the complaint."

Just then Cole walked back outside shaking his head.

"Karin, I don't know what you said to him, but he agreed to not file charges. He's ready to forget the whole thing."

"It really was a misunderstanding. Erich has always been a bit dramatic."

I could tell that Cole did not believe a word of what she was saying.

"Okay then, I guess I made this trip over here for nothing. Next time try and solve your family problems before I get a phone call."

"Cole, thanks for coming by yourself," I said. "I know you didn't have to."

"You're Joe's brother. I still miss him."

"Yeah, me too."

Karin and I watched as Cole lumbered over to his car and drove away.

"Thank you," I said. "If you wouldn't have pulled me off of him, I'd probably be in the patrol car right now and on my way to jail. I swear I could have killed him."

I felt sick and walked over to the curb and sat down.

Karin sat down next to me and held my hand. She knew what I was thinking without me having to say anything.

"Do not question yourself. I should never have left you alone with him. You would have stopped yourself even if I hadn't come back in."

I wasn't so sure about that, but it was something I would have to live with.

"Come on," I said. "We can't sit in front of Erich's house forever. He'll have us arrested for loitering. We need to talk, and I think we need some reinforcements."

Alma was seated in her office when we walked into the library.

"Let's see if Alma will let us use one of the empty offices," I said.

"Alma? You call Miss Jones Alma? Since when?"

"Since two days ago. We are now the best of friends. She's been helping me with some of my research. Wait here a second. I have Ben's portfolio in the car, and I want to show you some of his work."

When I walked back in, Karin and Alma were talking like they were long-lost pals, both smiling in my direction.

"I'll be back in a few minutes," said Alma.

"What was all that about?" I said.

"Oh nothing. Your new best friend just wanted to let me know what a nice young man you are. Her exact words were, 'Nice boys like Tommy Stern are hard to find. Don't you let him get away.'"

"Really, she said all that in the few seconds I was gone?"

"Yes, she did."

"And what did you answer her?"

"I think I'll let you keep guessing. Now, what did you want to show me?"

I let Karin pore through the drawings and stories herself. I had put them in chronological order. I wanted her to see how he grew as an artist.

"His work just kept getting better and better," she said.

"I know. It kind of blew me away when I saw the last few covers. I was around for a lot of it, but had sort of lost interest by our senior year. I had other things on my mind if you know what I mean."

"You must mean football."

"Football? Oh—that was a joke. Very funny. What I was trying to say is that a number of these are new to me too."

Karin had reached the last two mock-ups in the pile. She spent several minutes looking at the cover, the one that showed Stark standing over piles of dead bodies with the caption, "I couldn't save them." She had tears in her eyes.

"Ben drew Stark to look exactly like his uncle Bernhard, the relative who died at Dora," I said.

"How did you know?"

"I didn't, at least not until I visited the Lowes and I saw an actual photograph of him. I realized then that Ben was using his art to tell the story of his uncle's death."

Karin then looked at Ben's last book. I placed my hand on her shoulder.

"Oh my God. How can that be? My father was never on trial."

She had just turned to the page depicting the courtroom scene from the war crime's trial at Dachau. Karin immediately recognized her father sitting amongst the accused. The tears were now streaming down her face.

"I don't know if I can continue," she said. When I started all this, I had no idea that our digging into the past might incriminate my father as well. He was a stern, distant presence in my life, but never cruel. Oh God! What if I find out something awful about him? How do I live with that knowledge? Ben must have known something. What could he have possibly found out?"

"I'm not sure, but I do think that everything that happened at the barbecue is somehow wrapped up in what Ben had discovered about your father. He may not have been on trial, but I think Ben discovered he was guilty of something."

"Ben was such a decent, noble person. He didn't tell either one of us what he suspected," said Karin.

"He knew it would hurt you," I said.

"Instead, it may have gotten him killed."

# 23

# 1951

I HAD NO early warning sign, no ominous foreboding that prepared me for Ben's last day on earth. That Saturday morning started out like any other with the smell of freshly baked-biscuits wafting upstairs from the kitchen. When I sat down to breakfast, my mother gave me one of those hurry-up looks and reminded me that we were spending the day together. We were going shopping for my college necessities, as she liked to call them. I told her that we still had the entire summer, but she insisted we get a jumpstart on what I would need. Those were the days when you still needed a proper wardrobe for college, and she was determined that I would be as well-dressed as all those boys from the Northeast.

The end-of-the-year senior class barbecue was that evening, and I was looking forward to spending time with Karin and thinking about saying goodbye to my friends. I had been going to school with the same kids since kindergarten, and it was strange to think that I might not have much contact with them again.

At six o'clock, I picked up Ben and we drove over to the school together. Within minutes, we were immersed in the tradition of having our yearbooks signed. Most of our class was either going to the University of Alabama or not going on at all. Many of our friends didn't understand the shared desire that Ben and I had to leave the South. For Ben, it was because he never really fit in. He was always just a little too different. As the years rolled on, everyone got used to having him around, but aside from Karin, I remained his only good friend. I was set on leaving because I had become just plain tired of Jim Crow. An entire segment of our population was relegated to separate everything. Public accommodations, including drinking fountains, restrooms, and restaurants were all segregated. I did not have a single Negro friend. They all went to a school on the other side of town, and the only person of color I knew well was Selma, our maid. My entire community was inured to the everyday sights of the racial divide. Being friends with Ben had altered my worldview. Unlike the rest of us, he was not a silent observer of the unwritten rules and regulations that divided our population and governed our way of life. He would always compare what his family had been subjected to in Germany with the blatant prejudice that he witnessed in our town. He had opened my eyes, and I wanted out.

§

When I conjure up the images from that night, I can still taste the barbecue. All the mothers, including my own, had gotten together to cater the party, and the mingling of sweet, hot, and smoky aromas filled the air. My mouth was watering, and I hoped they would start taking off the lids and let us all eat. I was in the middle of talking to a few of my buddies when I caught sight of Erich and Karin out of the corner of my eye. She always looked miserable when he was around, and that night was no exception. I walked over, hoping to save her from her brother's hold.

"Hey, Karin, Erich. Glad you could make it."

"Why wouldn't we have come?" He replied. "We're part of the class, are we not?"

I didn't bother to answer. He was always looking for a confrontation, and the last thing I wanted was to make trouble at the final school-sanctioned event of my senior year.

By the end of that year, Karin and the three other German kids who joined our class back in September had all reached out and made other friends. Only Erich remained on the outside, as much by choice as by anything else. I would not miss him.

The barbecue was finally in full swing. The lids had been removed, and I was in line with my plate waiting for my first slab of ribs to be thrown on when

I heard shouting and the unmistakable sounds of a scuffle. I had little doubt that it was Ben and Erich who were slugging it out.

"What the hell?" I yelled, as I ran over to see if I was right. I was. The two of them were rolling around in the dirt, and I could barely tell who was who.

Some of the parents had started to come over, so a couple of my buddies and I pulled a still-swinging Ben off Erich and shielded the two of them from the chaperones, who would not have taken kindly to a fight on school property.

"Ben, stop swinging! You almost hit me," I said.

By this time, Erich had gotten himself off the ground and was brushing the dirt off his clothing.

"Karin, come, we are leaving," Erich demanded.

She ignored him and instead walked over to Ben.

"Are you okay?" she asked.

"Yes, I think so."

"Karin, I said we are leaving," Erich repeated.

I was ready to take a swing at Erich myself, but Karin stepped in front of me.

"Don't," she said.

She turned toward Ben, gave him a hug, whispered something in his ear, and left with her brother.

I thought about following her, but guessed Karin was in no mood for a confrontation and so I let her go. Instead, I found Ben standing alone, watching them leave.

"Hey, what was that all about?"

He shook his head and wiped away tears. He looked around to make sure no one was watching him.

"Don't worry. Everyone is back by the food," I said. "Come on, tell me what that prick said to you."

"Tomorrow. I'll come by and see you in the morning. I promise."

He said he would see me in the morning. He wouldn't have promised if he knew he wasn't planning on being there. Ben always kept his promises.

# 24

## 1968

"WHAT NOW?" KARIN asked.

Her eyes were still focused on Ben's comic book page showing her father as one of the defendants in the Dora war crimes trial held at Dachau.

"I'm not sure."

We were sitting in the small library office looking at the portfolio when Alma came in and pulled up a chair. We showed her Ben's last illustration. She looked surprised to see Hermann Angel sitting in the witness stand with a tag around his neck.

"That looks like your father, but as you know, it's not historically accurate. The first of these trials took place in 1947. Your father was never one of the accused. He was already at Fort Bliss in 1947."

For the next few seconds Alma studied the drawing. She was hesitating, trying to choose her words carefully.

"I think, and this is only conjecture, that Ben may have suspected that he should have been on trial with the rest of them," she added.

I nodded in agreement. We both saw that Karen was shaking. Alma and I reached for her hand at the same time and held on to her together.

"Karin, do you have any idea what your father's job or position was at Dora?" I asked gently.

"Whenever I asked, which wasn't often, he said he was involved with production. Once we emigrated, our time in Germany was rarely mentioned, at
least not in front of me. I don't remember hearing any of my parents' friends dis-
cussing the past. Perhaps they did when we, the children, were already in bed.
They must have all known what the others did during the war. They protected
each other. They still do. They are a close-knit group."

"I think you might be able to find out a little more about your father," said
Alma.

She was still holding Karin's hand.

"You just have to be willing to do a little digging. Do you know if he was a
civilian or if he held a military rank?"

"Military. Like von Braun, he was an officer in the SS. Many of the engineers were made honorary officers in the SS. By the end of the war, he had risen
to the rank of a *Hauptsturmführer*. I believe that is equivalent to a captain in the
United States Army. My father wore the uniform often. Mostly, I remember his
black boots. They never had a mark on them. That was one of Erich's jobs, to
keep the boots polished. The uniform was designed to strike fear in people—
all black with death's head insignia on the collars and shoulders. People would
cower when my father approached."

Karin wiped away her tears.

"Are you okay?" I asked.

"I was thinking about Mrs. Weiss."

"Your neighbor?" I asked.

"Yes, she would look away every time she saw him in it. I told her not to be
afraid. I told her my father was a kind man and no harm would come to her."

"Who is Mrs. Weiss?" asked Alma.

"She was a Jewish woman who lived in the same apartment building as my
family. She taught me how to play the piano. She was my friend, really more
like a grandmother, and like so many others she disappeared. I never found out
what happened to her."

"There are records," said Alma. "You can probably find out what became of
her but be prepared. The news will most likely not be good, and sometimes the
knowing is harder than the not knowing. Are you sure?"

"Yes. I owe her that much and more."

"It will be harder to find documentation covering your father's service," said Alma. "It appears that Ben found out something incriminating, so we know the information is out there and available. You just have to know where to look. Are you two ready to do a little traveling?"

I looked toward Karin. She had pulled her sleeves down. It was warm in the office we were sitting in, and she was still shaking. I placed my arm around her.

"It's just such a lot to take in," she said. "Most of the scientists and engineers the U.S. helped to bring over served the Reich in one way or another. If you didn't comply, the punishment was often severe. My mother always said that my father did what had to be done. But what did that actually mean?"

"I think it's time we find out," I said.

"If whatever my father did during the war had something to do with the why and possibly the way Ben died, I know I'll never be at peace until I find out. So yes, I guess I'm ready to do a little traveling. Where do we need to go?"

Alma explained that most of the records—the documents that held the answers we were looking for—were still classified. The Paperclip dossiers had been closed since the end of World War II. Those documents that were open to the public were housed at the National Archives in Washington, D.C. She suggested we start with the transcripts from the war crime's trial proceedings.

Once again, Karin blanched. I was worried. In the end, my need to prove Ben didn't commit suicide might destroy Karin, the one person I hoped to protect.

"It'll be okay," I said. But I wasn't sure it would be.

§

Once I booked our flights to D.C., I called my secretary to tell her to cancel the remainder of my week's appointments. Instead of being angry, Helen sounded worried. I wasn't sure if her concern was for my job or for hers, but she told me that Philip Greene, the managing partner of my firm, had left several messages for me. He was none too pleased with my absence. I could only imagine what awaited me upon my return to Atlanta. Oddly enough, I realized I no longer really cared.

We were leaving in a couple of hours, which gave Karin and me just enough time to go to our respective homes, pack our bags, and head for the airport.

"Are you okay?" Karin asked.

We were buckled in and had started to taxi away from the gate.

"Why?" I asked.

"You're sweating, your knuckles are white from holding on too tight, and you haven't stopped chatting since we sat down."

"Oh. Sorry. I guess I'm just in a talkative mood."

I wasn't quite ready to reveal my cowardly side to the woman I was trying to impress, but while I was deciding what to say, she unclenched my fingers from the armrest and held tightly on to my hand.

"It'll all be okay." She was smiling.

"Are you laughing at me?"

"A little. Your secret's safe with me. Besides, I get it. I may not be nervous about flying, but I've been afraid of one thing or another most of my life, and it's not all because of Erich. Our parents were distant and did little to make us feel safe. That's why a part of me, a very small part of me, still feels bad about the way Erich turned out. Mama and Papa were both so caught up in Hitler's vision of a new Germany that they forgot about their children. I told you that Erich always polished my father's boots. I'm sure he was just trying to get some attention for a job well done. It was pitiful to watch. Erich kept hoping for Papa's approval long after I had given up."

Karin had grown quiet and leaned her head on my shoulder.

"There's a part of Mrs. Weiss' story that I didn't tell you. I suppose I was too ashamed to reveal all the sordid little details about my relationship with my father. Now that I suspect the worst about him, it no longer matters. After my mother forbade me from visiting her apartment, I almost complied, but not because I cared about getting caught. It was because it had become so horribly painful to witness the wearing away of a once-proud, independent, and talented woman. She had turned into a frightened little mouse, terrified of every foot-step in the hallway and every knock on her door. I told her not to be afraid, that I would speak to my father and he would protect her. I believed it and I made her believe it too. I begged him to make sure she would remain safe. He promised he would try, but she disappeared regardless. I never asked him what happened and we never discussed it. He had failed me, and I never thought of my father in the same way again. After she was deported, my father and I rarely spoke. I was too angry, and at the time I supposed he just didn't care. Later, I thought or maybe hoped that he was too ashamed by his indifference, his apathy to her plight.

"You need to hold on to that. Maybe he did try to help her. You can't be certain. He must have known how disappointed you were in him. He did not forget about you. He probably couldn't face you. No one could ever forget about you."

"You did. You left Huntsville and forgot about me for a very long time."

"I never forgot about you. I'm hoping that the fact that I was an eighteen-year-old, frightened teenager might help to mitigate my guilt."

"You sound like you're in the courtroom, pleading a case."

"I'm sorry, I'm trying to explain. I was in pain and couldn't find a way to make myself feel better, let alone anyone else. I know I failed you, and if I could go back and change how I handled everything, I would. But forget you, no, never. I tried to build a new life away from Huntsville. I was even married for a short time, but when I was with my wife I always thought about you. I knew she sensed there was someone else."

"Tell me about her," she said.

"Really?"

"Yes, I'd like to know what she's like."

"Hmm, let me think."

I really did not want to do this.

"Donna. Her name is Donna. She's a little older than us. In fact she recently turned forty. We met at a fundraiser for the Atlanta symphony. We had both been wrangled into attending by our respective firms, and over a couple of drinks we discovered that we would have preferred seeing Willie Nelson, who was performing in another part of town. We started dating, got along reasonably well, and married. In retrospect, not a very good reason."

"How long were you married?"

"Just under five years, and not because of our devotion to one another, but more as a testament to our laziness. After a couple of years of pretending, we realized that we were really good at being friends and not so good at being husband and wife. Donna's easygoing, and we've remained friendly. I only wish we had figured out our incompatibility as a married couple before we sunk most of our savings into buying a house. Actually, it's a very nice house with a pool and a yard that backs up to the Chattahoochee River."

"You still own it?"

"I do. Once we decided to separate, she moved out and I stayed on. Donna wanted to sell it. Financially it would have been the better move, but every time I thought about it, I changed my mind. I eventually bought her out. It's really too big for me. I kind of ramble around in there, but it has a small, cozy library with floor-to-ceiling bookshelves. It's where I spend most of my evenings. I think you'd like it."

"I'm sure I would, and it sounds as if I might like Donna too."

"Yes, I think you might."

When the pilot announced that we were making our final descent into D.C., I was surprised.

"Thank you," I said.

"For asking you about Donna?"

"No, for keeping me preoccupied. I hardly knew we were up in the air."

"I'm glad I could help, but you do realize that we still have to land."

# 25

# 1968

THIS WAS KARIN'S first trip to D.C., and I wished I could have shown her the sights, but we were not on a pleasure trip. Neither of us had a clear idea about how much time we would need to research Hermann Angel's war record. We arrived at the National Archives, and after a quick look at the Constitution, the Declaration of Independence, the Bill of Rights, and my favorite, the Faulkner murals of the founding fathers, we filled out all the paperwork, presented our driver's licenses to the receptionist and were given clearance to do research.

Alma had suggested that we start with the microfilm, but once we were in the area housing it all, we realized we didn't know where to begin. It was daunting. The research room was filled with large wooden library tables, about twenty or thirty microfilm readers lining the walls, and metal cabinets with hundreds of drawers filled with thousands of reels. The deer-in-headlights look on our faces must have been obvious because, within minutes, a tall gangly archivist walked over and asked us how he could help.

"You look confused."

"Really, how could you tell?" I asked.

The man's smile went from ear to ear, and we were happy to put our search into his able hands and let him lead us through the maze of records.

His name was Donald Fitzgerald. In five minutes' time we learned that he had worked at the Archives for the last twenty-five years and that he probably knew more about its holdings than anyone else.

"So, how can I help?"

"My father is Hermann Angel. He was one of the Operation Paperclip engineers brought to the United States under that program in 1947."

I was surprised by how forthcoming Karin was.

"He died several years ago, and I've become curious about what his actual job was during the war."

I'm sorry, but the Paperclip documents are still classified. I'm not sure when they'll be made available to researchers. It will literally take an act of Congress to open them up.

"Oh, our local librarian sent us here," she continued. "She knew the dossiers were closed, but thought there would be other records to look at."

Karin sank into the nearest chair.

"Please, don't worry. I'm sure I can help," he added quickly. "I only meant that the actual dossiers were classified. We have the service records of German soldiers, trial transcripts, and interviews that should be able to shed some light on your father's service. Most of these records were brought back by the United States Army after the war, and deposited with us. What can you tell me about him?"

"He was an officer, a *Hauptsturmführer* in the SS, and an engineer. He was first stationed at Peenemünde, and later was sent to oversee the production of V-1s and V-2s at the Mittelwerk factory at Dora-Mittelbau. I always assumed he had minimal or no contact with the slave laborers."

"Why? Did he tell you that?"

"No, not exactly, but that's what most of the engineers said. Why else would the US government and the Army allow them to come?"

"How much do you know about the 'Paperclip project?'" asked Donald, turning toward Karin.

"Only that it was the program designed to bring German scientists, doctors and engineers, like my father and Dr. von Braun, to America after the war. The United States government wanted and needed their expertise."

"Right. All of that is true. What is also true is that when Hitler came to power, the Reich's leading doctors, scientists, and engineers were directed to channel their research toward advances that would benefit the military. Unfortunately— and I truly am sorry to have to tell you this—in most cases, moral and ethical concerns were set aside in Germany's quest to win the war. Areas of research once considered taboo were encouraged. You may already be aware that concentration camp inmates were used as human guinea pigs in medical experiments. The Nazis hoped that some of their findings would give them the military superiority needed to win the war. One such experiment forced inmates to sit in ice baths so the *Luftwaffe* could estimate the survival time of a flier forced to parachute into the freezing temperatures of the North Sea. Slave laborers, always expendable, became even more so at the Dora-Mittelbau complex."

Karin was eerily silent.

"Miss Angel, do you need a moment? This must be very upsetting for you."

"No, please continue, I'm fine."

She wasn't, but this was her decision. He was her father.

"Where was I? Oh yes. So, by the end of the war, the V-2s were believed to be Germany's last chance to stop the Allies. Production was stepped up and more prisoners died as conditions worsened. What is also true is that certain high-ranking officials in our government knew that many of the Paperclip doctors, scientists, and engineers had been complicit in war crimes. It no longer mattered. They decided to look the other way because they didn't want men like your father to fall into the hands of the Russians. As the war was winding down, the one-time Allies were not only in a race toward Berlin, but also racing to grab as many of these individuals as possible. Once hostilities officially ended, the Russians and the Americans were desperate to gain access to the same scientists, doctors, and engineers, even though some of these men had committed heinous crimes again humanity. So in the case of the US, if that included changing or eliminating a few lines or paragraphs in a potential subject's file to make an individual more palatable to the American public, then so be it. Everyone became a potential prize—a spoil of war, so to speak.

"The Joint Intelligence Objectives Agency, or the JIOA was established in 1945 as a subcommittee of the Joint Intelligence Committee of the Joint Chiefs of Staff to oversee the Paperclip project. Over a thousand five hundred dossiers were eventually compiled on prospective candidates in the postwar years. In 1962, the JIOA was disbanded, and all the records were sent here to the Archives. They're still classified and closed to researchers."

Thanks to my research in Huntsville, I already knew most of this, but this was all new to Karin.

"Give me a few minutes. I need to look through the manuscript catalogue to see what is open and available to researchers."

"Mr. Fitzgerald, please, I have one other request," Karin said. "There was a woman, a Jewish woman from Berlin, who was taken away, deported. Is it also possible to find out what happened to her?"

"Please, call me Donald, and what was her name?"

"Anna Weiss."

"That's a fairly common name. Can you tell me anything else about her?"

"I do not know when she was actually deported, but I do know the exact day she was taken from her apartment. It was March 10, 1943."

"You're in luck. As I said earlier, a portion of those records was deposited with us after the war and the lists from Berlin are complete."

We waited at one of the library tables. Nearly forty minutes went by before Donald reappeared. He was pushing a rolling cart filled with twenty or so identical gray boxes and one folder sitting on top.

"What's all this?" I asked.

"I brought out everything available. The boxes contain the trial records. I also have a transcription of an oral history I'd like you to read.

"An oral history?" Karin asked.

"Yes, sort of a verbal memoir. About five years ago, a World War II veteran visited the Archives. He was interested in the trial records from Dora. Turns out that he was with the 786th Tank Battalion attached to the Third Armored Division that liberated the camp. They entered Dora-Mittelbau on April 11, 1945. We started talking, and I asked if I could record him. Historians are just now starting to see the value in oral testimony. He needed to share the details of what he saw with someone else. The interview was emotional for both of us.

I transcribed the tape and sent him a copy. He wrote to thank me, but said he was not planning to listen to the recording. He gave the tape to his local library."

"And Mrs. Weiss, did you find out anything about her?" Karin asked.

Donald reached into his pocket and handed Karin a slip of paper.

"She was sent to Theresienstadt, a camp in Czechoslovakia. Several months later she was transported to Auschwitz."

Karin nodded.

"This only confirms what I already knew. I mourned for my *Tante* long ago and she is never far from my thoughts. I take comfort in the fact that if not for me, no one would remember that she existed at all. I will never forget her, and now, since I've shared her story with you, I hope you will also think of her from time to time. Now we should get to work, no?"

We started with the oral history.

This was not for the weak of heart or for those with a sensitive stomach. As Donald warned, Frank Battaglia broke down and had to stop several times through the telling. His anguish was evident in every line. Karin read one passage out loud.

*The smell is what I still have nightmares about. I wake up in the middle of the night and I swear I'm back there, looking at all the bodies stacked high, brittle, and exposed to the elements. But it's the smell and the taste of the camp I can't seem to shake. It felt like I had arrived in hell. There weren't many survivors, only a couple of hundred skeletal stick figures wandering aimlessly or laying on the ground. We wanted to help, so we gave them a part of our rations. We heard, later, that some of them died from eating more than they were used to. So much for helping. We also found out that the rest of the prisoners had been marched away, to God knows where. What was the point in that? We could have saved so many more. We were only there for a day, but the memory of those few hours has stayed with me for the rest of my life.*

Donald waited until we looked up. "I'm sorry, but I thought you should read this before you started going through the other documents. Are you okay?"

We nodded.

"Okay then, have either of you ever used archival records before?"

We both shook our heads.

"I thought we would be going through microfilm," I said.

"You're in luck. In a few months time we're going to be filming all our unclassified records from the war. When that happens, researchers will no longer be able to view and touch the originals. I don't know about you, but reading the typewritten words on actual paper makes me more aware of the historical significance than when I'm scrolling through a reel of microfilm."

Donald explained the rules for handling the originals and offered us each a pair of white cotton gloves from a basket sitting on the table. He also confiscated our pens and handed us each a pencil, just in case we inadvertently made a mark on one of the documents. When he opened the first box, the scent of old paper wafted into the air.

"What's all this?" I asked.

"The trial documents."

I couldn't summon up a response. The sheer number of boxes on the cart overwhelmed me, and by the look on Karin's face, I knew she was feeling the same way.

"Okay," he said. "Let's get started. Here's the inventory from the collection. Spend some time going through it, and then I can help you retrieve the files that may answer some of your questions."

I reached for Karin's hand under the table and gave it a quick squeeze. She smiled back. Not so daunting after all.

Donald got up and left us with the twenty-page inventory.

The boxes on the cart contained everything from the trial, including interrogation reports (in German with English translations), witness lists, investigative reports, summaries of camp functions, atrocity photographs, casualty lists, pretrial exhibits, camp maps, diagrams of the chains of command, administrative authorizations, and autopsy reports.

We decided to start with the list of defendants. There were nineteen in the first trial. In Ben's rendition, he had placed Dr. Angel in the witness box, but we already knew he had never been on trial or accused of anything. There was not one high-ranking officer listed among any of the accused.

"Look at this," said Karin. "The government is charging the defendants with being involved in a common design 'to operate the Nordhausen complex from 1943-1945 in order to result in wholesale starvation, beatings, tortures, and killings." In addition, she read, "the prosecution maintained that the rifling of inmates' mail, black-market trade in food, the lack of proper toilet facilities, the exposure of inmates to the elements without providing adequate clothing and shelter, and the callous disregard for medical needs constituted criminal behavior."

"This is insane," she said. "The highest ranking officer on the list was an SS first lieutenant. Who was giving the orders? They were getting them from someone. Why weren't any of those people on trial?"

"I don't know," I answered.

Who was in charge? Who were the officers ordering these nineteen defendants to starve and to work the prisoners to death? I was beginning to accept that some of them were now safe and secure and sitting in cozy little offices in the United States.

For the next several hours we continued making our way through the boxes. We gained a lot of knowledge about the running and functioning of the Nordhausen-Dora-Mittelbau complex, but we still didn't have a reason to condemn Hermann Angel for any of the atrocities committed there.

"Let's go talk to Donald," I finally said.

His office was nearby. He looked up as soon as we knocked.

"How's the research going?" he asked.

"That's hard to say," I answered. "We've learned more than we probably wanted to know about camp atrocities, but not a thing about the scientists or the engineers who must have been in and out of there all the time. We have no idea where to look next. We know we're missing something. We're pretty sure that twenty years ago a friend of ours from our hometown found something that incriminated Karin's father. We think that information may have gotten him killed."

Donald paled.

"Give me a minute."

We watched as he walked back into his office and retrieved a large binder.

"These are research request forms from 1945 until 1952. What was your friend's name?"

"Benjamin Lowe," we answered in unison.

"Unfortunately, the forms are not alphabetized. They're filed by date. Do you have any idea when, in 1950, he may have visited?"

"He wouldn't have visited. He would have written a letter requesting the information. We were eighteen and living in Huntsville, Alabama. We would have known if Ben suddenly went on a trip to D.C. Half the town would have known, and then they would have told the other half."

"Okay, then. That helps. I'm an archivist. I have every single letter written to me since I started here after the war. I have a niggling feeling about this. You said he was from Huntsville."

"Yes," I answered.

"Okay. You start looking through this book and see if you can find his research request form, and I'll start looking through my correspondence files."

"Donald," said Karin. "I think he might have written the letter sometime in May or June."

"Why?" I asked.

"Because the comic book with the illustration of my father seated with the other defendants was the final one in Ben's portfolio. It just makes sense that he found out right before we graduated."

"She's right. It had to be late in the school year."

"Okay then," said Donald as he walked back into his office. "I'll start looking and you two do the same."

Using Karin's reasoning, it didn't take us more than a few minutes to locate Ben's research request form. It was like striking gold. We were about to signal Donald that we had found it when he walked out holding a folder.

"I've got it. The second I read the opening line I remembered the inquiry. The war had only ended five years earlier, and it was the first time I had received a request from anyone whose family members had been victims of the Holocaust. Since then, I've received hundreds, but this one was special."

Karin and I sat down and opened the folder.

*Archivist*                                          *May 19, 1951*

*National Archives*

*Washington, D.C.*

*Dear Sir or Madam:*

*My name is Benjamin Lowe, and I emigrated from Germany to the United States with my parents in 1938. As you may have guessed, we are Jewish and except for the three of us who now reside in Huntsville, Alabama, everyone in our family perished during the war.*

*In 1946, my father discovered how and where his brother, Bernhard Lowe, died. He was among the thousands of slave laborers who were worked and starved to death at the Nordhausen-Dora-Mittelbau complex where the V-1 and V-2 rockets were manufactured. At the beginning of my senior year of high school, over one hundred scientists and engineers who worked for the Reich on the rockets were transferred from Fort Bliss, Texas, to the Redstone Arsenal in Huntsville to continue their work.*

*I am writing to try and discover if any of these men committed war crimes and if they are responsible for the death of my uncle and for thousands of others who perished at Dora. I understand that this is an unusual request, but I am living in a city where my parents are walking the same streets and breathing the same air as individuals who may have been complicit in the death of my uncle. All of the men now in Huntsville were a part of Wernher von Braun's team. They all surrendered as a group to American troops at the end of the war.*

*I am especially interested in any information you may have on Hermann Angel. I believe he was an engineer.*

*Thank you for your time and consideration,*

*Sincerely,*

*Benjamin Lowe*

I could picture Ben sitting with pen in hand at his too-small wooden desk trying to compose a letter to the archivist at the National Archives.

"I remember wanting to help this kid. I served in the Pacific. I didn't know the extent of what happened in those camps until I came home," said Donald. "I'm sorry that the name Hermann Angel didn't ring a bell when you first came in," he added, turning toward Karin. "It was a long time ago. I remember writing him back, telling him I would look into it."

"And did you?" I asked.

"Yes."

He then pulled additional sheets of paper out of the folder.

"I was plain lucky, I guess. There was no way this interrogation report should have ended up in the records from the Nordhausen-Dora trial, but there it was. I'm sure it was an oversight, a mistake made by one of the clerical workers who gathered all the documents and filed them neatly into their Paperclip folders. The Joint Intelligence Objectives Agency was pretty careful about not leaving incriminating evidence lying about, but there it was, a document about the war service of your father Hermann Angel."

"Is that what you're holding in your hand?" I asked.

"Yes. Only the summary of the interrogation is in English. The rest is in German. They used interrogators who were fluent in the language. I don't speak German, so I never read the full report. I Xeroxed the original pages and sent them off to your friend. I was hoping to hear back from him, but I never did."

"When did you send the material to Ben?" I asked.

"Looks like it went out on May 27, 1951."

"Ben died on June 2nd. I guess we'll never be sure if he got it in time."

"He must have," said Karin.

Donald then passed the pages over into her shaking hand. She placed them on the table and began to translate as she read:

"The witness was Dieter Schmidt. He was an *Untersturmführer*, or second lieutenant, and served under my father at the Mittelwerk factory at Nordhausen-Dora. This interrogation took place on May 20, 1945. The interrogator was a United States Army lieutenant by the name of Henry Steinberg."

She continued reading silently for a few more minutes.

Karin then said, "Steinberg began the questioning by asking Schmidt about his job and about some of the engineers and scientists who he saw coming in and out of the factory. He then asked him how often he saw von Braun at Mittelwerk. Schmidt answered that he saw him there more than a couple of times. Steinberg also asked him about the role of Hermann Angel at the factory.

"Schmidt said my father had an office at Mittelwerk, and that he was there regularly. He was in charge of the production schedule and in that capacity was responsible for supplying enough laborers to meet the deadlines imposed by *Reichsführer* Himmler.

"Schmidt also claimed that when he objected to the working conditions and the treatment of the prisoners, my father threatened him with arrest. He said he kept quiet after that."

Once again she paused as she read the next couple of paragraphs.

"What! What does it say?" I asked.

"Tommy, please, give me a minute."

"He said that there was another engineer that tried to intercede on behalf of the prisoners."

"Karin?"

"My father reported him for anti-regime remarks. He thinks he was shipped off to Dachau. Schmidt said he never saw him again."

"Can that be checked out?" I asked.

"Yes, of course. What was his name?" Donald asked.

"Johann Franks," she answered.

"I'll take a look. Be back in a few minutes."

"You okay?" I asked.

"Not really. I'm trying. It's just so hard to take in."

"I think Fitzgerald got lost," I said. Another thirty minutes had gone by. Karin was preoccupied with her own thoughts and hadn't noticed.

"I think in my heart I always knew," she said. "My parents were never truly relaxed. They rarely spoke about the war in my presence, but in 1960, when the Mossad, the Israeli version of the CIA, arrested Adolf Eichmann in Argentina and brought him back to Israel to stand trial, my parents acted as if there were Israeli agents lurking on every corner of Huntsville."

While I was mulling over Karin's newest revelation, Donald reappeared at our table.

"I found it," he said. "Johann Franks was an engineer. He worked at the Mittelwerk factory at Dora. In the winter of 1945, he was arrested for treasonous remarks and was sent to Dachau."

"Did he survive?" I asked. "Can we check?"

"I already did. The Nazis were methodical about record keeping. They had lists of who was being transported in, who was being transferred out, who died, etc. Since this camp was liberated by US troops, the documents were collected by the military and civilian units in Europe and deposited with us."

"Well?"

"Oh, sorry. Good news, it looks like he made it. It's hard to say where he went after the camp was liberated. The records only indicate that he was originally from Potsdam. Maybe he went back home after the war."

"Potsdam. That's near Berlin in East Germany. It's almost like a suburb," said Karin.

"Things have loosened up a bit. Maybe there's a way we can call and see if he's still alive and living there."

"No, they haven't loosened up that much," said Karin. "The Stasi monitor every telephone call from the West. I'm not even sure how we would locate a directory without going there. Besides, I'm going to have to come up with some kind of story so he'll agree to see me. I'll have better luck in person."

"There is no way I'm letting you go there by yourself. I seem to remember a rather large barbed-wired wall separating the East from the West."

If I hadn't already been fired from my firm, I soon would be. I needed to give the managing partner a call and try to explain.

"You don't need to come. You've already missed so much work. I can do this."

"Look at me," I said. "I am in this for the long haul. I am not the same frightened eighteen-year-old kid who skipped town because he was scared. You are not going alone. I love you. I've never stopped loving you. I was hooked the first time you walked into our classroom."

And there we were, all three of us—me, Karin and Donald. It was awkward, to say the least.

"I think I need to do a little work," Donald said. "Call me if you need anything. Anything at all."

Karin barely acknowledged Donald's departure.

"You love me?"

"Isn't that obvious?"

I reached across and softly touched her cheek.

"You haven't said whether you love me back."

The kiss was enough. I didn't need the words.

We stood there for a few seconds until we heard one of the other patrons clearing his throat.

"I think it's time for us to go," said Karin.

We stopped by Fitzgerald's office on the way out.

"Somehow a mere thank you doesn't seem adequate," I said.

"No, it was my pleasure. Today is what we archivists consider a great day. I helped someone solve a mystery. Let me know how the trip to Potsdam turns out. I'll be interested to hear if you locate him."

"We will," said Karin.

And then she reached over and hugged a clearly embarrassed archivist goodbye.

# 26

## 1968

Once we finished at the Archives, we headed back to the Washington Hilton where I had booked a room. As soon as we entered, I kicked off my shoes and plopped onto the bed. Karin just shook her head and laughed.

"You could at least pull back the spread," she said.

I could tell she wanted to talk. I was still thinking about the kiss at the Archives and hoping we could discuss our plans in the morning.

"Stop looking at me like that," she said. "I promise, I'm worth the wait."

"You are, are you?"

I had always loved her smile. I had forgotten how much.

"Yes, I promise. Now come over here and sit in this chair so we can make some plans."

"I cannot talk to you here in this room with that bed staring at me. I really can't."

"Tommy, how old are you?"

"I think that's the second time in two days that you've asked me that."

"Okay then. If you can't stay in the room like a big boy, lets go downstairs to the hotel restaurant and plan the trip. I'll tell you all about Potsdam. It was once a very romantic city."

"And then we'll come back up."

"Yes, and then we'll come back up."

§

The only things I knew about Potsdam was that it was the site of the last meeting of Stalin, Truman, and Churchill, the "Big Three" allied heads of state at the end of World War II. Karin had visited Potsdam as a child and remembered the city with fondness.

"Potsdam was once very picturesque," she said. "Unfortunately, much of that beauty was destroyed when the old market square was bombed during the war. The city also had the misfortune of lying just outside of West Berlin after the construction of the Wall, so we will need visas to go back and forth from the West."

Karin didn't seem to be interested in or worried about the logistical problems we might encounter, but I was. Besides the visa issue, I didn't have my passport. For whatever reason Karin always carried hers in her purse, but mine was tucked away in a drawer at my house. I had already called my mother to send it, but it was going to take at least two days to get it.

"The accommodations in the East are not good, so I think we should stay in a hotel in the West and cross over. I have heard that restrictions have eased up a bit lately and it is relatively easy to get permission to cross over. Those stuck on the eastern side are not so lucky."

This was sounding better and better.

"Is there any place or anyone you want to visit while we're over there? A relative or an old friend?" I asked.

Karin sat there for the next minute or so, sipping her drink and deciding.

"You are such a good man and I appreciate the offer, but I think not. I do not need to reconnect in that way. Berlin no longer holds any happy memories for me. Besides, even if I wanted to, my home is long gone. It was obliterated during the bombing along with most of the other houses on the street."

Finally, Karin finished the last bit of cognac in her glass and I motioned for the waiter to pay our bill. I almost sprinted to the elevator.

The following morning I called TWA and booked our flights to Germany. We were scheduled to fly out in two days' time. After breakfast, we walked over to the West German Consulate and were told that visas for day trips into East Germany could be arranged at the checkpoints. They were usually granted without any trouble, but one never knew what kind of mood the border official might be in.

Next, we walked over to Garfinckel's, one of D.C.'s oldest department stores, and bought a few essentials that we might need for the trip. I headed for the men's area and Karin went over to the lingerie department. We planned to meet up in an hour.

In a matter of minutes, I finished buying my extra BVDs and shirts and proceeded to do some shopping in another department. I had just enough time to waylay Karin as she was handing over the money for her purchases.

"I thought we were meeting by the front doors," she said.

"I finished early and wanted to surprise you."

"Come on, let's go back to the hotel and drop off our packages. It looks like we're going to be able to do some sightseeing in D.C. after all."

Neither one of us said much on our walk back to the hotel. I didn't know what Karin was thinking about, but I was holding on tight to the little jewelry box that was tucked away in my pants pocket and thinking about how much time I had wasted running away from my past.

# 27

## 1968

Since Karin made it clear that staying in Potsdam was really not an option, I made reservations at the Savoy, located on a quiet side street near the Kurfürstendamn, one of the largest thoroughfares in Berlin. I had opted for old-world elegance instead of something more modern, and once we entered the lobby I knew I had made the right choice. The room was small but had a quaint charm. The canopied bed looked like a claustrophobic's nightmare, but Karin loved it so I kept quiet. After checking out the rest of the room, she walked toward the balcony and opened the heavily brocaded draperies to reveal the city of her childhood.

"Come look. You can see a portion of Berlin from here. I honestly never thought I would return, but as long as we are here we might as well enjoy the view. The last time I was here most of the buildings were draped in Nazi flags and banners. That dreadful swastika was everywhere and the beauty of the architecture was lost. So much was destroyed during the bombing, but I think that was a good thing. Germany needed to be cleansed. We needed to pay for the crimes we committed. Still—so many, like my father never answered."

Karin turned away from the window, took my hand, and led me over to the bed.

"Are you nervous about crossing over to the East tomorrow?" she asked.

"A little. To tell you the truth, I almost feel like I'm a character in a spy movie."

She leaned against me.

"Okay, you can be Robert Mitchum and I'll be Deborah Kerr. Wouldn't it be nice if we really were playacting in a movie, or simply on a vacation? Unfortunately, this is all too real and a little scary."

"I'm with you there. Honestly, when we registered with the man at the front desk I felt the hairs on my arms spring into action. I mean, he's probably in his mid-to-late forties, and I couldn't help but wonder what he did during the war."

"I thought about that too. Did you notice how his demeanor changed when he realized I spoke the German of a Berliner. He cracked that little smile and became slightly more accommodating, like we shared some sort of secret kinship. I almost came out and asked him where he served, but I didn't want to end up making some sort of scene in the lobby. He was so officious. I expected him to click his heels as he went back to retrieve our room key."

"Thank you for that," I said.

"For what?"

"For not getting into a brawl in the hotel lobby. I would have had to come to your defense, and then the two of us would have most likely been hauled off to jail, and we'd never get back to what I want to do before we go down for dinner. And don't you dare ask me how old I am again."

Her laughter was infectious and within seconds we were stripped of our clothing and lost in something else, something better.

Two hours later we were seated in the hotel dining room ordering drinks and talking about our plan for the next day. This was her bailiwick. The only German I knew was from watching *Hogan's Heroes* and listening to the incompetent Sergeant Shultz and the bungling Colonel Klink bark out orders. I had no idea where to begin and expected that we needed to go to yet another archives or library to do an exhaustive search.

"I'm hoping, if he is still alive that he has a phone and is listed in the telephone directory," said Karin.

"That's your plan. The telephone directory?"

"Yes. How many Johann Franks in Potsdam can there be?"

§

The next morning, with my eyes still closed, I patted the bed beside me expecting or maybe hoping for a continuation of the fun we'd had the night before. I did not expect to find the space empty. Just then, the doorknob turned and in she walked, grinning like a Cheshire cat. I was not smiling.

"Were you worried about me?" she asked. "You know, you're very cute when you're worried."

"No, of course not."

"Yes you were. Admit it, you were worried about me."

"Okay, maybe I was a little worried. Where were you by the way?"

She was still smiling when she jumped onto the bed and wrapped her arms around me.

"I used my flawless German and my feminine wiles to wrangle the only telephone directory for East Berlin away from the hotel manager. He told me I could keep it for several hours and would allow us to place multiple calls without the exorbitant fees the hotel usually charges."

"Feminine wiles, hmm?"

"Yes, I do have them, you know."

"Really, I haven't noticed."

"Well if you sit here quietly while I make these telephone calls, I promise to show them to you."

That was an offer I couldn't resist.

Who knew there were seventeen Johann Franks in East Berlin? So much for narrowing the search. The directory was five years old, and my pessimism about ever finding Franks was growing.

The first three Johann Franks were in their twenties. The fourth, we learned from his still-grieving widow, was deceased and fortunately not our Johann. By the tenth call I was beginning to zone out and had picked up Karin's copy of *Rosemary's Baby*. I was reading the back cover when Karin snapped her fingers to get my attention and gave me the thumbs-up sign. When she got off the phone she was once again grinning.

"I found him, and he's willing to see us."

"Who did you say you were?"

"I made up a name. Karin Schmidt. I said my father, Dieter Schmidt, served with him during the war and asked me to look him up on my trip to Germany."

"Didn't he question the name?"

"No. Do you have any idea how common the name Schmidt is in Germany? It's like Smith in the US. Besides, it was so long ago I'm sure he couldn't remember whether he knew a Dieter Schmidt or not. Regardless, he said we could come."

"We can walk to the Friedrichstraffe and cross there, then we will have to take a taxi. It's about thirty-four kilometers to Potsdam and his apartment."

"The Friedrichstraffe. Isn't that Checkpoint Charlie?" I asked.

"Yes, it is the only place foreigners can cross."

My heart was racing as we approached the guard. I was certain he would deny our request and send us packing, but moments later we were seated in the taxi on the way to the home of Johann Franks.

As we got closer to Potsdam, we passed a few homes that had survived the bombing. Some had been renovated and were sitting between the drab cement-block high-rise apartments put up by the East Germans. They were sterile, ugly, and identical. Franks happened to live in one of the old buildings, and as we walked up the steps Karin pointed out the intricate architectural embellishments above the windows and along the roofline.

"Before the war this was probably a single-family home. They have now all been subdivided into apartments."

She was right. Frank's building had been converted into separate units, and unfortunately, the interior of the front hall did not share the prewar elegance still in evidence on the exterior. The walls hadn't been painted in years and none of the fixtures had been modernized. One overhead bulb was all that remained to guide us over to the mailboxes to search for his name.

Once we pushed his button, we were buzzed in immediately. We took the lift up to the fourth floor and knocked on the door of apartment 4B.

Johann Franks was nothing like I had imagined. For some reason, I expected a much older man, but he was clearly somewhere in his fifties. He must have only been in his early thirties when he served at Dora. He was shorter than I had imagined too, grandfatherly looking with a twinkle in his eye. I liked him immediately.

"Miss Schmidt told me you don't speak any German," he said in perfect English.

"Nary a word," I answered.

"Then we will all converse in English. Did you have any trouble at the crossing? Sometimes the Stasi can be quite unpredictable."

"No," I answered. "It was surprisingly easy."

"Do not be surprised if they ask you the nature of your visit to me on your return. There is little that gets by them."

The pounding inside my chest picked up a notch.

We followed him into a room off the main hallway. Immediately, I felt as if I had stepped back in time. The furniture, the draperies, the lighting, in fact, everything looked like it hadn't been changed or updated in over thirty years.

He saw Karin admiring one of the paintings.

"My parents owned a summer home, miraculously untouched by the war. Most of the furnishings are from there."

He then led us into a small library, richly filled with shelves of colorful leather-bound books. Most of the titles were in German, but there were others in English as well as French. Johann Franks was obviously a well-read and educated man.

"I'm a bibliophile. I've been collecting books since the early 1950s. They are not so easy to come by in East Germany, but some of my old friends in the West do my shopping for me. All the packages are opened, so you wont find anything the least bit subversive on these shelves. Do you like books, Mr. Stern?"

"I enjoy reading. But no, I'm not a collector."

I immediately thought back to my childhood collection of Scribner's Classics and the shelf my father had built to hold them. I wondered what became of them. Maybe my mother still had them stored in her hope chest for a grandson who might one day enjoy them the way I did.

"I did collect books as a child. They were more companions, friends really. I haven't thought about them in years."

"I am glad my library has sparked some pleasant memories for you."

"Now, Karin. May I call you Karin?"

"Of course," she answered.

"You told me very little over the telephone. You said that your father often spoke of me and that we served together. I must be honest with you. I have searched my memory and I do not remember anyone by the name of Dieter Schmidt."

Karin could barely make eye contact.

"Please, *Herr* Franks, I am so sorry and embarrassed. I lied to you. I needed to speak with you in person, and I was afraid if I revealed my real name you would not have agreed to see me."

"And why is that, *Fräulein?*"

"Because my father was Hermann Angel."

His expression hardened, and he slowly walked over to the sofa to sit down.

"What do you want from me? I'm sure your father can answer your questions about the war."

"He died several years ago."

"Ah, so I outlived him after all."

I noticed that he did not offer the obligatory, "I'm sorry for your loss."

"I came here, to you, because I need to know the truth. I need to know the circumstances of your arrest and why my father sent you to a concentration camp."

"And why is that?"

"Because I think his actions during the war may have been a factor in our friend's death and neither of us will rest."

I reached for her hand and finished for her.

"We suspect that Karin's brother may have permanently silenced our friend when he discovered the truth about their father's war record."

"Please, sit down."

We did as directed and took the two chairs facing him.

"Tell me what you think happened," he said.

"I believe my father turned you in for trying to get better conditions for the slave laborers at Dora. I think you ended up at Dachau because he sent you there."

"Who told you this? Your father?"

"No. He never discussed the war."

"No, I suppose he would not have. Then how?"

His eyes narrowed.

"We did some digging at the National Archives in Washington and discovered that he had you arrested."

"Ah, your father, he became an important man—a national hero in the States, no?"

"I suppose he was to some."

"Sometimes the truth is not very pleasant. Are you sure you are ready to hear it?"

She reached for my hand, and held on tightly.

"Yes."

"This is not easy for me either. I rarely speak about the war. Like most, I have tried to forget those years. The victims, and yes, I sometimes still question whether I truly am one, construct walls to keep the demons at bay during the day, but they are very clever and often tiptoe in during sleep to infiltrate our defenses. The perpetrators don't speak of the war either. Why would they want to remind anyone of their crimes? So the stories from those years remain hidden away. No one speaks, no one asks. You are the first."

"Please, I know I am stirring up the past, and the last thing I want to do is to bring you more pain, but this is the only way I have to be certain. He was my father. I won't condemn him until I have proof."

I thought he would ask us to leave. Instead he took another sip of coffee and began to speak.

"My father was a physician, a pediatrician. His partner was a man by the name of Heinrich Dreyfuss, a Jew. They met at the University and became friends. When they finished their medical studies, they decided to open a practice together. Our families became close and we were often together. The Dreyfusses had two daughters—Liesl, who was the same age as me, and Katrina, who was three years younger. I did not have a sibling, so I found companionship with the two girls. When we were small, I use to enjoy playing pranks on them. Katrina always cried, but Liesl would laugh and try to find ways to get back at me.

"I have a photograph of her. Liesl's parents, they now live in the States and sent me this portrait along with some other mementos after the war. They still keep in touch with me, and I with them. They are forgiving people. I doubt I will ever see them again. They refuse to ever return to Germany and I, of course, am a prisoner of politics."

Johann walked over to his desk at the far end of the room and brought back an elaborate silver frame holding Liesl's portrait. I understood the attraction.

"She was beautiful," said Karin.

"Yes, she was. The photograph does not do her justice. In life, her eyes sparkled, her skin was radiant, and her smile was infectious. When she laughed you could not help but laugh with her."

He looked at the portrait again and held it on his lap while he continued.

"You said the Dreyfusses were forgiving people," she said. Why did they need to forgive you?"

"Karin, you are eager for your answers, but I'm afraid you must wait for the entire story to be told. Now that I am finally speaking about the past, I find myself not wanting to leave out the slightest detail.

"In 1935, only two years after Hitler came to power, my father—the more pragmatic of the two partners—encouraged his friend to begin thinking about emigrating from Germany. Heinrich, however, was one of the many who thought the Nazis would pass from power and the German people would return to their senses. The following year, Jewish doctors were barred from practicing medicine in German institutions. They had already been stripped of their citizenship, but Heinrich could still not bring himself to consider starting again in a new country. Besides, he was German through and through. Publicly they dissolved their partnership to avoid arrest, but privately, Heinrich was still seeing all of the Jewish patients. Both men knew that if he attempted to see any of his old Aryan patients, he would eventually be turned in and arrested. Those were treacherous days. We feared everything and everyone. Amidst the dread and uncertainty Liesl and I fell in love. The new restrictions also barred marriage between Jews and Aryans. Only our two families attended the very private ceremony.

"That same year, I began my engineering studies at the Berlin Institute of Technology and graduated in 1938, two months after the *Anschluss*. The annexation of Austria by Germany finally opened Heinrich's eyes, and he began the tedious process of finding a safe haven for his family. Luckily, because of my father's badgering, their papers were all in order and within two months time their quota numbers were called and they sailed to America. My Liesl refused to go with them. Her parents begged her to reconsider. They came to me pleading. They wanted me to insist that she travel to safety with them. They pled their case to deaf ears. I could not bear the thought of her leaving, so I did nothing to support them. I naively thought I could protect her. I thought my prominent family could save her from the abyss. I was wrong. If I had not been so pigheaded, if I had listened to my father-in-law, then my Liesl would have escaped the carnage. And now you see why I said they are forgiving. For whatever reason they don't blame me. Ah, but now I am getting ahead of myself.

"Before I was called up, in the last year before the start of the war, I worked for the Nazis in a civilian capacity at Peenemünde under the command of Major General Walter Dornberger. We were developing the A-4 rockets, but by 1940, I like everyone else was conscripted into the military. The pressure was also mounting to join the Nazi Party. We resisted, but in the end, my father and I believed that if I joined, I could offer Liesl even more protection. She moved in with my parents and we wrote daily. I could hear the fear and despair in every one of her sentences even though, for my sake, she tried to remain positive.

"I believed she was safe. I thought I had anticipated and accounted for every possible danger. I have since learned that there are moments in life that no one can anticipate. I have also accepted that good men can never truly comprehend the malevolence that lies in others. In late 1944, she was turned in by a neighbor and sent to Bergen-Belsen. My parents barely escaped being deported along with her. They continued to let me believe she was safe. They were afraid of my reaction. When I stopped receiving letters from her, they told me that she was ill but recovering. I suspected the truth, but a part of me wanted or perhaps needed to believe them, so I did.

"We were losing the war. We all knew it. When the RAF bombed the facility at Peenemünde, it was decided to move the rocket production to an underground facility. It was then, when I was transferred to Dora-Mittelbau, that I first came to be under the command of your father.

"I have no words to adequately describe the assault on my senses when I first arrived at Dora. Horror, shock, revulsion, none of those adjectives can truly describe what I witnessed. Surely, reasonable men could not have created something so monstrous. But I was wrong. Reasonable men, my countrymen, did just that and worse."

"Do you need to stop?" asked Karin. "Would you like more coffee or perhaps some water?"

"*Nein*, I am almost to the end. It is best to continue."

He was now looking directly at Karin.

"*Fräulein*, although we have just met, I feel you are sincere in your pursuit of answers, but as I already warned you, the truth is not always pleasant to hear. Your father, he was a true believer, a Nazi. If he told you he only joined the party under pressure, or in fear for his own life, then he was lying. He was a loyal soldier of the Reich and a supporter of the *Führer*. He wore his uniform with pride. There were those who were forced to join out of a real fear of reprisals. Your father was not among them.

"*Hauptsturmführer* Angel was in charge of production, and I was one of several engineers assigned to supervise the mostly Soviet, Polish, French, and Jewish prisoners from Buchenwald, who were assembling the rockets. The conditions were deplorable. The flimsy, threadbare uniforms did nothing to protect them from the cold. He expected these skeletons to complete complex tasks, ones that required concentration and steady hands. It was impossible."

Tears had begun to well up in Karin's eyes, and her grip on my hand intensified. I didn't interrupt and neither did she.

"Your father never saw the laborers as human beings. To him, they were the means to an end, a disposable commodity. If someone grew too weak or too sick to continue, then he would be sent to Nordhausen to die. I had heard from one of the guards that in prior months, the ill and dying were sent by rail back to Auschwitz to be gassed, but by the time I arrived, it had become more cost- effective to simply have them die from starvation and lack of medical treatment at the nearby camp.

"I was only there a few days when I first suggested that perhaps more would be accomplished if the prisoners' situation were improved. I thought if I could show that better conditions would increase production and lead to a higher quality product, they would give the workers more food and better clothing. I didn't anticipate that there was always a steady stream of replacements. No one cared how many died. I was reprimanded and warned by the *Hauptsturmführer* to keep my opinions to myself or face the consequences of my insubordination. I was in a strange universe, where good was punished and evil rewarded. For the next several weeks I tried my best to alleviate some of the suffering. Without your father's consent, I told the kitchen to increase the daily rations of food and the guards to allow the laborers more time to rest between shifts. I understood I would be caught, but in what other way could I live with myself?

"I was arrested in the middle of the night, unceremoniously stripped of my rank, and transported to Dachau. I suppose I am fortunate that he didn't send me to Nordhausen or on a train east to Auschwitz. At least at Dachau, we were still given a few rations and a chance to survive.

"Dachau was liberated by American troops on April 29, 1945. By then, I had joined the ranks of the walking dead and needed to be hospitalized for several months. Germany was in chaos, and I had no idea if my family was, somehow, still in Potsdam, or had even survived. It was not until August that I received a letter from my father, forwarded to me from the International Red Cross. My parents were well and had survived the Allied bombing. It was then that they finally revealed that Liesl had been deported. God forbid one Jew should have escaped the carnage.

"For years, I hoped she would miraculously find her way back to me. She was young and strong. Over time, a few survivors trickled back. Why not my Liesl? Hope was all I had left. That is why I stayed in Potsdam, and that is why I was still here on August 12, 1961, when overnight we East Berliners were sealed in behind concrete and barbed wire. I ended up trading one totalitarian regime for another. The Gestapo for the Stasi. Different uniforms, same mindset."

"Did you ever find out what happened to her?" I asked.

"Yes. For years I waited even after I knew it was hopeless. I finally wrote to the International Red Cross. Their response was short and to the point. It mentioned the transport number of the train she was on and listed her as one of the thousands of Jews who had succumbed to typhus at Bergen-Belsen in the last days of the war."

The tears were now visibly streaming down Karin's cheeks, and I unclenched her hand from my own so I could place my arm around her.

"*Herr* Schmidt. I am so sorry for all that you have lost," she said. "How could my father have done such a thing and then go on to pretend he was not a Nazi?"

There was nothing else to say. We all knew the answer: self-preservation and selective memory.

"Karin, sometimes the answers we are seeking are more painful than the false reality we were living in," he said. "In the end, I hope you find the peace of mind you are seeking."

"Thank you, *Herr* Franks. I hope so too."

# 28

## 1968

"Hey, talk to me," I said on our walk back to the hotel. Silence. She shook her head and kept walking.

I couldn't get a word out of her, and I was beginning to believe that our quest for the truth was the worst idea I'd ever had. What was that old adage? Let sleeping dogs lie, or something like that.

I decided not to push her. *She'll talk to me when she's ready.*

Once we were in our room, Karin started to pace.

"Erich killed Ben. I'm sure of it. He killed him to cover up my father's war crimes. It's the only thing that makes sense."

I had already come to pretty much the same conclusion, although something else about Erich was still bothering me. I needed more time to think it through before I voiced it to Karin.

"Are you ready to talk about it?" I asked instead.

"I don't know what else to say."

"How about how you're feeling about all this."

"I'm not really surprised about Erich. I always knew he was capable of monstrous acts."

"And your father?"

"I think I always suspected something. It's going to take me a while to sort out all of my feelings about him. I'm equally upset about my mother's complicity. I'd like to think she didn't know the truth. I'd like to believe that she wouldn't have stayed married to a man like that, but I also suspect if that particular truth was revealed, I would be sorely disappointed. She met Hitler once. Did I ever tell you that?"

"No."

"No, of course not. Why would I have told you? Who in their right mind would reveal such a thing? After meeting the *Führer,* she hung his portrait in a place of honor in our living room. I haven't thought about that horrible picture in years. I wonder what she ever did with it. Certainly, she did not ask if she could bring it along when they were packing for America. It was probably tossed into the fireplace with some of my father's other Nazi regalia. Can you imagine the look on the interrogators' faces if she had asked to bring along the portrait? Perhaps then they would have removed his paperclip from his file."

She looked so miserable.

"Come here," I said.

She walked over to the bed and I pulled her onto my lap where we sat for several minutes while I held her.

"Are you sure you can love the progeny of two such people?"

"Not only do I love her, but I'd like to marry her, if she'll have me."

I reached for my overcoat that lay at the foot of the bed, then pulled the small box out of its pocket and handed it to her. She looked startled and a little confused.

"What, when did you do this?"

"In D.C., when we were shopping at Garfinckel's."

She opened the box, and I placed the simply set, round diamond on her finger.

"Tommy, are you sure? Even after all that we learned today?"

"I've never been more sure of anything in my life."

We sat there for what seemed like an eternity. I didn't know what she was thinking, but she hadn't removed the ring.

"I love you," I said. "Nothing else matters."

§

We stayed in bed the rest of the day.

"Are you going to ever stop looking at that ring?" I asked.

"I love it. I really do. It's exactly the style I would have chosen."

She snuggled up against me.

"We should think about getting dressed and finding a place for dinner. We could ask the concierge for a few suggestions," she said. "Since we're not flying out until tomorrow night, perhaps we could rent a car and drive out to the countryside."

"I actually have another idea for tomorrow."

"Really? Does it involve staying in the hotel room all day?"

"Hmm, now that you mention it, good idea, and I wish I would have thought of that, but no. I've been mulling this other thing over ever since we arrived in Germany."

"What?"

"Walter."

"Ben's cousin, Walter?"

"Yes. The Lowes searched for him after the war and could never find him. What if he's still alive? What if we could locate him?"

"Tommy, you cannot fix everything."

She snuggled closer.

"Am I that transparent?" I asked.

"Yes. I know you are on a mission to give the Lowes some peace, but do you have any idea how difficult it will be to find one individual so many years after the war? Were the Lowes even sure that the parents found a hiding spot for Walter?"

"No, but in Bernhard's last letter he said that they were working on getting him to safety. He actually implied that the Lowes would know where they were taking him."

"Did they?" asked Karin.

"No. I mean they wrote to everyone they could locate. Germany was in such shambles. So many people had died; others had just vanished. It's possible the Lowes' letters never reached their intended recipients."

"That's not a lot to go on. Do you even know where to start?"

"I thought we could put an ad in the newspaper. I know Frank and Helen checked various registries, but I don't think they ever actually advertised. I was also hoping we could enlist the help of a private investigator. Did you just roll your eyes?" I asked.

"Tommy, our flight leaves tomorrow tonight. Do you really think we can accomplish all that in one day?"

"I'd like to try, and I can't do it without your help. In case you haven't noticed my German is not quite as good as yours. I'm really quite good at making you smile, aren't I?"

"Yes, you are—and okay."

"Okay?" I asked. "Did you just say okay?"

"I did," she said. "Now let's go find a restaurant. I'm starving,"

In the end, it was Karin who did most of the work. She found out the name of a reputable private investigator and she was the one who composed the advertisement for the newspaper.

The man we hired said he would try his best, but added that the search would be difficult and more than likely unproductive. According to him, many children were lost in the chaos following the war and few were found. For whatever reason, I still believed we would find him.

# Part III

## Absolution

# 29

# 1968

WHEN THE WHEELS of our plane touched down at Atlanta's Hartsfield Airport, we were almost too tired to get out of our seats. I hadn't been able to sleep, and my endless nervous banter had kept Karin up for most of the flight home.

"What now?" she asked.

"Now we go get our bags, and we drive over to my mother's so she can hug and kiss you. Then I will be forced to stand there while she tells me that I better not screw this up."

"I mean after that?"

"I suppose we drive back to Huntsville and then we…"

"That's just it. Then we do what? If we confront Erich, he'll just end up denying everything. We can't go to the police. We don't have anything to offer them other than our suspicions. I can just imagine the expression on Cole's face when we try and explain."

"Let's go see my mother and then we'll decide what our next move is. At least we know the truth, and that's more than we had before."

By the time we got our bags, went through customs, and got in the car, we were exhausted. We decided to surprise my mother in the morning and instead, drove to my home.

"You have that look on your face," Karin said. "The same one you had when we were crossing the border into East Germany. Are you having second thoughts?"

"About what?"

"About us."

"Is that what you were thinking? Giving you that ring was the best decision I ever made."

"Then what is going on?"

"I'm nervous about you seeing my house."

"Tommy, that is silly. Why in heaven's name are you worried about that?"

"I'm not exactly sure."

We were pulling in the driveway before I finally answered her.

"I suppose I want you to fall in love with the house the same way I did. I want you to sell your bookstore and your home and move here to Atlanta, to live with me in this house for the rest of our lives."

Once again, I was startled by the spontaneity of the kiss.

"I don't care where we live as long as we're together."

§

We were both up bright and early. Jetlag was no joke. Karin was sitting outside on the back deck, watching the river flow by, and I was putting on the coffeepot when I heard the telephone ring. It was Helen. I should have let it ring.

"Thank God I found you. Mr. Greene is on the warpath. I think he's ready to fire me since he can't fire you without the approval of all of the other partners."

I was strangely calm. I could see Karin through the window and I suddenly realized that I didn't really care what Philip Greene thought. My job had always been a means to an end. It allowed me to buy my house, to drive around Atlanta in fancy cars, and to eat dinner at The Coach and Six, my favorite Buckhead restaurant, whenever I had a craving for their famous lobster ravioli. The few times I actually believed that my client was innocent were few and far between.

"I'm sorry I've been such a pain in the ass. I'll fill you in later, I promise. Tell Phillip that I'll be in this afternoon to talk."

I hung up before Helen could ask me any more questions. I had made my decision. Now I just had to figure out what to do with the rest of my life.

Karin had walked back in while I was hanging up the telephone, and I handed her a cup of coffee.

"Who was that?" she asked.

"Helen."

"How did she know you were home?"

"She didn't. She's been calling every hour for the last day and a half."

"Oh. Are you in trouble?"

"Well, I suppose it depends on what you consider trouble."

I paused and continued, "I'm looking at the fact that the managing partner of my firm is more than a little put out with me as an opportunity of sorts. I'm thinking about handing in my resignation."

"Do you want to talk about it?"

"Yes, but first I want to give you a tour of our house."

As I led her through the rooms, I hoped she could see past the imperfections, water stains, and peeling wallpaper and imagine the house as it was once and could someday be again.

"It was built in 1930 and needed a lot of work when Donna and I first bought it. I've been a little lax in fixing it up, and thought you might give me a few pointers."

"It must have been quite grand at one time."

"It was. I went over to the Atlanta Historical Society and found some photographs that were taken of the house when it was first built. All the original woodwork was painted over at some point. It's going to take a long time, but I plan on removing every coat."

The stairs creaked on the way back upstairs reminding me of yet another part of the house that needed repair. We had spent the night in the master bedroom, but had fallen asleep in a matter of minutes. This time I pointed out the high ceiling, mullioned windows, and fireplace, hoping she could see the rooms former beauty.

"I know it's not in the greatest shape, but it's the only room that doesn't leak when it rains. The roof is missing a few tiles."

"Tommy, it's beautiful."

She sat down on the window seat.

"What a great place to read and unwind."

I began to relax too. I could sense that Karin was visualizing a future with me here, in this house.

"The formal dining room and living room are in the worst condition. I'm hoping that once I remove the carpet, I can salvage the floors."

"It's a special house. I can see why you fell in love with it," she said.

"I've saved the best for last."

I took her hand and walked her downstairs and into the library.

"It's the only room I've restored. What do you think?"

"Oh, Tommy, it's so warm and cozy."

Karin reached out and touched the burled mahogany paneling that I had discovered hiding beneath more coats of paint. After the divorce I'd worked on it in the evenings. I had little else to do.

"You told *Herr* Schmidt that you didn't think of yourself as a bibliophile, but look at all the titles on your shelves. I wish he could see it."

"Most of these were my father's. I guess I never thought of myself that way, at least not since I built that little collection of Scribner's Classics when I was a kid. I really need to ask my mom if she kept them for me."

"I plan on spending a lot of time in this room," said Karin.

She plopped down in one of the leather chairs facing the fireplace.

"With me?" I asked.

"With you, forever. Now come on, I'm not letting you off the hook. Let's go outside and have that little talk."

We sat down on a small wrought iron bench left on the back lawn by the previous owners. The yard sloped down toward the river, and watching the current with a morning coffee or evening drink had become a ritual. It was a new and even better experience sharing the moment with Karin.

"Are you stalling?" asked Karin.

"No, I'm just gathering my thoughts."

"Take your time. I'm not going anywhere."

"Before Ben died, I was the embodiment of the outraged Southern liberal born and bred in the Jim Crow South, who thought I would one day be part of the movement to change it. I fancied myself as some kind of avenger, a righter of wrongs, cut from the same cloth as my brother."

"Sort of a superhero?"

We both smiled.

"Yes, I suppose so. Ben grounded me. Without him, I lost my way. I didn't care much about anything, so after law school, when a job became available at the prosecutor's office in Atlanta, I jumped at the chance. At first, I thought putting away criminals would give me a sense of purpose, and maybe it did in the beginning, but then when a murderer got off on a technicality, I started thinking that if the justice system was that unpredictable, I might as well work for the other side and make a lot more money. I forgot how good it felt to think about someone other than myself. These last couple of weeks have changed all that for me. You've helped change all that. Trying to prove that Ben didn't commit suicide has reminded me that there are causes out there that are worth fighting for, and I want to be a part of that."

"So, in other words, what you're trying to tell me is that instead of marrying a high-priced, rich, defense attorney I am now going to be marrying someone who wants to do volunteer work."

I didn't know what to think.

"Oh Tommy, I was kidding. You were so serious, and I just couldn't resist. Don't you know how much I love you? I've never stopped loving you. I don't care if we live in this house or an apartment as long as we live together. Besides, I think you'll make a very handsome superhero. I plan on personally designing your cape."

I got up from my seat and pulled Karin into my arms.

"Thank you."

"For what?"

"For listening and for letting me have a second chance. Since that day in the coffee shop in Huntsville, when you asked what had happened to the boy you knew, I've been trying to figure it out. After Ben died, I shut myself off from everyone and everything except school and then work. I didn't ever want to feel anything again. It was all too damn painful. You were collateral damage, and I'm sorry."

"You're forgiven."

I held her even closer. I could have sat with her on my lap watching that river forever.

"There is one more thing I'd like to talk about, actually a promise I'd like you to make," Karin said.

"What? Anything."

"It's about Joe."

"What about him?"

I knew I sounded defensive.

"I understand how much you loved him and how you still miss him, but promise me that you'll stop making decisions about your life based on what you think your brother would have wanted."

"Is that what you think I do?"

"Honestly, I do. I wish he was still here, but Tommy, live your life for yourself. I never had the chance to meet Joe, but from what you've told me about him, I believe that's what he would have wanted for you."

"I'll have to think about that one, but thank you."

"For what?"

"For sitting here with me while we watch the river and for loving me enough to tell me something I might not want to hear."

§

I called my mother to make sure she was home, and told her I had important news and would be there shortly.

"What, what. You tell me what it is right now! I'm still your mother."

"Mom, I live ten minutes away. I know you can wait ten minutes. See you in a few."

I hung up while she was still talking. No sense ruining the surprise.

She was waiting on the front steps when I pulled into the driveway. When she saw Karin open the passenger door, her look of curiosity broadened into a smile.

"Karin Angel, I haven't seen you in years, and you are as beautiful as I remember."

"You haven't changed either, Mrs. Stern."

"Tommy, this is a nice surprise."

I could tell my mother seemed a bit perplexed about why I had brought Karin Angel over to her home with such a buildup. There was no point keeping her in suspense.

"Mom, I have big news. Karin and I are engaged. We're planning to marry."

We all stood there for several seconds, no one saying a word, and I worried that perhaps my mother was thinking back to those days when the Germans first arrived in Huntsville, and how she felt about how their presence had affected our town, our lives. Karin's grasp on my hand grew tighter.

"Karin, then why in the world are you calling me Mrs. Stern? You're going to be my daughter-in-law for darn sakes. My name is either Elizabeth or Mom. You can choose. Now come over here and give me a hug."

I think I felt more love for my mother at that moment than I ever had in my entire life.

"Now let's go inside, and you and my son can tell me what in the hell has been going on with the two of you."

So for the next couple of hours, while my mother set out plates of food, we talked about our discoveries at the National Archives, about our trip to Germany, and our meeting with Johann Franks.

"Mr. Franks sounds like a remarkable man."

"He is, and I plan on sending him a few books to add to his library," I said. "I only hope the East Germans will let them through."

My mother then turned to Karin and reached for her hand.

"I hate asking, but how sick is that brother of yours?"

"I'm not really sure. He's lost a lot of weight over the last couple of months, and I don't think he's getting any more treatments. When I asked, he said he had six months to a year, but he could be lying. He is a very proficient liar."

"I'm sorry, honey. I know you think he's done something horrible, but he is still your brother."

"Mom, I know you're trying to help, but honestly you have no idea what Erich's like."

"Tommy, please. It's okay. I understand what your mother is saying."

Turning toward my mother, she continued, "my relationship with my brother is complicated, to say the least, but you are right. No matter what, he is still my brother. I'm not sure how I will feel when he is gone. For the moment though, I want to do everything I can to discover the truth about how and why Ben died. The guilt, the remorse about that night, those emotions have never left me. I'm still living in Huntsville because I can't give myself permission to leave Ben alone in that graveyard. If Erich had something to do with Ben's death then he is the only one who has the power to grant me absolution."

My mother was uncharacteristically silent.

"What can I do?" she asked.

"I don't know. I honestly don't know how to get him to talk about that night. He's dying and will never see the inside of a prison, but for whatever reason he still cannot find it in his heart to give me some peace."

"It seems to me you only have one card to play. You need to tell him that you'll expose your father's wartime activities unless he comes clean," said Mama.

"Come clean?" I said.

My mother was watching way too many episodes of *Hawaii Five-O* and *Starsky and Hutch* on TV.

"I doubt if the newspaper in Huntsville will publish anything negative about her father," I said. "The town reveres all the Germans who settled there."

"No, you're probably right," answered Mama. "But the *Journal* and the *Constitution* here in Atlanta will and so will some other large papers and news outlets once they get wind of the story."

"I could beat it out of him," I said. "I've been wanting to knock the shit out of him ever since the first day I met him."

Their looks were identical. *Oh my God, I was marrying my mother.*

"I was just kidding," I hastily said. "Besides, I already did that, and I almost got arrested."

"What did you just say?" asked my mother.

"It's a long story. I'll fill you in later."

"Tommy?"

"Mom, I promise nothing happened. I'll tell you later."

"Well, if you're going to Huntsville, I'm going with you. We can leave this afternoon."

"We? What do you mean we? You haven't been back to Huntsville since the day you left for Atlanta."

"Then there's no time like the present. I should have gone back years ago, and a visit to Al is long overdue."

"Mom, come on. Erich's erratic. I don't want you anywhere near him."

"And if he's that unpredictable, I don't want you and Karin anywhere near him. A united front is the best approach. Why don't the two of you go back to your house and pack, and then pick me up in an hour?"

"There is no arguing with her," I said to Karin.

"I can see that," said Karin, "but I would never forgive myself if Erich did anything to harm you."

"And neither would I," I added.

"Fine! I'll stay at Al's when you go see him, but honestly, if you're that worried, you should take someone from the police with you. You're both beginning to terrify me. This is not some game you're playing."

She was right, and honestly, I didn't know how to proceed. I had no idea how Erich would react. We had done all the research. We thought we knew the truth. We believed that Erich had something to do with Ben's death. But now what? Would Erich really tell the truth in exchange for our silence about his father's war record? Did his father's legacy mean that much to him? And then a worse thought occurred to me: What if we had it all wrong? What if the Lowes were right all along and Ben did commit suicide? What then? Then, I would have to finally admit that I had failed my friend and that I was oblivious to his pain.

"Tommy, don't forget Ben's art portfolio. You should bring it along," added my mother. "Seeing his father seated with the other defendants might shake him up enough to talk."

I could tell by the look on Karin's face that she had her doubts and honestly, so did I.

# 30

---

# 1968

My mother hadn't been back to Huntsville since the façade of Stern's had been painted over. I saw her quickly look away as we drove by the old store.

"I think I'll have Al take me over to the cemetery while the two of you visit with Erich."

"Are you sure, Mama?"

The few times my mother had visited Joe's grave she was out of commission for days.

"Yes, I'll be fine. I promise."

We drove over to Al's, and, once again he was waiting for us on the front porch. He nearly bounded off the steps when he saw us drive up.

"Elizabeth, you look wonderful. How long has it been?"

"Too long, Al, too long."

His bear hug left my mother breathless.

"Come in, come in. There's someone inside waiting to see you."

"Lord, Mrs. Stern you is as pretty as the day I met you."

"Selma, this is a surprise," she said as the two women embraced.

"Tommy said you were still working for Al."

"I come by and make him his meals. He just loves my cooking."

"I can understand why. You look well. It's so good to see you. We have so much catching up to do."

I knew my mother well enough to see that the return to Huntsville was playing more havoc with her emotions than she cared to admit.

Selma was putting on her sweater and heading for the door when Mama stopped her.

"Please, Selma, join us. I have so much to say to you and Al, and I'd like Tommy and Karin to hear it too."

"I don't know Mrs. Stern. It don't seem right."

"Selma, don't be silly. It's 1968. I'd like to believe that those times have changed, at least in our family."

Selma removed her sweater and took a seat at the table. Al removed the cellophane from the platters and we all sat down to eat.

"Selma, this is as good as it gets," said my mother. "You haven't lost your touch."

"Thank you. You was a pretty good cook yourself by the time you moved to Atlanta."

"You were a patient teacher. I'm sorry I didn't keep in touch. After Tom died and I buried him over at Maple Hill, I couldn't wait to leave this city. Everywhere I walked I was assaulted by what once was and could never be again. I needed to start over and leave Huntsville behind me. I should have stayed in contact and for that, I am deeply sorry."

Selma reached over and held Mama's hand.

"You is a good woman Mrs. Stern. No need to apologize. We all loved Joe and we all loved Mr. Stern. You had a right to grieve anyway you knew how."

"Thank you," whispered my mother. "Al, after lunch, I was wondering if you'd drive me over to the cemetery. I'd like to spend some time with my husband and son."

"I'd be happy to, Elizabeth."

After several minutes of silence, the conversation reverted to the good old days. It was a time to eat and an opportunity to avoid talking about the real reason for our visit. We waited until Selma was on her way home before we discussed our next move.

"I'm very uncomfortable about the two of you going over to Erich's without a police presence."

"Mom, all we have is our suspicions. What do you think Cole's going to say? First of all, Karin's father is respected in Huntsville. No one is going to believe he was a Nazi without a lot of proof, and even then, who knows? All we have going for us is the threat that we'll expose his father's activities to the news media."

"Do you have extra copies of all of the documents you discovered at the National Archives?" asked Mama. "If you do, they may prove enough to convince Cole to accompany you over to Erich's."

"We have them, but I'm not sure Cole or anyone else will believe us," I answered.

Karin had not uttered a word throughout our conversation. Her silence spoke volumes. We were intent on exposing both her father and her brother, and that had to be affecting her in ways I couldn't possibly imagine.

"Karin, any thoughts?" I asked.

"I think your mother's right. We should bring Cole into the conversation. He was a good friend of your brother's and holds a lot of respect for your family. He's at least going to listen to what you have to say. Besides, I really should go check in at the bookstore and see what's going on over there. I dumped everything onto my manager when we took off for D.C. Al, can you drop me off on the way to taking Elizabeth to the cemetery. I'll have my manager drive me back. How about if we meet back here, in let's say two hours, and then we can pay my brother a visit. I'll breathe a lot easier if Cole knows we're going over there."

"And so will I," added my mother.

"Okay, it's three o'clock now," I said. "I'll see you back between four and four-thirty."

§

I should have checked with Cole to make sure he was available. He wasn't. He was out on a call and wasn't expected back for another forty minutes or so. I took the front desk sergeant at his word and decided to wait. When I finally saw him enter the building, I realized the forty minutes had turned into an hour and ten. I would have to summarize quickly.

"Tommy, back again? You don't visit for years and now you're here every time I turn around. What's going on?"

"It's a long story."

I looked at my watch.

"Can I use your telephone for a minute? I have to call my cousin to let him know I might be delayed getting back to his house."

"Sure, be my guest."

Luckily, Al and my mother had returned from the cemetery. Al said he would let Karin know as soon as she walked in.

"Okay, Tommy. What's on your mind?"

I decided to start at the beginning. I told Cole about my initial conversation with Karin, her discovery of Erich's journal and the revelations found therein, and about my visit with Ben's family in New York. I then showed him Ben's art portfolio. Cole didn't say a word until he started going through the illustrations. He was as amazed as everyone else who had been given the privilege of seeing Ben's work.

"Whew. Who knew the kid was so talented? What a waste."

I waited, not wanting to say anything else until Cole finally came to the last few drawings in the pile. I saw his eyebrows go up.

"This guy looks familiar. Is this who I think he is?" he asked.

I nodded.

"Ben thought Hermann Angel was a war criminal, and you say you found proof of that? Where?"

"In the National Archives in Washington."

I was losing my patience. I pulled the document out of the folder and pushed it across the desk.

"And that's why he killed Ben. To keep him quiet," I said.

"Tommy, Ben committed suicide, and besides, he wouldn't have known about this report. He was a kid. It was 1951."

"He did know. He wrote a letter to the archivist in D.C., who found this document just by luck. Believe it or not, he sent a handwritten copy of it to Ben.

Who knows, it could still be mixed up in some of Ben's old papers at his parents'. I suppose I should have called and asked, but I didn't want to upset them by having them look through his things."

"Give me a minute."

I looked at the clock above Cole's desk. I was already twenty minutes late.

"Okay, tell me if I have this right. You and Karin believe that when you were all just eighteen years old, Ben wrote a letter to someone."

"The archivist!"

"Okay, okay, the archivist at the National Archives in Washington asking him to check out the activities of some of our town's newly-claimed citizens to see if they were war criminals. And that he was particularly interested in their activities at the Dora concentration camp because that is where Ben's uncle died. Am I right so far?"

"Yes."

"Then, lo and behold, this archivist miraculously discovered the one document that would incriminate Hermann Angel, the father of the boy who Ben despised. Once the discovery was made, Erich murdered Ben to cover up his father's crimes and then made it look like a suicide. That is what you're saying, right, Tommy?"

"Yes," I said again.

Was that pity I detected in Cole's eyes? Cole picked up the document from the National Archives again.

"Tommy, look. Try and understand. I can't go and arrest Erich Angel on the basis of this information, and I can't go around soiling the memory of one of Huntsville's most respected citizens either. All this says is that a witness claimed to have known that Dr. Angel arrested another engineer for anti-regime remarks. He could have been lying."

"He wasn't. The man's name is Johann Franks, and Karin and I just got back from Germany where we interviewed him. He corroborated the entire story."

"You actually got on a plane and went to Germany to talk to this guy?"

"Yes, we just got back."

I thought I finally detected a flicker of interest.

"Look, Cole. I admit it, I'm no fan of Erich Angel, but my gut is telling me that he killed Ben and made it look like a suicide. I'm asking, no, I'm begging you to at least consider the possibility."

I looked at the clock again and realized I was now almost an hour late.

"I'm meeting Karin at Al's and then we're heading over to Erich's. We're hoping he'll tell us the truth in exchange for our silence about his father's wartime activities. If he's as sick as he looks, he won't even make it to trial. We could use a little backup when we confront him. To tell you the truth, the guy frightens us, and I know he won't try anything with you there."

"All right. I'll go along for the ride."

"Thank you, Cole. I mean it."

"But, remember, I don't want another fight breaking out like it did the last time you and Karin spent a little time with Erich."

"It won't. I promise, and thank you. By the way, did I mention my mother drove up with us? She's staying at Al's and I'm sure she'd love to see you."

"I'd like to see her too. I used to spend as much time in your house as I did in my own."

"I remember."

For a second, I thought Cole was going to reach out and ruffle my hair like Joe used to do when I was a kid. I almost wished he had. Instead, he put his arm around my shoulders and led me out to his car.

No place was too far in Huntsville, and the ride over to my cousin's took under five minutes. When we walked in, Mom and Al were engrossed in a couple of old photograph albums and were oblivious to our return.

"Hey," I shouted. "I brought someone to see you."

"Cole Preston, as I live and breathe. How long has it been?"

"I'd say at least fifteen years. You look exactly how I remember you."

I am sure I was the only one who detected her amusement when she answered.

"Why Cole. Y'all haven't changed a bit either."

My mother was the quintessential southern woman, always polite with a little bit of devilish mirth poking through.

While they were getting reacquainted, I went into the kitchen expecting to see Karin. I didn't.

"Where's Karin?" I asked.

"Not back yet," answered Al. "She must have had a lot of catching up to do over at the store."

"It's after five. Did she call?"

"No, we haven't heard a thing."

"I'm calling the store. What's the name of it again? Do you have a directory?"

"The Book Nook, and follow me. The telephone is in the kitchen."

I could barely thumb through the pages. I dialed and let it ring at least ten times before finally giving up.

"She probably stayed to help her manager close up. I'm sure she's on the way," said Al.

He was probably right, but I kept wondering why she hadn't called to let everyone know that she'd be late. That wasn't like her.

"Come on, Tommy. Let's go out to the porch. We'll watch for her there," said Al.

I waited as another fifteen minutes slowly ticked by. I listed and discarded all the reasons for her delay because, even if she and her manager had stopped for gas or had run a quick errand, they should have been back by then.

"Something's definitely wrong," I said.

"Honey, I'm sure she's fine," said my mother.

I hadn't even realized that she and Cole had joined us on the front porch. I was done waiting.

"Cole, can we take a ride over to Erich's? I have a sinking feeling that Karin is over there."

"Sure, hop in."

# 31

## 1968

B EFORE GOING TO Erich's, Cole insisted we drive by the bookstore just in case Karin was still inside and ignoring the phone. The shop was dark and locked up tight. I hadn't realized until then how close Erich's house was to Karin's shop. She could have easily walked there after Al dropped her off. Why would she go there without me? We had a plan. When we pulled up to the curb, I hoped I'd see Karin coming out the front door, but no such luck.

"Come on. Let's go check it out," said Cole. "She's probably inside having a long-drawn-out conversation with her brother and didn't realize what time it was."

I wasn't sure which one of us Cole was trying to convince.

There was no answer when we rang the doorbell, and I could feel the dread creeping in, ready to devour me.

"Where in the hell is she?" I yelled.

"Tommy, calm down. We don't even know that she was here. Erich's probably out running a few errands."

"You need to break in."

"I can't. There's no probable cause and I don't have a warrant. I will not break the law, not even for your family."

"Then I will."

I moved back to take a run at the front door when Cole grabbed me and physically lifted me off the ground. By the time I knew what was happening, I was halfway back to his patrol car.

"Cole she's in there, I know it. He's hurting her. He used to hit her all the time when they were kids."

"Try and calm down. The first thing we need to do is go back to the car to radio the station. I'll have the desk sergeant call Penny."

"Who?"

"The manager over at the Book Nook. Come on. Karin was probably delayed."

I paced outside the car while Cole radioed in.

"What's taking so long?" I yelled.

Cole held his finger up.

"Are you kidding me?" I muttered.

"What! What did she say?"

I waited as Cole stepped out of the car. Could he move any slower?

"Karin never went to the bookshop."

"Now can we break the door down?"

"Tommy, listen to me. I know you're worried, but Karin could be any-where. Maybe she did go visit him and they're on their way back to your cousin's house right now."

"You don't get it. He's dangerous. He's hurt her before. Karin's in trouble and if you won't break the door down, I will."

I shook off Cole's grip on my shoulder and ran toward the front door with Cole sprinting directly behind me.

"Tommy, wait!"

It was too late. I threw myself at the door, readying myself to be met with fierce resistance. Instead, I flew into the front hall, landing solidly on the floor.

"Tommy, what the hell? I ought to arrest you right now."

"For what? The door was open. Aren't you even curious why? Because I am."

"Okay, okay, the door was open, so I don't suppose it would hurt to look around a little bit. Erich is sick. He could be in need of some help."

Cole said it loudly enough for Erich to hear, if he were actually inside. He was still worried about unlawful entry, and I was praying that Karin's psychopathic brother was not torturing her.

"Erich, you okay? Are you in here?"

While Cole was yelling Erich's name, I started searching through the rooms. I knew it was a waste of time. The house was empty. Neither Erich nor Karin was there.

I sank down on Erich's couch trying to think. Cole sat in the seat across from me.

"Look, Tommy. There's no reason to expect something happened to Karin."

"Come on, Cole. You and I both know something's going on. While I'm trying to convince you, she could be…"

I couldn't finish the rest of the sentence.

"Let's look around the place again," he said.

I didn't have far to look. When I stood up from the couch my hand brushed against something sticking up from the back of the cushion. It was an earring, and it was Karin's.

"Cole, look, it's Karin's. She put this pair on this morning. She was here! If Karin was okay, she definitely would have called by now."

While Cole continued his hopeless search through the rooms, I called Al. He still hadn't heard a word from Karin, and I could hear my mother in the background demanding that they get in his car and start searching for her.

"Do not leave the house," I yelled. "She may return, and I need for you to call the police if she does. They'll radio it in to Cole."

"Okay, Tommy. I'll try and talk her out of it, but she's already heading outside."

I slammed the phone down.

*Where is she? Think, think. Where would he have taken her?*

Nothing was coming to me. Cole was still thrashing through the house and I went out front to try and clear my head. *The schoolyard. He's taken her to the schoolyard.*

"Cole, come on. I know where she is."

§

Cole drove with his flashers on and the siren off.

"On the off chance you're right, I don't want to warn him," he explained. "We'll park on the side street across from the school and approach on foot."

"Do you have a plan?" I asked.

"Let's just see if they're even there."

The darkness had started to settle over my old high school building and the parking lot where the senior barbecue had taken place twenty years earlier. We had yet to see another car, and I think Cole was beginning to question my sanity.

"There, over in the corner," I said.

We both saw the distinct outline of the front of a 1966 Chevrolet Impala before the entire car came into view. It was parked in the corner, near the woods that surrounded the back of the school.

Cole grabbed his rifle and we started walking toward the spot—the place where Ben was once found hanging from a one-hundred-year-old, live oak tree. I could taste the bile as it settled into the back of my throat. In the months before I left Huntsville for good, I'd avoided the area at all costs. As we got closer we heard voices, or to be more precise, one voice.

"Ah, the party can finally get started. I was expecting you earlier. You had us worried. Right, Karin?"

There was no answer.

"I was beginning to think you might not figure out where we were. Ben was always the smarter one of the two of you."

Cole had disappeared into the shadows and was no longer walking with me. I had positioned myself near one of the trees.

"Where's Karin?"

"Oh, you don't see her. You need to come a little closer."

"Tommy, stay where you are," she yelled. "He has a gun."

"Karin?"

And that's when I saw her. She was standing on a bench beneath the tree of my nightmares. A rope was wrapped around her neck and her hands were tied behind her back.

"Oh God, Erich, please. What are you doing? She's your sister. Your twin sister. Please let her go."

The breeze had picked up and the branches were swaying above Karin's head. She looked tired. One false step, and she would fall. Erich was next to her, too close for Cole to have a clean shot. My breathing had quickened, and my heart was on high alert.

"Karin and I have been catching up," he said. "We haven't had a meaningful conversation in years. I finally told her that I was the informant who reported our upstairs neighbor to the Gestapo. Mama never liked the fact that she was so close to that old Jewess, so I took care of the problem. I explained that it was actually her fault. My sister knew the law and yet she was still sneaking upstairs to take piano lessons from her. Karin, did you think it was one of the other neighbors? I believe you always suspected Hans Gundermann. He lived in the apartment next to her and made no secret of his hatred of the Chosen People. I was home when the Gestapo came. I watched from our doorway and waved farewell. She walked right off with them. Not a peep. Karin, do you remember all the lovely things in her apartment, especially the piano? I did miss her play-ing, so much better, than that of those brats who moved in afterward."

Karin's knees began to buckle.

"Karin, I'm right here," I said. Karin, look at me. Don't listen to him. Keep your eyes on me. Erich, your secrets are safe. You need to let her go. I promise we won't tell anyone."

"Karin has already promised to not say anything about Papa's war record. It no longer matters. I tried to protect his legacy, but now he's dead and I will be soon. Karin and I came into the world together. We will leave the same way, though this time she will have the honor of being first."

That's when I saw the gun protruding out of the waistband of Erich's pants. I realized that no matter what I said, he was going to kill her and then turn the gun on himself. He had nothing to lose. I needed to keep him talking long enough for Cole to position himself and get off a shot. I had no idea what kind of marksman my brother's old friend was, but like most of us, he grew up hunting and knew how to down his prey.

"I wasn't talking about that secret. I was talking about the other one that you've been trying to cover up all these years."

I hoped I hadn't gone too far. *What if I was wrong?* I needed to keep Erich talking and this was my only play.

"What secret?" he shouted. "I have no other secret."

"Girls, Erich. We all knew you didn't like girls. You never showed the least bit of interest in any member of the opposite sex the entire time we were in school. I used to think it was because you were always so wrapped up in your schoolwork. But that wasn't it, was it? The only one you did show any interest in was Ben. Was that it, Erich? Were you in love with Ben all those years ago?"

Erich's features became twisted. There was fury in his eyes, and I knew I had guessed right.

"Did you kill him because he wanted to be with your sister and not you? You were always trying to prove how much you hated him, but I think it was a cover-up. You were afraid someone would find out how you really felt. It must have been horrible loving another man, and a Jew no less. According to the racial laws of the Reich, you were committing a crime. You would have ended up in one of the camps along with the rest of the homosexuals and other subhumans."

I hoped I hadn't gone too far.

"LIES! YOU ARE TELLING LIES! SHUT UP!"

"How long have you known?" I asked. Did you know since you were a little boy? Did your father suspect and send you off to Hitler Youth to toughen you up? Did someone there pay extra-special attention to you?"

"Is that true Erich?" Karin asked. "I didn't know. It must have been horrible for you, to pretend all the time in front of the other boys, and in front of our parents. I'm so sorry. I would have helped you."

He turned toward his sister.

"I don't want your pity. I never wanted it. You didn't help me. No one tried to help me. Not when I was being beaten and not when that youth leader pig forced himself on me. Now stop talking! All of you just stop talking!"

"Erich, what did they do to you?" Karin pleaded. "Please talk to me. I didn't know. I swear I didn't know."

"It doesn't matter anymore."

"Tell us what happened the night you met up with Ben at the schoolyard," I said.

Erich fumbled for a cigarette in his pocket and managed to light it while still standing menacingly close to Karin. The change in Erich's posture was barely noticeable, but he seemed slightly more vulnerable, or maybe just plain tired. *Finally*, I thought. *Finally, he's going to tell us.*

"I found him sitting on this very bench slumped over, his face buried in his hands. I started to leave. I thought he hadn't noticed me, but then he asked if he could have one of my cigarettes. I asked him when he started to smoke. And he answered, 'Tonight.' He smiled and I smiled back and I walked over to hand him a cigarette. He took a puff and began to cough. He smiled again and tossed it on the ground. I told him that maybe smoking wasn't his thing.

"We were alone, and I thought maybe things could be different. I sat down on the bench next to him and he showed me Karin's note. She didn't love him— she never had. She was in love with you. He was devastated, but in a way re-lieved. He said he had been riddled with guilt about seeing my sister behind your back. So I asked him if one Angel sibling could replace another. He just stared at me. I reached over to take his hand."

Erich was crying. I didn't care. All I could think about was how tired Karin must be. I had no idea how long she'd been standing on that bench. Her legs were trembling. I was terrified that they would give out and I wouldn't be able to get to her in time.

"I have never forgotten the look on his face. I could have taken his anger, or maybe even his revulsion. Instead, all I saw was pity. The Jew was feeling sorry for me. FOR ME! He pushed me away and started to leave. I couldn't let him. I grabbed him. He swore he would tell no one, but I didn't believe him. I knew he couldn't be trusted. He would tell Karin and then she would have told you and my parents. I couldn't let that happen. Ben thought he could just walk away. He didn't understand. I had no choice. He didn't see me take off my belt. He was still walking when I caught up to him from behind and threw the belt over his head and around his neck. He was so startled. He tried to break free, but I held on pulling the belt tighter and tighter. Afterward, I drove home and brought back the rope. It was the only way I could hide the marks on his neck."

Karin was whimpering, and Erich had finally moved slightly to the right of her. *Where in the hell was Cole?*

"Karin and I thought you killed Ben because he discovered that your father was a war criminal. He found out exactly what your father did during the war. He knew your father should never have been given clearance to come to America. His Paperclip file was full of lies. He was a war criminal. He turned in one of his own men for the crime of wanting better treatment for the slave laborers. That last night, he could have told you what he knew, but he didn't. Ben could have destroyed your family, but he chose not to. You didn't do the right thing twenty years ago. You can still do something good. Please, Erich! I'm begging you."

"He knew about my father?" asked Erich.

"Yes, and he still couldn't bring himself to hurt you."

Erich turned to look at Karin. I could no longer see his face. For a brief moment their eyes met. I heard the crack of a rifle and saw Erich falter, stumbling against the bench.

§

I had fallen asleep in the chair next to her bed. I woke up stiff, remembering little of the events from the night before. Snapshots really. I heard Cole radio for the ambulance, and I remembered sitting next to Karin as she clung to me, whimpering like an injured animal. Erich was moaning, rolled up in a small ball, obviously in pain from the gunshot wound to his shoulder.

"You're up," said Cole. "I peeked in a little earlier and you were sound asleep. Thought you might need the rest."

He handed me a cup of coffee and sat down on the only other available chair.

"Your mother and cousin are in the waiting room down the hall. They've been here all night."

"Have they? They should go home and get some rest."

"I'll relay the message when I go back out. Mind if we spend a couple of minutes together first?"

"Nope."

"Why don't we take a walk down the corridor so we don't disturb Karin," said Cole.

"I can't leave her. I don't want her to be alone when she wakes up. They gave her a sedative last night, but it should be wearing off soon."

"Okay, we'll talk quietly. How's she doing?"

"I'm not sure. Her throat and neck are badly bruised, and she was in shock when they brought her in. Other than that, I just don't know."

"You saved her, you know. I never saw anyone run so fast. You got to her just in time. One more second, and I…"

"I know. I'm trying to forget that look of absolute terror on her face. And by the way, nice shot."

"Thank you. I keep in practice. I spoke to Erich's doctor. The bullet was a through and through, but in his weakened state, the doc doesn't expect him to live too much longer. Apparently, he hadn't been coming in for his treatments. I've posted an officer outside his door, but honestly, at this point, he's too weak to even go to the bathroom let alone escape from his room. If he lives, he'll be charged with murder, kidnapping, and attempted murder."

"At least I know the truth. That's all I wanted when this got started. I wanted to know what really happened to Ben on that last night."

"And now that you know, does it help?"

"Yes, actually, it helps a lot. For years I thought I had failed him. I was wrapped up in Karin, planning for college. You know, not really paying attention to what was going on around me. Hell, I didn't even know that Ben was in love with my girl. Now I know that Ben had no intention of taking his life. That it had nothing to do with Karin, his parents, or me. Absolution for all of us, and it feels pretty damn good."

# 32

## 1968

"Tommy?"

I had been standing by the window staring out at the parking lot when I heard Karin trying to croak out my name.

"Hey, Sleeping Beauty. How are you doing?"

"My throat hurts."

"Honey, I know. I'm so sorry."

"I remember a gunshot. Is Erich dead?"

Tears welled up in her eyes and she tried to get up.

"No, he's not dead. He's here, just down the hall. You can see him later. Now you should rest."

Apparently, that was all Karin needed to hear, and she settled down on her pillow and once again closed her eyes. I propped the extra pillow on the back of my chair hoping for sleep, but not expecting it to come. I was wrong. When I awoke, Karin was sitting up staring at me and smiling.

"That is the prettiest smile I've ever seen," I said.

I unfolded my aching body from the chair and climbed into the bed beside her.

"Nurse McKenzie is not going to approve," she said. Her voice was slightly stronger.

"The hell with Nurse McKenzie. I need a hug and you need one too."

We were still there, in bed, sound asleep with our arms around each other, when we heard the shrill voice of the nurse.

"You!"

"Me?"

"Who do you think I'm speaking to? Get out of that bed this very minute. Oh my. You actually still have your shoes on. Do you have any idea how unsanitary that is?"

Just then my mother and Al walked through the door.

"And do you have any idea what these two have been through? Go find some other patients to yell at and leave them alone," said my mother.

Nurse McKenzie had finally met her match.

"Mom, it's okay."

I got out of bed and apologized. The two women were still staring at one another.

"I'll see what Doctor Nolan has to say about this," the nurse said.

"You do that. I've known Charlie Nolan all of his life. In fact, I was at his christening. You tell him Elizabeth Stern says hello."

"Okay, ladies. Mom, sit down. Nurse McKenzie, I'm sorry for breaking the rules. Can we please call a truce?"

The nurse nodded toward me, fortified her exit with all the dignity she could muster, and walked out the door.

"Mom, really. That woman is taking care of Karin. We don't want her to hate us."

She ignored me and walked over to sit on the bed next to Karin.

"How are you doing, sweetie? Can we get you anything?"

I rolled my eyes, and Al was trying hard not to bust out laughing. My mother had withdrawn her protective talons and was back to being a charming, gracious southern lady.

"No, I have everything I need right here in this room, but I would like to go home. Has anyone asked the doctor when I might be discharged?"

"He said if you're up to it, there's no reason why you can't leave in the morning," I answered.

She smiled, but I could tell something else was going on, and perhaps it was time for my mother and Al to say their goodbyes. Mom obviously sensed the same thing.

"I think we're tiring you out," said my mother. "Al and I are going to grab some lunch and then I could use a nap myself."

Al leaned over and kissed Karin on the forehead.

"You've been through a lot—give yourself some time to heal."

"Thank you. I will."

I waited until the door closed behind them.

"Okay, what's going on? Talk to me."

"It's Erich. He not only killed Ben, but he also sent my *Tante* to her death in Auschwitz. What kind of person is capable of such evil? He didn't just take Ben's life, he covered it up and allowed all of us to believe that our beautiful gifted friend committed suicide. What kind of person could do that?"

"One who spent most of his life guarding a very deep secret, and who was trying to prove himself to your father and to the other little Nazis."

I couldn't believe I was defending Erich, but a small part of me, a very small part, understood how horrible it must have been to have known that he would have been sent to the camps along with everyone else had they discovered his sexual preference.

"He was probably terrified that someone would find out," I said.

"Yes, I suppose. Who knows what abuse he suffered? Something must have happened to him all those years ago, but I don't believe that mitigates his guilt. Bad things happen to a lot of people and they don't commit murder."

"No, they don't. You have all day to think about whether or not you want to see him. If it makes it any easier, I'll go with you."

"Thank you. I love you. And by the way, thank you for saving my life."

"My pleasure."

§

Later that day Karin and I walked down to Erich's room accompanied by a police officer. She had decided to say goodbye to her brother. She would not be coming back for his funeral. The doctor told her it would only be a matter of days.

When we approached his bed, Erich opened his eyes, and I could tell that he was surprised to see us.

"I am leaving tomorrow morning. I'm driving back to Atlanta with Tommy and his mother."

He nodded.

"I loved you once, you know."

Erich shut his eyes, but I sensed he was listening.

"I understand that in some ways you were also a victim. I am sorry for that, but I cannot forgive you for what you did to Anna Weiss and to Ben. I want you to know that. I've tried, but some sins are unforgivable."

He nodded again and turned his head toward the windows.

"Goodbye, Erich. Rest in peace."

# 33

# 1968

COLE CALLED ME with the news. Erich had held on for only one more day. Karin heard the telephone ring and must have noticed the expression on my face when I walked into the bedroom.

"Is it over?" she asked.

"Yes. He died this morning."

"We should call the Lowes."

That's all she said. Not one other word about the death of her twin brother.

"I know, but it's not the kind of conversation I want to have over the telephone. I thought I'd fly up to New York and tell them in person."

"I'd like to come."

"I thought you'd say that. We'll go as soon as you're up to it."

They had waited this long; a few more weeks wouldn't matter. I watched as she closed her eyes again and fell back to sleep. She was exhausted physically and emotionally. *Did time really heal all wounds?* I had my doubts but hoped so.

Over time, as I hovered, Karin began to recover. Once in a while I even made her smile. Slowly we were falling into a routine. She directed the day-to-day activities of her bookshop by telephone, and I went to the office, where I tried to patch up all the problems I had created by my absence. Every evening we shared a bottle of wine, ate dinner and tried to figure out what to do with the rest of our lives. Karin had decided to sell the Book Nook and planned to open a similar shop in Atlanta. I was no longer interested in defending high-priced, often guilty clients, but I had no idea what to do next.

Later, I wondered why it had to take a monumental tragedy for me to come to a decision. On April 4, 1968, while I was staring out the window of my downtown Atlanta office, Martin Luther King was assassinated while giving a speech at a hotel in Memphis. The next day, I finally stopped sitting on my ass and handed in my resignation at my law firm. I then placed a call and offered my services to the Civil Rights Division of the Justice Department. Thankfully, they were interested. I had once been an able prosecutor, and the division head felt I had a unique perspective being a born and bred Southerner.

My discoveries about the Paperclip scientists—individuals like Karin's father, who had actually perpetrated war crimes, and those like von Braun, who had claimed they had seen and heard nothing—had changed me. I didn't know if I'd ever be able to bring any war criminals to justice, but for now, I was anxious to get started with the Klansman and White Citizen Councils members who were still causing problems throughout the South.

A month had passed since the night at the schoolyard, and although Karin and I had been successfully sorting out our respective careers, we still hadn't spoken about what had finally pushed Erich over the edge, and the emotional toll it had taken on her. Karin was holding back, and even though my mother kept telling me to give her time, I was getting impatient.

"Are you ever going to talk to me?" I asked.

We were sitting on the back deck, nursing our wine and watching the river.

"We talk all the time."

"Karin, I think you know what I mean."

She took another sip.

"I do, and I want to. It's just that whenever I try, whenever I let my mind go back to that night, those images come back. Me standing on that bench, the gunshot, Erich, everything."

"Baby, don't cry."

I got up and pulled her over to sit on my lap.

"My mother warned me not to push you. I should have listened. I'm sorry."

"I promise. As soon as I'm ready."

"I know, darling. I know."

§

The next day I made our reservations for New York. The official notification from Cole's office finally arrived. The medical examiner had changed the cause of Ben's death from suicide to homicide. I called to let him know it came, and asked if he thought the local paper would pick up on the story.

"There's already been an article," he answered.

That seemed odd. Alma was calling often to check in on Karin, but she hadn't mentioned seeing anything in the paper.

"Can you mail me a copy? What did it say?"

"It's over, Tommy. Let it go. You got the answers you were looking for."

"Damn it, Cole. What did it say? I can always send for a copy."

"Okay, okay. I'll read it to you. Give me a minute. It's somewhere on my desk."

Within seconds, Cole came back on the line and started to read.

*SURPRISE DEATHBED CONFESSION IN EIGHTEEN-YEAR-OLD CASE*

*On March 10, one day before his death from complications associated with his battle against leukemia, Erich Angel confessed to accidentally killing his fellow classmate Benjamin Lowe eighteen years earlier. The two boys were graduates of East Clinton High School. Lowe's death was originally labeled a suicide. Angel said that the boys, both born in Germany, had an altercation earlier in the evening. Hours later, when they met up in the schoolyard, another fight erupted, resulting in the Lowe boy's unintentional death. Fearing repercussions, Angel staged the scene to make it look like a suicide.*

"What the hell! Nothing but half-truths and lies! That article is a travesty. It wasn't an accident and you know it. You were there, damn it! You heard the confession! How dare they simply report that both boys were from Germany? One was the son of Holocaust survivors and the other one was the son of a Nazi."

"Tommy, I told them the truth. All of it, but do I need to remind you which folks this would have affected? Erich and Karin's father was revered in

Huntsville—still is. There's been talk of naming a street after him. Did you really think the local paper was going to besmirch his good name because of something his crazy son went and did eighteen years ago?"

"Yes, foolish, stupid, trusting me. I actually believed someone might care that the life of a kind, intelligent, artistic boy was snuffed out by a pitiful excuse for a human being."

"Tommy, I'm sorry, I really am, but in this town, no one cares or wants to remember what happened to Ben Lowe. And besides, Erich Angel was a homo. I can't imagine Karin wanting that spread all over town. Maybe you could try and put something in the Atlanta paper."

"Cole, the fact that Erich was a homosexual is beside the point. Oh, never mind, just forget it."

I knew I was wasting my breath.

I hadn't noticed that Karin had walked into the library and had been listening.

"I have to go."

"It was nice reconnecting," he said.

"Bye, Cole."

"I take it that the Huntsville newspaper didn't exactly report the facts," said Karin.

I shook my head and walked over to the nearby chair. I now knew why Alma hadn't forwarded the article. She was trying to spare us.

"Come sit with me," I said.

She moved to my lap and placed her head on my shoulder. I breathed in her scent, and my anger began to slip away.

"You know, it really doesn't matter," she said. "We know the truth and by tomorrow evening the Lowes will too. I finally feel that Ben can rest in peace. It's the crimes of my father and others like him that I cannot forget. Outside of a very small number of people, most of them government officials, no one is even aware that Operation Paperclip happened. Who else besides my father was guilty of war crimes and brought to safety under the guise of national interests?"

"Alma knows."

"Alma knows what? I'm beginning to think I might have some competition."

"Don't make fun of my relationship with Alma. She's been calling every week to see how you're doing."

"You know I'm just teasing. I like and respect our old librarian."

"She's been collecting information for years. Someday, when the dossiers are unclassified and I'm more established at Justice, I'll be able to talk the department into looking into some of these guys with a little more scrutiny. Right now, they're still being protected."

We sat there a while longer. There was nothing more to say.

# 34

## 1968

"KARIN, HURRY UP. We'll miss our flight."

She was upstairs, still packing.

"We're only going for one night. How much are you bringing?"

"Tommy, we have plenty of time."

I looked at my watch. She was right, but flying always maxed out my stress levels, and today was no exception.

"I want to stop at my old office first. Helen called and said she'd been holding onto some mail for me. It's probably a bunch of junk, but I'd better check it out. The office is on the way. Did you hear me?"

"Yes. I heard you. I'm coming. Relax. You can hold my hand and talk to me all the way to New York."

"Very funny."

"I'm not trying to be funny."

"Good, because I'm planning to do just that the entire trip."

The stop at my office only took a few minutes, and we were back on the road in no time at all.

"Will you go through the mail and see if there's anything I need to look at?" I asked Karin as I drove.

"You were right. Mostly junk. Ah, but here's an invitation to a fundraiser for the Atlanta Symphony. Interested?"

"It's a pet project of my mother's. She and Henry Sopkin, the first conductor, were good friends. We should probably go."

"There's a letter addressed to you from Berlin. I recognize the name on the return address. It's from that private detective we hired when we were there last month. Maybe we should pull over."

"We'll be late. Just read it to me."

"Are you sure?"

"Yes."

Silently, I was praying it was good news.

Karin started to read.

*Dear Mr. Stern:*

*Sadly, I am writing to report that after an exhaustive search I was unable to discover the boy's fate. I understand that this is not the news you were hoping to hear. Of course, there is no way to way to know for sure. After the war very few children turned up. Berlin was in ruins, and if that was where Walter found sanctuary it is likely he did not survive the Allied bombing. Again, I wish I had better news.*

*Sincerely,*

*Klaus Huber*

"Damn, I'm a fool." I said. "I really thought we'd find him and give the Lowes a happy ending."

"I know you did," said Karin.

"Will you tell them that you searched and couldn't find him?" Karin asked.

"No, I don't think so. Why reopen the wound?"

"Even though you didn't find Walter, you tried, and that is what makes you my most favorite superhero."

"Better than Batman?"

"Yes."

"Superman?"

"Yes."

"Captain America?"

"Are we done yet?" she asked laughing.

"Yes, we're done."

§

The ride to the airport took longer than expected, and the race to the gate was the last thing I needed. As promised, Karin was holding my hand as we taxied onto the runway, and I was trying my best not to cut off her circulation.

"I'm ready," she said.

"Ready for what? I know you can't resist me, but, honey, we're on an airplane."

She let go of my hand long enough to punch me in the arm.

"I'm ready to talk about what happened. Erich, Ben, all of it."

"You sure?"

"Yes, I'm sure. It will keep you occupied."

She squeezed my hand harder.

"That day, I know I promised to wait for you and Cole back at Al's house, but I felt so responsible for who my brother was, for what he may have done, for the sins of my father, for everything. I could not allow you or anyone else to be hurt. On the drive back to Huntsville, my sense of impending disaster intensified with each and every mile. Erich was unpredictable, but I still believed I could get through to him. When I got there he let me right in. I gave him a hug. It was not returned. I was trying so hard to reconnect, to rekindle something— a memory, a once upon a time of loving me.

"When we sat down, I told him what we had discovered in Washington and in Potsdam. He seemed to be listening. I begged him to tell me the truth about that night. When he did turn toward me, I was stunned by the vacancy of his expression. He had barely spoken, but I finally understood. My brother, my long-ago playmate, despised me. I should have left then, but I was paralyzed by an overwhelming sadness. He still hadn't said anything. He walked over to a small desk, pulled out a handgun from a drawer and told me to get up and to follow him into the bedroom. There, in a little box on his dresser was the note I had written to Ben all those years ago. He had kept it. I was stunned.

"I stopped looking at the gun and reached out to touch the crumpled paper from so long ago. 'But why?' I asked. His answer was to call me stupid. He said, 'You ignorant little fool. You still don't get it.' He then pushed me out to the garage, where he picked up the rope and forced me into his car. The rest you know."

"Do you have any idea how courageous you are?"

"I'm not courageous. I'm protective. I could not allow him to hurt you."

"Instead, you almost died."

"For the last few weeks, it's all I've been thinking about. I sit outside watch the river, and wonder why he hated me so much."

"He was jealous. You were the normal one, and in his warped sense of right and wrong, that just wasn't fair. He must have struggled his entire life to fit in. Here, in America, it's still considered a crime to be a homosexual. Sodomy laws are still on the books in most states and homosexuals who have the courage to live openly are often fired from their jobs and ostracized by society. I can't begin to imagine how terrifying and confusing it must have been for him to have had those feelings in a country that didn't tolerate differences of any kind. At least in America, you're generally not killed for loving someone of the same sex."

"And then, later, Ben fell in love with me instead of him."

"Yes, then Ben fell in love with you."

"I am glad the Lowes will finally know the truth, but maybe I should wait back at the hotel when you go over to see them. My brother murdered their son, and my father was complicit in the death of Mr. Lowe's brother, Bernhard. They probably hate me. I would hate me if I were in their shoes. I don't know what I was thinking—I should never have come."

"No one hates you. Do you remember what you said about absolution? How discovering the truth about Ben freed you of guilt? You're delivering that same gift to them."

"You think?"

"I know."

"I'm still terrified."

"I know, but for the moment let's concentrate on me. I just heard the wheels go down."

§

By the time the taxi pulled up to the Lowes apartment building, Karin's nervousness had rubbed off on me. I hoped I wasn't kidding myself. Would they understand that Karin had nothing to do with the crimes of her brother and father? I hadn't given them any details over the telephone. I told them that Karin Angel and I had gotten back together and they seemed pleased. They sounded excited about our visit.

Once again, the doorman knew we were expected and directed us to the elevator that would take us to the Lowe's apartment. By the time we arrived at their front door, I wasn't sure who was holding up whom.

"We can still cut and run," Karin offered.

I smiled and knocked.

Helen and Frank embraced us both with equal intensity and, in that instant, my fears were washed away. I hoped Karin's were as well.

The dining room table had been set up for lunch and Helen invited us to sit down to the type of feast I remembered as a child: juicy brisket, noodle *kugel*, and homemade dill pickles.

"Tommy, two visits in less than a few months. This is such a pleasure," said Helen. "Karin, it is a delightful surprise to finally meet you."

"Yes, it is right that the four of us finally are together," said Frank. "We should have apologized to you years ago."

"To me? I don't understand."

"Why yes. We pushed our son to commit that horrible act when he told us of your love for each other."

"No. Oh please, you don't understand."

The tears had already started to form in Karin's eyes.

I needed to step in. I placed my hand on top of Karin's and looked into Frank's and Helen's bewildered faces.

"It's a long story. I hope you don't have any plans for later this afternoon," I said.

I told them about our research, our discoveries about Hermann Angel, and finally about Erich's admission of guilt. They sat quietly through the telling.

"So our son was murdered?" asked Frank.

"Yes. That's what I've been trying to tell you. Ben had no intention of killing himself. He loved you and he was looking forward to college."

"My brother strangled him and then made it look like a suicide. Erich was sick, but there are no excuses for what he did. I cannot change that fact anymore than I can absolve my father for his crimes. I would never ask you to forgive them—their sins are unforgivable—but if you could ever find it in your heart to forgive me."

Frank and Helen remained silent.

Karen pushed herself away from the table and began walking toward the door. I got up to stop her, but so did Frank.

"Karin. Child."

Frank took her by the hand and led her back to her seat at the table. Helen got up and the two of them stood before her. Helen spoke for the two of them.

"Our son, he recognized the goodness in you, and Ben was always a good judge of character. We all make choices in life. Your father and brother chose hatred and self-preservation, while you chose decency and kindness. It is because of what you and Tommy uncovered that Frank and I might actually have a decent night's sleep. There is nothing to forgive you for. There never was."

Helen and Frank pulled Karin up from her chair, and the three fell into a tight embrace.

§

Karin was better after our trip to New York—happier and more content. We both were. Weather permitting, we spent our mornings and evenings in the backyard enjoying the river. We made wedding plans, worked on our house, and made love. In between we imagined children, perhaps boys to be named for Ben and for Joe and a girl to be named in memory of Karen's *Tante*, and we also imagined nightly bedtime stories filled with the escapades of my heroic brother, my courageous friend, and a superhero named Stark.

Made in the USA
Columbia, SC
16 June 2020